W9-CLC-569
8604 9100 004 281 7

ALPENA COUNTY LIBRARY
211 N. First St.
Alpena, Mich. 49707

# The Misfortunes of Others

*By the same author:*

FRIENDS TILL THE END

GOING OUT IN STYLE

AS THE SPARKS FLY UPWARD

# The Misfortunes of Others

## A Bernard & Snooky Mystery

*by*

*GLORIA DANK*

A Perfect Crime Book

DOUBLEDAY

New York London Toronto Sydney Auckland

A PERFECT CRIME BOOK
PUBLISHED BY DOUBLEDAY
a division of Bantam Doubleday Dell Publishing Group, Inc.
666 Fifth Avenue, New York, New York 10103

DOUBLEDAY is a trademark of Doubleday, a division of
Bantam Doubleday Dell Publishing Group, Inc.

*All of the characters in this book are fictitious, and any resemblance to actual persons, living or dead, is purely coincidental.*

*Book design by Dorothy Kline*

Library of Congress Cataloging-in-Publication Data

Dank, Gloria.
The misfortunes of others: a Bernard and Snooky
mystery / by Gloria Dank.—1st ed.
p. cm.
"A Perfect crime book."
I. Title.
PS3554.A5684M57 1993
813'.54—dc20 92-27139
CIP AC

ISBN 0-385-46808-3

PRINTED IN THE UNITED STATES OF AMERICA
April 1993
FIRST EDITION

1 3 5 7 9 10 8 6 4 2

*We all have enough strength to bear*
*the misfortunes of others.*

*—François, duc de la Rochefoucauld*

*To Leif and Jacob*

# ONE

THE PHONE rang at seven o'clock in the morning. Maya put down her pencil and took off her reading glasses.

"Hello?"

"Collect call for Maya Woodruff from Jean Jacques Rousseau," said the operator, her voice made tinny from the distance.

"I accept the charges."

"Thank you. Go ahead."

"Maya."

"Snooky, you beast."

"Did you know that Rousseau was born in Switzerland? Here I always thought he was French."

"Did you call me at this hour to tell me that?"

"This hour? What time is it there?"

"It's early in the morning."

"Well, it's early in the morning here too."

"Where are you? What part of the planet?"

"I'm in St. Martin," her younger brother said. He sounded cheerful. Of course, Snooky always did sound cheerful. "French Antilles. It's beautiful here, Maya. You would love it. Sun, sand and surf. I'm visiting friends."

"Well, of course you are. When's the last time you ever paid for a hotel room?"

"You sound grumpy, Maya. It's not like you. Is everything okay?"

"Yes, everything is fine."

"Where's Bernard?"

"Snooky, I can't believe I'm paying for this conversation. Think for a moment. It's seven o'clock in the morning. Bernard is asleep."

"Oh."

There was silence, broken only by the crackle of the telephone line.

"You don't sound like yourself, Maya. You sound extremely grumpy. Usually you're delighted when I call, no matter what time of day. I had a psychic intuition I should call you, so I did. Something is wrong, isn't it? Is it you and Bernard? Are you getting divorced? I always thought you were such a solid couple."

"Bernard and I are not getting divorced."

"Are you ill? Is one of you sick? Should I come immediately?"

"Neither of us is sick."

There was a brief silence.

"You're pregnant, aren't you?"

"Snooky, you are amazing. You can tell whether or not I'm pregnant over a telephone line long-distance from the Caribbean?"

"You are pregnant."

"Yes."

There was a pause. "I'll be there later today. Don't bother to pick me up. I'll rent a car in New York."

"Snooky—"

Maya was left talking to a vacuum. The telephone crackled and hummed ethereally, the sound of the electronic muses. She sighed and placed it back on its hook.

"Snooky diagnosed my pregnancy in a two-minute telephone call from St. Martin," Maya told her husband later that day.

Bernard, a large man with dark hair and a bristling beard, took a sip of coffee from the oversized coffee cup which he favored. He looked grumpy. "I assume we paid for that call?"

"He knew right away, Bernard. Don't you think that's . . . well . . . unusual?"

"Everything about Snooky is unusual. Unusual, you understand, in the sense of not quite normal."

"He really is psychic. Mother always said he was."

Bernard folded his newspaper. "How are you feeling today?"

"Really awful."

"I'm sorry. Can I get anything for you? How about some decaf?"

"I don't want to look at coffee." Maya scribbled irritably on a large legal pad she was holding on her lap. "I don't want to look at tea. I don't want to look at anything except maybe some celery. And in about two minutes I'm going back to bed for the rest of the day."

"I think we're running out of celery." Bernard cocked a worried eye toward the kitchen.

"Go get some more."

"I never knew celery was a miracle drug for pregnant women."

"It's not a miracle drug. It happens to be the only thing that settles my stomach and keeps away that awful fainty feeling. That blackout low-blood-sugar thing. Now leave me alone for a little while, Bernard. I'm struggling to get this article done, and it's not easy." Maya worked for a small magazine called *The Animal World.* "I don't see how I can possibly write anything decent while I'm feeling like this. I'd like to see you work under these conditions."

"I haven't gotten anything done for the last two months either, you know, sweetheart."

"Well, at least you don't feel like this." Maya leaned her head wearily against her hand. "I have no joy of living. I've lost my esprit. I have no good cheer. I am no longer a happy camper."

"You're in your first trimester. You're not supposed to be a happy camper."

"I don't see how something that's only a few thousand cells big can make a person feel this way."

"Can I do anything? Can I give you a back rub? Can I bring you some herbal tea?" Bernard hovered lovingly over her.

"You can call all my so-called friends and tell them that when they told me the first few months weren't so bad, they were wrong. Oh, by the way." Maya lifted her head. "Snooky is coming. He'll be here later on today. He didn't say when."

"He never does say when. He just crawls up to the front door, like a cockroach."

"We'll need stuff for dinner. I can't think about it. Do you mind doing the shopping?"

"No. I'll make up a list."

"Get celery. And salad stuff. Oh, and Bernard—?"

"Yes?"

"Get about a million shrimp. I think I could go for some shrimp tonight."

---

Bernard was standing in the kitchen later that afternoon, watching the shrimp, cleaned, shelled and deveined, doing a macabre and ghostly dance in the pot of boiling water, when there was a hollow banging sound from the vicinity of the front door. He glanced at his watch, which read 5:00 P.M., and made his way slowly down the hall to the foyer. There were more loud banging sounds. Bernard did not hurry. When they had bought the old blue-and-white Victorian in a state of ill repair, worn down by the centuries and by the casual abuse of previous owners, there had been an elderly doorbell which chimed loudly when a button was pushed. Bernard had disconnected it shortly after he and Maya moved in. He loathed doorbells—agents of the devil, he called them. He hated jumping every time the bell sounded, he hated those particular chimes and he hated the artificial cheeriness of it. To Bernard, someone at the front door was not a cause for celebration. For a long time he had left the button there untouched, and many visitors and deliverymen had spent hours pushing it before going away unanswered, but finally Maya had persuaded him to put up a brass lion's-head knocker of impressive weight and stature, which leered into a visitor's face and (Bernard felt) made them think twice before knocking. It produced a very satisfactory brass clanging sound which, unlike the doorbell, he could ignore with equanimity. He had spent many happy hours ignoring it, closeted away in his study upstairs.

Now as he came into the foyer, it became apparent that the banging sound was not coming from the lion's-head knocker, but from an area several inches above the floor. Bernard grimaced and slowly unlocked the door. It opened to reveal a giant brown teddy bear.

Bernard contemplated the teddy bear for a moment.

"Snooky."

His brother-in-law's head appeared next to the bear's, an unlikely Medusa. "Bernard. So good to see you."

"Did you have to kick the door?"

"I couldn't reach that very impressive brass knocker you have there with my feet. I'm sure you understand."

"Come on in."

"Thanks so much."

Snooky put the bear down carefully on an antique hat stand with a wooden seat in a corner of the foyer, placed his suitcase on the floor, and turned to embrace Bernard in a tearful hug.

"Bernard, I . . . I can't express how I feel."

Bernard stood woodenly, in pained amazement.

"I'm so happy for the two of you, I could cry."

"Please take your hands off me."

Snooky wiped his eyes and stood back. "I brought you a bear."

"So I see." The bear was hard to miss, lolling drunkenly on the hat stand.

"I know I've been an uncle before"—Snooky and Maya's older brother, William, a corporate lawyer who lived in California, had two small children—"but as I guess you know, I can't stand Anna and Buster. They drive me crazy. I'm hoping to have a better relationship with your child. I know I could be a good uncle if I tried. I'm starting now. I don't want Maya to do anything. I'm going to take over running the house. She'll sit for nine months with her feet up. You'll see, I'm going to do everything."

Bernard stared at him gloomily. "Seven months."

"Seven months. I would have been here the first two months if you had told me. Did she tell you I knew over the phone? Do we have a connection, Maya and I, or what? Did she tell you I was coming?"

"She warned me."

"Where is she now? I want to show her the bear."

"Snooky, she's pregnant. Don't show her the bear. It might scare her, and that would disturb the child." Bernard stared at the plain brown suitcase Snooky had brought with him. "Since when do you have luggage? I've never seen that before."

Snooky, on his wanderings across the country and to various foreign lands, visited them often in the little town of Ridgewood, Connecticut. He had graduated from college several years before and had never yet held a job, so it made visiting very easy. He had inherited enough money from his parents' untimely death to get by in the style to which he had always been accustomed—as his older brother William said, "He spent his life in training to do nothing"—and part of that lifestyle was to wander from place to place, never staying anywhere too long, renting instead of buying, visiting instead of settling down. The one place he returned to year after year was his older sister's rickety old Victorian house in the idyllic suburb which was Ridgewood, a town of winding lanes, crystalline lakes surrounded by woods, and houses of every shape and color, from thatched cottages to modern steel-and-glass geodesic domes, tucked away into the scenic landscape. Snooky usually traveled light, which in his case meant weightless, *i.e.* no luggage at all, showing up at Maya and Bernard's front door with grand plans to borrow a toothbrush and wear his brother-in-law's clothes—not that they fit him, but he would wear them anyway, Bernard's oversized outfits draped luxuriously on Snooky's gangly frame.

"Don't tell me you brought your own clothes," Bernard said.

"No, no, don't be ridiculous. It's presents, Bernard—gifts. Small bits of this and that for Maya. My sister. My pregnant sister."

"Where'd you get the suitcase?"

"I bought it at the airport. Nice, isn't it? I'll leave it here when I go. No point in traveling with luggage, it just means more waiting in line when you get off the plane."

Bernard led the way into the kitchen. "Maya's asleep right now. At least she's lying down. I don't want you disturbing her, Snooky. She hasn't been feeling well for weeks."

"So I gathered on the phone." Snooky flopped down at the big oak table in the middle of the room. He glanced around in satisfaction at the big country kitchen, with gleaming pots hanging from the ceiling, ceramic tiles on the walls and vining plants tumbling in graceful green loops from the shelves. "This kitchen never changes. Nothing ever changes here. You fixed this place up nicely when you moved in, and now nothing is ever different. I love it here."

"I hope you don't love it too much." Bernard stirred the shrimp gloomily. "Maya said she wanted shrimp tonight. I've never made shrimp before. Is an hour too long to cook it?"

"An hour?"

"Too long, isn't it?"

"It depends. Is it the four-foot-long, twenty-pound jumbo shrimp of the Frisian Islands?" Snooky got up and leaned over the stove, to be greeted by a gust of steam from the pot. "No. Well, in that case, an hour is too long. By a factor of twelve."

"I don't trust shrimp. You can get sick from it. I wish Maya wouldn't eat it, but when she wants to eat, I want her to have whatever she wants, as long as it's not obviously poisonous. Do you think it's safe by now?"

"Yes. I think it's safe. It's not edible, but it's certainly safe. What else do you have in the fridge?" Snooky opened the door. "What is this, Bernard? A festival of celery?"

Bernard shrugged.

"Do you have any rice?"

"I think there's some in the cupboard."

Snooky rummaged around. "This is the most pathetic thing I've ever seen. This pantry looks like . . . well, like you've been doing all the shopping for two months. Never mind, I'll find something for dinner. But for now, let's talk, Bernard. We so rarely get a chance to talk, just the two of us. Tell me, how does it feel? How does it feel, knowing you're about to become a father? I know how excited I am about being a new uncle. How do you feel?"

Bernard stared at him in glum silence. This was what he hated most about Snooky's visits—this, and the trail of misfortune and sudden death which always seemed to accompany his appearances. Bernard shared his soul with few people, and his brother-in-law was not one of them.

"I feel pretty," he said at last.

"No, really."

"I feel frightened."

Snooky was interested in this. "Frightened? Is that so? Increased responsibility? The care and feeding of a helpless newborn on your hands?"

"The prospect of you and William coming to stay permanently."

"Well, you don't have to worry about William." Snooky took out a dog-eared package of brown rice and inspected it from all sides. "This should be okay. Anyway, you don't have to worry about him. You'll be lucky if he flies in from the West Coast to inspect the newest member of the family, see if the baby is up to his high standards. Has Maya told him yet?"

"No."

Snooky was gratified. He flashed Bernard a pleased smile. "I was first, then," he said dreamily. "The first one she told. William doesn't even know. That's wonderful."

"She didn't exactly tell you."

"No. I guessed. It's a little gift I have. Psychic, you know. I can foretell the outcome of horse races, too. That's why I don't gamble. It wouldn't be fair."

Bernard was not impressed. "Can you foretell when you'll be terminating this visit?"

Snooky turned back to the cupboard. "The future is hazy, Bernard. Hazy, and unexpected. Certain things are difficult to predict. It depends a lot on my sister. If she's really not feeling well, I may be here for a long time. A very long time."

"Everyone says she should feel better in the second trimester. That's in a few weeks."

"Could you tell me when she wakes up?" Snooky lifted the cover again and peered doubtfully into the pot. "I have a few little things I brought for her. I don't think you have to worry about these shrimp, Bernard, they're definitely dead."

When Maya opened her eyes an hour later, she was confronted by the sight of an enormous brown bear leaning over her, its flat button eyes gazing at her sympathetically. She smiled.

"Thank you, Snooky. I love it."

"Well," said her brother, putting it down on her bed and sprawling beside it, "it's big, at least. It's the biggest one they had."

"I love it. Have you named it yet?"

"No. I left that up to you. I was too busy planning the games I'm going to play with my new niece or nephew. Do you know which it is?"

"No, and if I did, I wouldn't tell you." Maya caressed the soft fur. "How about . . . hmmmm. How about Mabel?"

"Mabel? Maya, this is a boy bear."

"How do you know?"

"Of course I don't know, but—well, aren't they all?"

Maya looked stubborn. A faint crease appeared between her eyebrows. "I want to call her Mabel."

"Mabel it is. And a good name, too. A fine name. Mabel. Yes. I hope the baby likes her."

"I'm sure Mabel will be a big hit."

"How are you feeling, Missy?" Missy was his pet name for her, from his childhood. Maya was five years older and had practically raised him after their parents died. He patted her shoulder and took her hand in both of his own. "You don't look any different."

Maya's gaze softened as she looked at her reprobate younger brother, the black sheep of the family. "I feel different, Snooks. I feel really terrible most of the time. I have my good moments and my bad moments. I'm just so tired that sometimes I feel like crying. I lie on my side and look out the window at the weeping willow on the lawn, and I think things like, 'Someday winter will come and the snow will cover the ground,' stuff like that. My brain doesn't seem to be working. I feel much stupider than I used to."

"Hormones," her brother said sagely. "Hormones. Hormones make you stupid."

"I suppose so." Maya stuffed two pillows behind her and leaned back. "It's just that Bernard and I were so excited about this whole thing, having a baby and everything, and now that it's happened I sometimes wish we had never started. I feel like I'm trudging uphill on a long road leading nowhere. I lie on my bed and I feel like saying, wait a minute, I didn't know it would be like this, but I know the universe doesn't care. Nobody cares. Everybody thinks it's so cute when I feel bad, because I'm not really sick. I'm just pregnant. Just pregnant!" She scowled. "You and Bernard wouldn't last a day, feeling like this."

Snooky looked at her thoughtfully. "You have it bad, Maya."

"Yes."

"You've allowed yourself to become bitter. I blame it on Bernard."

Maya bristled. "Bernard? Why Bernard? He's been terrific, slaving away downstairs for me, doing all the shopping and running the house."

"I blame Bernard. Bernard, as you apparently have not noticed, is not a good slave. He has too independent a spirit. He is not a good cook and, even though he loves you, he has his own work and cannot wait on your every need. What he did to the shrimp tonight, Maya, no poor helpless invertebrate should have suffered."

Maya smiled at her brother. Looking at his face was like looking into a mirror, a younger, male reflection of her own. They had the same thin crooked nose, hazel eyes and pale skin. They had the same golden-brown hair, which Snooky wore brushed back casually and Maya wore sweeping her shoulders in a pageboy. They even shared the same aristocratic bone structure. "And you feel you can correct this situation?" she said.

"I, Maya, am the perfect slave. If this were an eighteenth-century English mansion, I would be the butler. You will do nothing; I will do everything. I am used to that from my previous visits."

"You are a good cook, I'll give you that. Not that I feel like eating anything."

"That will change. I have noticed that most pregnant women, after the first few months, seem to have no trouble eating."

"I suppose so."

"Come on downstairs. I have a few things to give you."

In the living room, a large open area with a high ceiling, exposed wooden beams and a picture window overlooking the willow tree in the backyard, Maya sank into an overstuffed chair while Snooky opened the suitcase. It was filled to overflowing with stuffed toys, rattles and mobiles.

"A stuffed platypus," Snooky said, lifting it up for inspection. "You don't get to see this every day, do you? Pink and blue matching stuffed bears. A dinosaur." The dinosaur was an attractive forest green. "The trendiest kind of mobile. They say these black-and-white designs are good for the baby's ocular system. I think they're a little hallucinogenic, myself." There was also a very charming little rattle shaped like a star, a mobile with stuffed animals that played "Send in the Clowns," a newborn outfit covered with smiling cows, a tiny pair of socks ("the baby will be born in the fall"), three receiving blankets in pale blue, green and yellow, and a jack-in-the-box.

"Very nice," said Maya, when Snooky was finished. "Thank you very much. How in the world did you manage to buy all this stuff today?"

"I rented a car at JFK Airport and stopped off in a baby store on the way up here. I told them I was expecting to become an uncle soon and I wanted the best of everything."

"We don't even have a nursery yet to put this stuff in," Maya said fretfully. She picked up the tiny pair of socks and gazed at it. A cold fear gripped her heart. "I don't think I can handle this, Snooks. All this responsibility. Look at these socks. They frighten me. They frighten me, Snooky."

"Don't worry, Maya, I'm here now. I'll take care of everything. I'm wonderful with babies."

"Since when are you wonderful with babies?"

"Since you decided to have one. Hello, Bernard."

Bernard had wandered into the room, sweating slightly from the heat in the kitchen. It was the middle of March, an unseasonably warm day. He was followed by a small red mop whose tail beat furiously when it spied Snooky.

"Misty!" cried Snooky, picking up the dog and dangling it in front of his face. "It's little Misty! How are you? Ready for a little brother or sister? Give me a kiss, Misty."

The dog licked his face luxuriously.

"I don't see how you can let her do that," said Bernard. He went to the picture window and cranked open one of the glass panels.

"Misty loves me," said Snooky. "I have a way with women. They come under my spell, and all is lost for them."

"Sweetheart," said Maya, "look at what Snooky brought for the baby. It's really too much."

Bernard looked over the pile of pastel animals, clothing and blankets scattered over the floor. "You're right. It really is too much."

"It frightens me, Bernard. It makes the whole thing seem so . . . so *real.*"

"It is real," said Bernard, in his pragmatic way. He stood next to the window, hoping for a breeze. "You can take over in the kitchen now, Snooky. I'm done in there. What's this?"

"It's a jack-in-the-box, Bernard. Didn't you ever have one?"

"Of course I had one," Bernard said irritably. He sat down on the floor and tentatively wound it up. The box played a manic "Here we go round the mulberry bush" several times in succession, then the top sprang open and out popped a little clown in Scaramouche attire, all gaudy tatters and purple velvet scraps. It bobbled there in front of Bernard's face, giving him a poignant lopsided grin.

Bernard, for the first time that day, smiled. It was a slow smile that seeped over his face like sewer water.

"I like this," he said. "It's the first thing you've ever brought us that I've liked, Snooky."

"There's no telling what it is you'll like, Bernard. There's simply no telling. I try my best."

Bernard put his hand on top of the little clown's head, pushed it gently back into the box, and cranked the handle again. Once again the tune played, the top sprang open, the Scaramouche popped out.

Bernard smiled. He pushed the clown back in, closed the top, and happily cranked the handle.

On the fifteenth repetition, Maya motioned to Snooky and the two of them left the room. Behind them they could hear "Here we go round the mulberry bush" played in an uneven, clanging tone, then a clatter as the doll sprang out. Maya could imagine Bernard's smile.

"No waste," said Snooky, clearing the table in the kitchen and getting down to work.

"No waste?"

"Yes. Whatever the baby doesn't like, Bernard will play with."

Dinner, when Snooky finally served it an hour later, consisted of a Creole shrimp and rice dish ("I had this in a tiny little restaurant up in a tree house in the middle of a palm tree grove—good, isn't it?"), a French bread which he had dug out of the freezer and drizzled with garlic, and a large eggplant which he had cooked, split down the middle and sprinkled with herbs. Maya ate one small portion of the shrimp dish, a few bites of the eggplant, and turned slightly green when offered the garlic bread.

"No garlic, thanks, Snooks. I'm not up to it. I have morning sickness all day long if I eat the wrong stuff."

Snooky was penitent. "I didn't think, Maya. I'm so sorry. It won't happen again. Garlic, how stupid of me."

Bernard happily consumed three large helpings of the shrimp casserole, most of the garlic bread and at least two-thirds of the eggplant. He said little. Bernard never did say much, particularly at meals. Snooky passed him what remained of the bread.

"Finish it off, Bernard. Finish what you've begun. God, watch him eat, Maya."

"I don't like to watch anyone eat these days."

"I don't think you have to worry about putting on a lot of excess weight with your pregnancy, Missy. I don't think you'll get the chance. Who's been cooking for you the last couple of months? Not Bernard?"

"Yes, Bernard," said Bernard.

"Pitiful. What's it been, Maya? Canned beans every night?"

"You underrate him, Snooky. You've always underrated him. Bernard can be quite a good cook, when called upon. He's made me some delicious meals."

"Oh, please. What does that mean? Scrambled eggs?"

"I make very good scrambled eggs."

"Anyone can make very good scrambled eggs, Bernard. It doesn't require any talent. What else have you served? TV dinners?"

Bernard bristled. "I wouldn't serve Maya TV dinners. There are a number of things I make that are good. Things I learned how to make when I was living on my own."

"Name one."

"Beef Stroganoff."

Snooky was surprised. "Really? Beef Stroganoff? Is it edible, Maya? Yes? I owe you an apology, Bernard. I didn't realize you had such hidden talents. I've never seen you make beef Stroganoff."

"I've never made it for you," said Bernard pointedly.

"And—correct me if I'm wrong here, Bernard—I bet you never will. Coffee, Maya?"

"No, Snooks."

"Bernard?"

"Yes."

Bernard grunted in satisfaction when Snooky served him coffee and dessert, bananas fried with brown sugar and honey. He settled down to eat, bearlike, a large dark bearded man hunched over the table, humming softly to himself.

Maya picked dispiritedly at her dessert. "I can't do it, Snooks. It looks delicious, but I can't eat it. My appetite isn't what it used to be."

"You never ate much, Missy. Don't worry. I know somebody whose appetite appears to be unaffected by the recent turn of events."

Bernard hummed happily to himself.

Snooky, who also never ate much, pushed his serving and Maya's across the table at his brother-in-law. "No waste," he said, and sat back to drink his coffee, watching Bernard with amusement over the edge of his cup.

After dinner Maya took Snooky upstairs to see the nursery.

"It's not in very good shape yet," she said on the way up the tortuous flight of stairs. "It's the extra bedroom on the second floor."

"The one that always had all the junk in it?"

"That's right. Bernard cleaned it out. Now we're trying to decide what color to paint it."

They passed Bernard's study, Maya's study, and the master bedroom. Maya went to a door at the end of the hallway and flung it open. "Here it is. What do you think? Use your imagination."

Snooky stood in the doorway for a long time, looking around the room. "Well . . . it's clean, at least."

The room was immaculately clean, all the boxes removed, the dust swept away. It was a small room with a slanting ceiling and a pretty view of the fir trees and sloping lawn at the side of the house.

"It's not so bad, is it?"

"The wallpaper will have to go."

"I know that."

The wallpaper, inherited from the previous tenant, was a loud splashy floral design in metallic hues of silver, orange and green.

"I've never understood what people will put on their walls," said Snooky. "I wouldn't wrap a gift in that paper. And what about the floor, Missy?"

The floor was covered with peeling silver-toned linoleum tiles.

"Bernard's going to pry up the tiles and refinish the floor. There's a nice hardwood floor underneath that, if you can believe it. Oak, like the rest of the house."

"And the curtains?"

"Well, of course we're going to replace the curtains," Maya said crossly. The curtains in question were a faded chintz which managed to clash with both the wallpaper and the floor. "You're not being very appreciative, Snooks."

"I'm sorry, My. It's a beautiful room. Look at that view. It's just that it's going to need a lot of work."

"We know that. Bernard's going to do it himself."

"Bernard?"

"That's right."

"Bernard, in his spare time, when he's not waiting on you or writing his books, is going to strip the wallpaper, paint the room, take up the tiles, refinish the hardwood floor, buy fabric and make nice new curtains?"

"That's right."

Snooky crossed his arms. "It's too bad that the human gestational period is only nine months, Missy. You're going to need a lot more time than that before this baby arrives."

---

Snooky moved his stuff, what little of it there was, into the third-floor bedroom under the eaves which was always his when he came to visit. The bedroom was hot in the summer and freezing in the winter, poorly insulated and completely primitive, but it had a beautiful view of the surrounding countryside, a wooden four-poster bed and a dormer window with a comfortable window seat, all of which helped (in Snooky's mind) to make up for the inconvenience. True to his word, he danced attendance on his sister, cooking her meals, making her little snacks to tempt her appetite, doing the shopping for the household and running errands. Maya relaxed gratefully into this pattern. Bernard, as Snooky had pointed out, was, despite the best will in the world, not a good servant; he did not enjoy doing the shopping and was not a gifted cook. After a few days of pro forma protests, Bernard also relaxed into letting Snooky run the household. He steamed off the wallpaper in the nursery—a long and laborious task—and then began to spend more time in his study, wrestling with his latest book, the story of a wayward lobster who gets lost during the annual migration.

"A tragedy, really," said Snooky when he heard the plot line. "A tragic tale. Not unlike Hamlet."

Bernard glanced at him sullenly.

"What made you decide to switch to arthropods?"

"Nothing."

Bernard's books were for children ages three to seven, and were mostly concerned with kindly sheep and dashing, daredevil rats.

"There must have been something," Snooky pointed out reasonably. "Some precipitating cause."

"I read about the lobster migration. It sounded interesting."

"We went out for seafood one night," Maya told her

brother later. "Bernard saw the lobsters in the tank and felt sorry for them."

"He's a good man, Maya. Strange, but good. What's the lobster's name?"

"I don't know if it has a name. Bernard hasn't been able to concentrate on his work, because of the baby and everything. And I haven't been in the best of moods. It affects his work when I'm not feeling well."

"Oh, come on. As far as I can tell, the tides affect Bernard's work. I've never seen him work well. He's always complaining about something or other."

Maya was complacent about this. "That's true. That's the way he is. It's not easy, what he does, you know, Snooks."

"It's easier than working for a living."

"How would you know?"

"I wouldn't. The observer's point of view, that's all. And how about your work, Maya? What are you doing these days?"

Maya looked grumpy. "I'm supposed to be doing an article on Exocoetidae."

"On what?"

"Exocoetidae. Flying fish, you moron. You took science in college, didn't you? You did go to college, right? Didn't William and I pay for that?"

"In more ways than one." Snooky's college career had been less than illustrious. His older brother William, who had graduated summa cum laude, president of the senior class and valedictorian, had watched in disbelief as Snooky edged his way nervously through his college years, doing poorly in some classes and brilliantly in others, a seemingly random pattern of success and failure. He had graduated with no fanfare, no awards, no speeches to give and a set determination never to attend an institution of higher learning again.

Maya smiled. "You were awful. You used to skip classes

and come to visit me instead. William would call your room at school and you were never there. Remember the answering machine you rigged up for him?"

"With the message that said, 'I'm not here, William, I'm out cutting classes and sleeping around'?"

"You are an awful brother to him. You both know exactly how to drive each other over the edge."

"That's a fraternal privilege, Maya. Something you wouldn't know about, would you? We've both spared you over the years."

"Bernard doesn't think I've been spared. He thinks both of you are good for nothing, and I'm caught in the middle."

"Well, maybe he's right. You were born in the middle, and you're sort of stuck there now."

"I guess so."

"So you're doing an article on flying fish? How fascinating."

"It would be if I could finish it. So far I've written, 'The flying fish, family Exocoetidae, live chiefly in tropical waters and possess long pectoral fins which resemble wings.' That's it."

"A short article, but a good article."

"I'm going to lose my job," Maya said fretfully. "Lose my job, lose my health, lose my sanity. Lose my mind."

"I think," said Snooky wisely, "that it's time for some celery."

They went downstairs to the kitchen, which was filled with shifting diamonds of sunlight from the old-fashioned leaded glass windows which lined the walls. Snooky made his sister a cup of herbal tea and gave her a plate of celery stuffed with cream cheese and sprinkled with paprika. "Here you go."

"Before you arrived, Snooks, I used to eat my celery plain."

"Unbelievable. And you, pregnant. This is my point about Bernard not taking care of you properly."

"Poor Bernard." Maya stirred her tea. "I told him to go out to the paint store and choose a color for the nursery on his own. I couldn't handle it, I told him. It's his responsibility."

"It's not exactly what I'd call a crushing one. Since you don't know whether it's a boy or a girl, avoid the obvious. White, for instance, is always good. Yellow. Peach. Violet."

"I think he's been looking in the fuchsia family."

"Has Bernard ever been noted for his color sense?"

Maya shrugged. Snooky, gazing at her, was filled with wonder and pity. There were dark smudges under her eyes, and her fine white skin looked sallow, creased with exhaustion. "For somebody who's creating life, Missy, you look pretty awful."

"I know. What time is it? Ten A.M.? Is it late enough for me to go back to bed yet?"

"It's always late enough to go back to bed, no matter how early it is."

"Thank God."

Bernard came into the kitchen, a gallon of paint clanking against his legs. He looked grim.

"Sweetheart," Maya greeted him. "Any luck at the paint store?"

Bernard hefted the paint can onto the table. "Number four thirty-one," he said. "Otherwise known as Balboa Mist."

"Balboa Mist?"

"A very pale green."

Maya tapped her teacup doubtfully. "Oh, I don't know, Bernard. Pale green? That's not at all what I saw for that room."

Bernard sat down at the table. "Perhaps those of us who saw something could share that knowledge with me *before* I go to the store."

"Pale green? Well, I guess you can try it. Will they take it back?"

"I doubt it very much."

"Well . . ."

"I'm going upstairs to paint the room." Bernard heaved himself to his feet. "If anyone calls for me, I'm busy."

"All right, sweetheart. We'll be up in a little while to see how it's going."

Bernard looked over at his brother-in-law. "I don't suppose you'd like to help me out with the painting?"

"Of course I would, Bernard. I'd be delighted to run the house for you and paint the nursery for you and buy all the baby clothes for you. Can it wait until after my mid-morning nap?"

Bernard took the paint can and left the room. They could hear him treading heavily up the stairs, the paint can clanging by his side.

Maya put her head in her hand. "Balboa Mist. It's going to look awful."

"Don't worry yourself, Missy. It's not your concern. Bernard will take it back to the store if it's no good. Maybe he should just go for primary colors, blue or red. You haven't told me, by the way. Do you want a boy or a girl? Do you have a preference?"

"I do, but I'm ashamed of it, and I'm not telling anybody."

"Why?"

"Well, what if it's a girl, and I've been telling everybody for months that we want a boy, for example? Wouldn't that be awful?"

"I'm not everybody. I'm your dearly beloved younger brother, who's known you all his life. And I know you well enough to guess which kind of baby you want, anyway."

"What's that?"

"You want a girl, don't you?"

Maya gazed at him, bemused. She brushed a lock of golden-brown hair out of her eyes. "Why do you say that?"

"Because you have an older brother and a younger brother, and you're tired of boys. You'd like to have a little girl, Maya, I know you."

"Well, all right, so I'd like a girl. And so would Bernard. But we'd be happy with either. Right now I'd be happy if I could get through the day without feeling so sick. Nobody ever told me morning sickness could last all day long. It doesn't seem fair, does it?"

"Do you want to go upstairs and lie down for a while?"

"No, no, Snooks. You sit there and talk to me. Tell me about your adventures in St. Martin. And make me another cup of that tea."

Snooky was still telling her about St. Martin ("I woke up after a little nap on the beach and this sand lizard was sitting on my chest, staring at me. Gave me the chills") an hour later when they could hear a heavy footstep on the stairs. Bernard came into the room, carrying the can of paint. There was paint on his shirt, his pants, his canvas shoes and his face. He looked at his wife glumly.

"Balboa Mist sucks," he said.

"Well, I told you."

"I'm going back to the store."

"Should I go with you?"

"No. It's my responsibility."

The kitchen screen door slammed behind him, and they could hear the car starting up.

Snooky smiled. "I can see this is going to be hours and hours of entertainment," he said, putting up the pot for coffee.

---

Over the next few days, Bernard painted portions of the room Lambswool, Victoriana, Butter Cream, Gray Wisp and Mexican Tile. After painting a section, he would stand back and gaze at it, his arms folded, for a while. Then he would put the top on the can, carry it out to the car and return it to the store. His expression grew increasingly more glum and his mood more despondent as time went on. Snooky watched all this with enjoyment.

"I think there's going to be a storm," he said to his sister finally, as Bernard drove away with a can of Pistachio Cream on the seat next to him.

"It's getting worse and worse, isn't it?"

"I think his head is going to explode if he goes on like this. And he hasn't managed to pick a decent nursery color yet, if you ask me."

"I know." Maya crunched miserably on her dry, crumbly toast. "I know."

"One of us—I won't say which one, My—one of us remarked days ago that color schemes were not Bernard's strong suit. One of us."

"That wouldn't be you, would it?"

"And now my advice to you is to call in an expert. Somebody who can look at a color on a one-half-inch-square piece of paper and tell what it will look like covering a whole room. A gift which Bernard clearly does not possess."

"True." Maya chewed thoughtfully. Her face lit up. "Oh, Weezy. Of course. I should call Weezy in. She has the most marvelous eye for that kind of thing. I was going to phone her today anyway."

"Now you're thinking, Maya. Weezy would be perfect for this job. Give her my love when you talk to her."

"I will." Maya reached for the kitchen phone and dialed. "Weezy? It's me . . . fine, thanks. Well, not really, but

Snooky is feeding me toast and I'm not feeling too terrible. Do you think you could do me an incredible favor? We have a bit of a problem here . . ."

When Maya hung up the phone, she had a pleased expression on her face.

"You look like a Siamese cat that just ate a bowl of cream," said Snooky. "I assume she said yes?"

"Of course. She'll be over this afternoon."

Weezy Kaplan—her real name, which no one who knew her even casually ever used, was Louise—was one of Maya's few childhood friends who had remained a friend throughout life. She was an artist with a small but growing reputation, and had moved to Ridgewood during the past year to get away from the frantic pace of life in Greenwich Village.

"You can always count on Weezy."

"Yes." Maya sounded relieved. "Thank you, Snooks. It was a good idea. It's been years since you've seen her, hasn't it?"

"Five or six years. Maybe even more. How's she doing?"

"Great. Did you know there was an article on her work in *The New York Times*? About six months ago, in the Arts and Leisure section. All about how she's an up-and-coming young artist. You know the kind of thing."

"Well, that's wonderful. Famous Weezy. She must have been thrilled."

"Oh, she was, she was." Maya tapped thoughtfully on her teacup with one finger.

"What's the matter?"

She looked up, startled. "What?"

"I said, what's the matter?"

"Oh . . ." She laughed. "Nothing, really. It's just that since then . . . well, right around the time the article came out, she started getting these weird phone calls. She picks up, and there's nobody on the other end. It's strange, if you ask me."

"Nobody on the other end? The caller hangs up?"

"I don't know. Nobody ever says anything."

"Maybe her phone line has a glitch or something, Missy."

"That's what she keeps telling me, except that the phone company can't find anything wrong. And it started happening right when that article came out on her. She says it's not related, that I'm making too much of a fuss."

"I see. You know, they say pregnant women can get very paranoid and suspicious. That protective maternal thing, you understand."

Maya leaned her head on her hand. "Is that what they say, Snooks?"

"Yes, it is."

"Pregnant women get a lot of bad PR, if you ask me."

A little while later the door banged and Bernard thumped through the kitchen, a surly look on his face, a paint can clanking against his legs. "I'm going upstairs."

"What is it this time, sweetheart?"

"Milk Shake. Sort of a pale brownish color."

"Sounds good," said Snooky. "And you know, if it doesn't look right on the wall, you can always drink it."

"It won't look good. I know in advance that it won't look good. And yet I feel compelled to try it."

"Personally, I thought Victoriana wasn't bad," said Snooky. "That smoky purple color. Not right for a nursery, of course, but at least not offensive to the eye."

"I really don't care what you think, Snooky. I'll be in the nursery. Hold my calls," Bernard said to Maya.

"You never get any calls, darling," she said mildly, but Bernard was already clunking his way up the stairs.

---

That afternoon a tall red-haired woman dressed in the most outlandish clothes—flowing red chiffon, a lacy scarf, several long necklaces and a pair of lace-up boots—let herself in at the door without knocking. She went straight upstairs to the nursery and stood in the doorway, watching Bernard as he determinedly painted the walls muddy brown. Bernard, absorbed in his task and trying not to cover himself with paint, did not notice her.

"This is the saddest thing I've ever seen," she said at last.

Bernard straightened up slowly. "Hello, Weezy."

"You may not be a visual artist, Bernard, but there's simply no excuse for this. You're painting the nursery dark brown?"

"It's not a dark brown. It's a pale—a very pale brown. It's called Milk Shake."

"Pitiful. No wonder Maya was in such a state on the phone. And with the pregnancy and everything. You should be ashamed of yourself."

"I've tried several other colors."

"So I see." Weezy regarded the walls, streaked with contrasting shades, with a disapproving expression. "Apparently Milk Shake is neither the worst nor the best of what you've tried. It's simply the most recent."

"Yes."

"I hate these food names for paint colors. This one here looks like it ought to have been called Lemon Meringue."

Bernard examined that section of the wall. "Very good. Lemon Twist, if I remember right."

"So pathetically predictable. You need my services, Bernard."

"Maya said you'd offered yourself as an interior decorator."

"And just in time. Just in time, before Maya leaves you and gives birth to the child elsewhere and raises it someplace where its innocent infant eyes will never see this color of paint. Stop putting it on the wall, will you? Put that brush down right now."

Bernard put the brush down. He drew his arm across his forehead, leaving it streaked with paint, and sat down with a dull whumping sound on a three-legged wooden stool which he had been using to get to the hard-to-reach spots. He sighed morosely, from the heart.

Weezy eyed him with a glimmer of sympathy. "It's not easy, choosing the right color."

"No."

"Particularly if you don't have an eye for it."

"No."

"And painting is hard work."

"Yes, it is."

"This could be a beautiful little room. Look at that view. And the way the ceiling slants. I assume that under this incredibly hideous tile, there's a nice oak floor?"

"Yes."

"Well, then, there's no problem. We'll stay away from blue or pink, so terribly boring. This purple shade you were trying here would be amusing if it weren't so tragic, Bernard. I see the walls in . . . hmmm . . . perhaps a light creamy color . . . with overtones of red or gold . . ."

She fell into a reverie, gazing around the room with a dreamy expression on her face. Bernard sat with his head in his hands. There was silence, broken only by the whistle of the wind through the fir trees.

"Look at that chintz," Weezy said at last. "I never will understand people. I never will. You and Maya rescued this house from the hands of a pedestrian soul with no taste."

"Yes."

"I see stiff white curtains, that bleached muslin look, a country look for this room. Thick enough to keep out the light when the infant sleeps. Which way does the window face? Southeast? Oh yes, you'll need thick curtains or the child will be up at dawn, which would not suit your lifestyle at all, sweetie. Which paint store have you been haunting?"

Bernard told her.

"And they let you return all this paint?"

"They let you return anything that's not a specialty color, and I didn't use any specialty colors."

Weezy threw him a look of withering scorn. "Just one of your many errors in judgment, Bernard. Here I always thought you had some visual imagination. Well, I was wrong. Now, you put the top back on Milk Shake or Egg Cream or whatever your last sorry mistake was called, and give it to me. I have some shopping to do."

On the way out the door, Weezy kissed Maya and gave Snooky a sisterly peck on the top of his head as he sat at the kitchen table.

"Hello, handsome boy."

"Hello, sexy lady."

"You're taller than you used to be."

"I'm not six years old anymore."

Weezy patted him on the head. "You'll always be six, Snooky. Inside, you know. Outside, you just get taller."

"You've been upstairs?" Maya said.

"Yes. It's unbelievable."

"You spoke to Bernard?"

"I'm not talking to Bernard. Did you see that lemon-yellow he tried? Is he not in full possession of all his senses?"

"Where is he now, Weezy?"

"I left him upstairs with his head in his hands, mulling over his lack of artistic talent. See you soon."

And she was gone, the screen door banging behind her.

When she returned, less than an hour later, Bernard was standing alone in the kitchen, holding a coffee cup and gazing anxiously out the window. He took the paint can from her and put it on the table.

"What color did you get?"

She gave him another one of her withering looks. "I told you, that's the first mistake you made, Bernard. I didn't get a color with a name. I had the paint store manager whip me up something special. A little bit of this and a little bit of that. And, in case you're wondering, we can't return it, because it doesn't have a name or even a number. But it doesn't matter, sweetie, because it's going to be stunning. Now, go out to my car and get the roll of fabric that's in the backseat. You still have that old sewing machine upstairs? Good. I'm going to need it."

"Fabric? You're going to do the curtains?"

"No. I'm going to lay the beautiful and, may I say, very expensive white muslin I got on the floor and use it as a drop cloth while I'm painting. Any more questions? Now, get the roll out of the car for me, there's a good boy, and bring it upstairs. Get me an old shirt of yours, something nice and roomy—that shouldn't be a problem, should it now?—and then vamoose. I'll do the painting myself."

"No, no, Weezy, you were just supposed to pick out the paint. I'll do the room."

"Thank you. Now do what I say, and then vamoose. I don't let anybody else do my painting for me. It's like coitus interruptus to buy the paint and not put it on the wall myself."

---

Maya was angry about this. She stormed into the nursery. "Weezy, you're crazy. I didn't want you to have to do the painting and make the curtains. I just asked you to pick out the right color for Bernard."

Weezy straightened up, paint dripping from the roller in her hand. Her wild frizzy red-yellow hair was tied back with a lacy scarf, and a child's plastic barrettes, red and yellow and green, held back different tendrils which threatened to escape and curl onto her forehead. She had narrow jewel-green eyes and an intelligent horsey face which was illumined by her smile. She was wearing an old white shirt of Bernard's, vastly big for her, which was rolled up to reveal her pale freckled forearms.

"Don't be silly, sweetie."

"I'm not being silly. I don't want you to do this. Bernard can do the work. He's happy to do it."

"I'm a full-service decorator," Weezy said, rolling the paint smoothly onto the wall with a practiced hand. "Curtains, walls, even furniture, we do it all."

"Weezy!"

"Go away, you're bothering me. Get out of here. You're pregnant, you shouldn't be smelling the paint anyway. Now, what do you think of the color?"

Maya looked around the room, seeing it for the first time. She smiled slowly.

"Oh, Weezy, it's . . . it's perfect. Like a dream."

"It's going to take two coats to cover those dark colors Bernard so obligingly put up here."

The wall Weezy had been working on was a pale creamy color with a suggestion of gold overtones in it. Awash in the afternoon sun, that part of the room glowed like a ripe juicy peach.

"Nice, isn't it? Of course it is. It's perfect for your dream child. Now go away and lie down or whatever you feel like doing. And keep Bernard away from here, I'm still not talking to him."

After a few days, having finished the walls, Weezy relented enough towards Bernard to order him to strip the linoleum off the floor.

"I don't do that kind of work," she announced.

"I'm happy to do it."

"I don't see why. It's boring and difficult."

"Why should it be different from the rest of my life?"

Weezy gazed at him in astonishment. "How can you say that? With your firstborn on the way?"

"Maya says it doesn't seem real."

"That's because she's not showing yet. She's always been sticks and bones, that girl, ever since she was little. Wait till she gets nice and round, and the baby starts to move. Then she'll believe it."

Bernard perked up at this, and went away to change into his work clothes.

For the next two days they worked happily side by side, Weezy in the hallway cutting fabric and sewing on the old Singer machine that had been stored away in the attic, and Bernard on his hands and knees ripping up the floor. When the tiles were gone, he laboriously sanded, stained and finally oiled and waxed the oak planks that were revealed underneath. When he was finished, the floor glowed a honey-gold that complemented the walls perfectly.

Weezy was approving. "Very nice. Excellent work, sweetie. Now take a breather, and we'll hang up the curtains. Look at these beautiful golden rods I picked up for a song at the thrift store. Take down those old curtains and rods, I can't bear to look at them one more second."

They hung the stiff white curtains which Weezy had made, and Bernard swept up the room. Afterwards they stood together in the doorway for a long time.

Bernard put his arm around Weezy and kissed the top of her head, an unaccustomed display of affection for him. "It's beautiful."

"Of course it is." Weezy's eyes were aglow. "It's divine. Almost good enough for your and Maya's baby."

"Let's go get her."

"Let's."

Maya and Snooky were dumbstruck when shown the results of their work. Maya became quite weepy over it.

"It's . . . it's so beautiful!"

"Hormones," said Snooky, patting her shoulder. "Calm yourself."

"It's just the way I dreamed it would be," said Maya, sniveling into a tissue.

"Remain calm. It's a room, Missy. It's not the Sistine Chapel."

"It's not a room. It's . . . it's my baby's nursery!"

Eventually she had to be led away protectively by Bernard.

"Perhaps you did too good a job," said Snooky, lounging in the doorway.

"She's pregnant. She's allowed to cry as much as she wants."

Snooky looked around in appreciation. "It *is* perfect."

"I know."

The muslin curtains swayed in a breeze which carried in the sweet smell of the pines. Snooky took Weezy's hand.

"Perfect," he said, kissing it.

---

Downstairs in the kitchen Snooky made a cup of brown rice tea and handed it to Weezy on a saucer with a shortbread cookie. Weezy gazed into the murky depths doubtfully.

"What is this shit?"

"Genmai-cha. Brown rice tea. Japanese. I thought artists liked that kind of stuff."

"Don't you have any real coffee?"

While he made a pot of coffee, Weezy sat back in her chair and looked around the kitchen with satisfaction on her face. "Beautiful room. Look at the dimensions. It looks like the golden proportion, honestly."

"I have no idea what you're talking about."

"The golden proportion, sweetie. The dimensions that look best to the eye. Didn't Maya send you to college?"

"Nobody seems to be sure. She asked me that herself the other day."

"You went in body, not in soul." Weezy chuckled softly to herself. "I mean that with all possible double entendres. I'm sure the women on campus will attest to it."

"Mind like a sewer. That's why you've always been my favorite among Maya's friends."

"We're two old reprobates, you and me."

"It's too bad you don't go for younger men."

"Younger men, perhaps," Weezy said, twirling a strand of red hair thoughtfully around her finger. "Children, no. Boys I've known since they were in diapers, no."

"A shame."

"You have to draw the line somewhere," she said, with what seemed like real regret. She accepted a cup of coffee gratefully and inhaled its aroma with a snort of delight. "Delicious. Nothing like real coffee. I assume this isn't the wimpy decaf variety?"

"No. Bernard drinks real coffee."

"Bernard is a real man." She drank deeply from the cup. "How Maya managed to unearth him when Bernard never meets or talks to anybody, I'll never understand. So how have you been, Arthur?"

"I insist—I must insist that you not use my real name, Louise. So few people know it, and I don't want the news to get around. I've been fine. I flew in from the islands when I heard about Maya's pregnancy."

"Don't be coy with me, Arthur. Don't try to impress me. I knew you when your only language was "dah dah" and you spat up three times a day."

"Still do."

"I'm sure. What's this feeble attempt to impress me with a reference to the islands? Which island? Or were you simultaneously on all of them?"

"I was on St. Martin. We also took a trip to a volcanic island called Saba."

"Which side were you on?"

"Which side of what?"

"Of St. Martin, you moron. The French or the Dutch?"

"Oh. The French side. I was staying with some friends there."

"I was on St. Martin years and years ago," Weezy said dreamily. "Lovely place. The St. Tropez Hotel. That little fresh-air market in Marigot. Conch stew under the stars."

"I was telling Maya about conch stew."

"I ate it every night. I couldn't get enough of it. Of course, I was young then." Weezy sighed and crunched into her shortbread wafer. "I'm sure now it would constipate me."

"You're hardly old." Both Maya and Weezy were in their early thirties.

"Old enough," Weezy said gloomily. "Old enough. Old enough to have avoided all the good relationships, and to have to eventually settle for something lousy or for nothing at all."

"Is that how it is?"

Weezy breathed heavily into her coffee cup. The steam rose luxuriantly around her face, dewing her forehead and frizzing her hair even more. "There's nobody, Snooky. There are no decent men."

"I'm a decent man."

"God, you're self-centered. What is this? Are we discussing you or me?"

"One day, Weezy, you're going to come to your senses. You'll turn around, and there I'll be, waiting for you."

"What a horrific thought," she said. "Promise?"

"I promise."

"No, you won't. You'll be married, just like they all are when they reach my age. You'll marry some little chickie."

"I hesitate to correct you, Weezy, but I'm never going to reach your age. I'm always going to be younger than you."

"Don't try to cheer me up. You'll marry some little chickadoo and go off to live somewhere exotic, like northern New Jersey."

"Why northern New Jersey?"

"Her family will come from there."

"A grim prospect," said Snooky. "Let me just clear up one point. Am I fated to marry a little chickie or a little chickadoo?"

Weezy exhaled into her coffee. "They all do. They all go off and marry some younger woman. You give them the best years of your life, and then they leave you and end up with somebody else."

"Who is this guy?"

"Oh, nobody." Weezy pushed her cup away. "Nobody. A man. One of the great race of men. As childish and self-centered and piggish as all the rest."

"What was his name?"

"Harold."

"Well, you should have known better, then."

"What's wrong with the name Harold?"

"Nothing, if you're an early Anglo-Saxon king. Otherwise, come on."

"True," said Weezy. This seemed to cheer her up. "True. Perhaps you're right. I should have known."

"Harold left you for a chickie?"

"Yes. Yes, he did." Weezy looked despondent. "It's too painful, Snooky. Too fresh. I can't talk about it."

"Try."

"Okay." The chair squeaked as she sat back in it. She took off one of her scarves, a filmy beige chiffon, and looped it around her head several times. "He was a doctor."

"Oh, God."

"I met him in the hospital."

"Why were you in the hospital?"

"Visiting a friend who had just given birth to the most adorable little girl you ever saw. Peaches and cream complexion, not at all like the scrawny red apelike things you usually see in photos. An angelic infant. Lay in her mother's arms and looked around peacefully while we visited."

"Sounds drugged."

"Oh, no, no, sweetie, you don't know my friend. No drugs. Nothing like that. Nothing at all, not even Demerol. Forty-two hours of natural labor."

"How did your friend look?"

"Radiant."

"I'm quite sure that's not true."

"All right. Terrible. But the infant was gorgeous. Wasn't I supposed to be telling you about Harold?"

"Go on."

"Harold was her baby's pediatrician. Wouldn't you think that would make him a nice person? A baby doctor."

"I don't know about that."

"He came in to check out Alissa while I was there. I don't know why all newborn girls seem to be named Alissa or Elissa or Elyssa, you know, with a *y*, these days," Weezy said fretfully. "It seems ridiculous."

"They should all be named Louise."

"Yes, and the boys should all be named Arthur. Anyway, he came in and looked the baby over, and talked to my friend, and somehow we got to talking, and after the visit was over he walked me to my car and asked me out. That was the beginning of the end."

"What did Harold look like?"

"A tall, dashing person. The kind I like. Dark hair, handsome features, a wonderful nose."

"A wonderful nose?"

"Roman. I itched to draw it. Dark eyes, fair skin. Wonderfully good-looking. After years of dating trolls, it was such a relief to be able to go out in public again."

"Trolls?"

"Oh, yes. Trolls."

"And then?"

"We went out for over a year. Such a sad end to a beautiful time together. Of course, we never did get along. We fought like cats and dogs. He was just divorced, and I think he was still a bit in love with his ex-wife. I was the rebound person, you know, the one they use up and throw away, like Kleenex. Eventually, of course—and how could I not have seen it coming, I ask myself—he met somebody else and left me for her. She was better for him, he said. Much more compatible. Well, as I told him, the Monster of the Black Lagoon would have been more compatible with him than I was. I mean, we fought constantly. But I was heartbroken. I'm still not over it. I may never get over it."

"A year is not exactly wasting your youth, Weeze."

"It's wasting a year of it."

"Is this Harold why you moved out of Manhattan?"

"I don't think so. Not entirely. I had had it with the city. So noisy, so dirty. People everywhere, the traffic, the car horns, the filth. It got unbearable, especially after Harold left."

"Are there any eligible men in Ridgewood?"

"I told you, sweetie. There are no more eligible men anywhere. It's a lost breed, a lost breed. The rest are all trolls. Deformed creatures from the bowels of the earth."

"As a man, speaking for my kind, I must object."

"It's true, I'm telling you. I've given up hope. I'll always be the bridesmaid, never the bride. Maya got the last good man."

"Now I really must object."

"It's so depressing, Snooky. I'm going to have to turn inward and get into meditation and find inward peace, all that shit." Weezy brooded over this. "I'll be one of those old ladies in Zen centers with gray hair sticking out of their ears, chanting and swaying. You know what I'm saying."

"Nothing wrong with Zen centers. I lived in one for a while."

"There are no good men left."

"I sense a theme to this conversation. How's your work?"

"Well, I have to say at least that's going well. I'm doing a show in the city a couple of months from now. It's quiet here, it's good for my work. I can hear the birds singing in the morning. I can go out on my deck at night and look at the moon. I've been painting like mad, except, of course, when I'm working on the nursery."

"Maya tells me you've become famous."

Weezy smiled smugly. "The article?"

"Yes."

"Well, it was fun, I won't deny that. My two seconds of fame. And it didn't hurt my career one bit. Frankly, I think this show in New York came out of it. The gallery owner said he had seen the article in the *Times*."

"Maya also told me that you've been getting some strange phone calls. There are a lot of nuts out there, you know. She says she's a little worried about you."

"Can I tell you a secret?"

"Of course."

"Maya is my best friend in the whole wide world. But just between the two of us, she worries too much. I pick up the phone and there's nobody on the other end, is that something to get flustered about? When I lived in Manhattan I risked my life just walking out on the street."

"How often has it happened?"

"I don't know. Four or five times, maybe."

"Does the line sound dead, or is somebody there but not saying anything?"

Weezy chewed her lip. "Well, I must admit it sounds like somebody's there. I say 'hello' a couple of times, and then I hang up. I figure if it's important and I couldn't hear them, they'll call back."

"But they never have."

"No. Is that really a cause for alarm? Maybe there's a faulty wire in the line or something."

"That's what I told Maya."

"There, you see. Great minds." Weezy glanced at her watch. "Oh, my God, I have to get going. I'm teaching these days, you know. I have a class of art students starting in half an hour."

"That's nice. You taught in Manhattan, too, didn't you?"

"Oh, yes. This class is culled from my best students in New York, so it's fun. Well, at least it's supposed to be. That's the theory behind it, that it's a wonderfully rewarding experience for all concerned. That's what we're all pretending is happening." She grimaced slightly.

"It's not wonderfully rewarding?"

"Well, they're artists, you know, Snooky. Artists. Touchy, flighty, unpredictable. Difficult to work with. The truth is, I discovered long ago that I hate all artists except for myself."

"So do I."

"Thank you. We artists are the lowest form of life on earth."

"That would make male artists the lowest of the low, I suppose."

"Oh, I don't know about that. I have one in my class who's a doll. A living doll. Difficult as hell, of course, but still a doll. Maybe you'll meet him, now that you're in town for a while. How long are you planning to stick around for, anyway?"

"As long as possible. Maya needs me. Bernard seems to have no idea at all what he's doing, taking care of her."

"Mysterious how they function so well in your absence, isn't it?" asked Weezy kindly.

"I don't understand how anyone functions at all in my absence."

"We limp by, Snooky. We limp by."

"Will you invite me over sometime to sit on your deck and drink your liquor?"

"Maybe. It's possible."

"I like gazing at the moon, too, you know. I'm a moongazer at heart. We have so much in common, Weezy. I really think you should reconsider what I've said."

Weezy patted him on the cheek. "Spend your time looking for your little chickadoo. And tell Maya I'll give her a call later. Tell her I hope she feels better."

Then she was gone, in a blaze of red chiffon.

# TWO

"WHEN YOU said you were going to sit on my deck and drink my liquor, I didn't fully realize how often you were going to sit here or how much you were going to drink," Weezy said.

"Surely a few glasses of wine isn't too much to ask?"

"Not of this wine, Snooky. It's Chassagne-Montrachet. Thirty-five dollars a bottle."

"I thought it was awfully good."

"You shouldn't have served it to him," said Maya. "He can drink like a fish and never show it."

"Drunk on life," said Snooky. "Drunk on life. Can I have one more glass of that indescribably delicious wine before you take it away?"

Weezy relented. "Well . . . because it's you."

They were sitting on Weezy's deck after dinner. The moon was in full view, hanging like a solemn eye in the night sky above them. It was early spring, and there was a chill breeze. Maya sat wrapped in several warm sweaters and scarves, a round bundle in her Adirondack chair. Snooky wore a blue scarf knotted loosely around his neck. Bernard, who never felt the cold, was in his shirt sleeves. He was sitting immobile, his head lolling back.

"I hate to say this, but I think your husband is asleep," said Weezy.

"He is asleep."

"He passed out as soon as he sat down," observed Snooky.

"I'm not surprised," said Weezy. "Did you see what he ate for dessert?"

"Did you see what he ate before that?"

"Cooking for him is like cooking for a large hotel full of people," said Weezy. "Which I did once, in my renegade past."

"Is that so?"

"Yes. I was twenty-one and didn't know any better. I thought I could handle it. I was wrong."

"What happened?"

"My sous-chef and I ended up sending out to various restaurants in town for the meals people requested. The hotel manager, when he heard of this, was not delighted. Still, have you ever tried cooking for a hundred and fifty people at once? I was beside myself."

"Well, you can certainly cook for four people. Four and a half, counting the baby," said Snooky.

"Four and two-ninths," said Maya.

Weezy had served them a whole fish split and baked with garlic, wine and herbs. She had thrown together a gigantic salad in an old wooden bowl, and dressed it with olive oil, lemon juice and more fresh herbs. There was a ceramic bowl ("I made it myself, in my pottery stage") filled with small red potatoes covered with melted butter and dill, and for dessert, a creamy cheesecake with a graham cookie crust. "I think I'm going to die of happiness," Snooky said when Weezy served the cheesecake.

"You are some cook," he said now, swirling the wine in his glass.

"Thank you so much."

"A cook and an artist. As I've said before, the perfect woman."

Weezy looked at him wryly. "Tell Harold that."

"Harold is obviously a fool."

"Men are all fools, Snooky."

"Not Bernard," said Maya.

Weezy glanced over to where Bernard slumbered happily on his lounge chair. "No. Not Bernard. Bernard is a teddy bear. I envy you so much for finding him, Maya."

"It wasn't easy. I looked a long time too."

"Not as long as me."

"It'll happen for you."

"I doubt it." Weezy looked up at the sky. "Still, I shouldn't brood. It's so boring for everybody. Look at that moon, how perfect it is. It looks like it's smiling tonight."

"How do you arrange not to have any insects?" asked Snooky.

"It's March, sweetie. The mosquitoes aren't out yet."

"Oh."

The sweet strains of a Mendelssohn symphony filtered out from the house. Weezy, upon arriving in Ridgewood, had gone straight to a real estate office, plunked herself down in front of a desk and said to the agent, "I want a house with light—plenty of light. That's my only requirement. Oh, and high ceilings. Someplace where I can paint and grow my plants."

Weezy's plants consisted of approximately a hundred and thirty different specimens, creepers, hangers, blooming and non-blooming, annual and perennial, fuchsias and orchids, purple passion and spider plants, dracaenas and begonias, a profusion of greenery which had filled her Manhattan apartment. She cherished them like children. On moving day, the one time she had lost her temper was when her monstera plant had been dropped, several of the large leaves bruised and the pot broken.

"No!" she had sobbed to Maya. "No! Not the monstera!"

The realtor, as directed, had looked through her lists and shown Weezy only two houses. The first was too far out of town for her taste; she wanted to live close by and be able to walk to the stores. The second one she bought as soon as she laid eyes upon it. It was a sprawling ranch house with a greenhouse addition and a large wooden deck. She moved her plants into the greenhouse, where they settled down happily, basking in the unaccustomed light, and converted one of the bedrooms into a studio. She filled the house with an eclectic mixture of new and antique furniture, some of it outrageously expensive and some found broken on the street, and covered the walls with art—her own work and that of others. She had been there for almost a year and had yet to tire of it.

"Weezy found a wonderful house," said Maya now, huddled in the depths of the chair.

"I was lucky about that. Are you cold, sweetie? Think of the child."

"I'm fine. It's beautiful out here."

"Once Snooky is finished draining my wine cabinet dry, and Bernard wakes up from his little nap, would you like to see my newest show? It's all new work, I don't think you've seen it yet."

"Love to." Maya smiled comfortably at her friend. Weezy's paintings were like her, flashes of temperament bathed in light. They were mostly abstracts which teased the eye with movement and bold color. Occasionally she painted from life, such as a seashore scene which had caught her interest, catching the waves about to spill with froth and the children at play in the sand. Since she had moved to Ridgewood, she had been trying her hand at still lifes of fruit and vegetables in a bowl or suspended in space.

"I'm finished now," said Snooky, putting down his glass.

"Are you sure? I don't want to hurry you."

"Delicious meal, Weezy. Soup to nuts."

"Have you gotten in enough moon-gazing for this evening?"

Snooky tilted back his head to see the moon, winking at him as gray clouds moved across its face. "I think so. I feel satisfied."

"Should we wake up Bernard?"

"No," said Maya. "Let him sleep. He could use the rest."

"Come with me, then."

They followed her through the house into the studio, a large room with a slanted ceiling in which she had installed two skylights. The room was scrupulously neat; the one time Weezy was compulsive about cleanliness was in her work. Her paints were stored in cabinets and canvases were stacked tidily against the walls. Weezy turned on the track lighting overhead and switched on a few lamps around the room.

"Here we go," she said, taking out the canvases and displaying them. "What do you think, Maya? Different, isn't it?"

Maya studied them in silence. The paintings were abstract, glowing with soft shades of pink, blue and violet. Small ink-drawn shapes danced in and out of the edges of the canvas.

"You must be getting over Harold," Maya said at last. "These are spectacular, Weezy. So much softer than before."

Weezy nodded, studying her work. "I suppose so. I must be feeling a little bit better. Everything I painted after Harold left me was red," she explained to Snooky. "Bright red. Red on red. Purple on red. The color of inchoate rage."

"I hear you. What's this one, Weeze?"

"What does it look like to you?"

"It looks like . . ." Snooky paused. "Like a fish having sex with an antelope."

"Thank you. Thank you very much. It's called 'Harmony III.' "

"How about this one? This looks like a fish having sex with a bear."

"Interesting." Weezy chewed her lower lip and studied the painting. "Interesting. Yes, possibly."

"And this one over here is Queen Catherine of Russia having sex with a horse?"

"Fascinating. Fascinating. Sad, of course, but fascinating. Have you ever done any Rorschach work?"

"Not really."

"I don't want to disappoint you, Snooks, but none of these paintings have anything to do with sex."

"Hard to believe."

"I mean, you can interpret them any way you want, particularly if you pay me large sums of money, but sex was not on my mind while I was creating them."

"I see."

"Sex is always on Snooky's mind," said Maya. "He thinks of nothing else."

"That's not true. Occasionally I also think about wine."

"Wine, women and song," said Weezy. "That's what a boy your age should be thinking about. You're right on schedule, Snooky."

"Weezy understands me. She understands me in a way you never have, Missy. Why couldn't she have been my sister instead?"

"A tragic accident of fate," said Maya. "Weezy, I love these new paintings. They're gorgeous. A whole different side of you, much softer and happier. You must be feeling better, and I'm glad to see it. Now please excuse me. I have to go outside and throw up."

Bernard was sitting in his lounge chair, his head bent back at an awkward angle, mouth open, snoring happily, when the phone rang. Weezy had rigged up the phone line so that it rang loudly in the greenhouse, next to the deck, and nowhere else in the house. This allowed her to work undisturbed in the studio. "Nothing worse than hearing the phone while you're working," she had told Bernard once. "Even if you don't answer it, you have to wonder who it was."

Bernard himself dealt with this problem by never answering his phone at all, at any time of day, whether he was working or not. He had never once wondered who it was. However, after the fourth ring he reluctantly opened his eyes and heaved himself out of his chair. Some vestigial impulse told him that Maya would want him to answer Weezy's phone.

He went through the greenhouse into the living room and picked up the receiver. "Hello?"

There was silence on the other end: a living, breathing silence. It was not the sound of a disconnected line. Bernard had the distinct feeling that someone was there.

He did not say "hello" again. Neither did he hang up. Instead, he stood with the phone to his ear and waited.

The person on the other end was silent. Bernard smiled grimly. Maya had told him about the strange goings-on with Weezy's phone. He figured that this time the caller was in for a little surprise. Unlike most other people, Bernard loved silence. He could wait for hours like this if necessary.

Finally, after several long minutes had crawled past, he could hear a faint hiss on the other end. It did not even sound human. It sounded alien and malevolent. Bernard felt a slight chill. There was a gentle *click* as the caller hung up.

Bernard put the receiver down. He stood for a moment, thinking. Then he picked it up and rapidly dialed *69.

There was a pause and a click. A recorded female voice came on.

*"This service cannot be activated because the telephone number is not in our service area."*

Bernard slowly put the receiver down. He was standing there, his mind far away, when Maya and the others came into the room.

"Sweetheart," said Maya. "I got queasy all of a sudden. It's not a comment on Weezy's paintings, they're marvelous. What's the matter?"

"What do you mean?"

"You're staring at the phone as if you've never seen one before."

Bernard fidgeted uncomfortably. "I'm sorry, Weezy. You got one of those calls just now."

"Oh, shit," said Weezy. "And you picked up?"

"Yes."

Maya stared at him. "But, sweetheart, you *never* answer the phone."

"I thought you'd want me to. I know you can't hear it in the studio."

"What happened?" asked Snooky eagerly.

"I said hello. Whoever it was didn't say anything. So I didn't say anything either."

"You hung up?" said Weezy.

"No."

"You didn't hang up?"

"No. I waited."

"You waited. How very interesting and strange of you," said Weezy. "What happened?"

"Nothing. Silence. Then, after a couple of minutes, the person hissed."

"Hissed?" echoed Maya.

"Hissed. A low kind of hiss. I think whoever it was was frustrated," Bernard said. "I think they were surprised."

"Hissed," said Snooky. "That's creepy."

"Was it a male or a female hiss?" asked Maya.

"I couldn't tell. Then, when they hung up, I tried to call them back."

"Pardon me?" said Weezy.

Bernard pointed to her phone. "I dialed star sixty-nine. You know. It calls back the last person who called you."

"How amazing. My phone will do that?"

"You've never done it?"

"Never done it? I've never even heard of it. Am I paying for it? Does it work?"

"Oh, it works all right. But the caller is outside our area code, so I got a recording. That's reassuring, actually, we know it's not someone next door. Are you sure that nobody's ever said anything to you before? No sound at all?"

"No, no. Not even breathing." She shook her head. "Of course, they never had the opportunity. I've never stayed on the line for more than a few seconds."

"So it isn't a glitch in your phone line," Snooky said. "I don't like this. I don't like this at all."

"Any idea who it could be?" asked Bernard.

"No. None. Probably just a prankster who got hold of my number somehow."

Maya sat down on the sofa. She looked faintly green. "I feel funny again."

"All this talk about phone calls and hissing is upsetting you," Weezy said, throwing an accusing glance at the two men. "Hissing, indeed! It was probably just static. I've never heard of such a thing."

"Can I get you something?" Bernard asked his wife.

"I'd like . . . I'd like a carrot. Yes. A nice carrot, and a glass of seltzer. Do you have seltzer, Weezy?"

"Of course. Give me a second." She vanished into the kitchen.

"I just want to go on record as saying that it's not the phone call," Maya said. "I mean, I'm upset about the phone call, but that's not why I'm feeling this way. I ate too much at dinner, I suppose."

"Punished for eating too much," her brother said sympathetically. He sat down next to her and patted her hand.

Weezy came back into the room. "One very nice carrot. And a glass of seltzer with ice."

"Thank you."

"How many of these calls have you gotten, Weezy?" asked Bernard.

She wrinkled her forehead. "Snooky asked me that the other day. I don't know. Four or five. Maybe five."

"When did they start?"

"I'm not sure, really. Six months ago. About that. Yes, last fall sometime. After that article came out. A couple of months after I moved here."

"You never got any when you lived in New York?"

She shook her head. "No."

"Any reason somebody might not have liked it when you moved away?"

Weezy stared at him in surprise. "No. None that I can think of. I mean, my students have to travel farther, but they don't seem to care."

"Are you sure?" asked Snooky.

She tapped one foot impatiently. "Yes, Snooky, I'm sure. My students are not the shy type—at least most of them aren't. If something was bothering them, they wouldn't be calling me up mysteriously on the phone. They'd tell me all about it in front of the whole class. That's usually how they share their innermost thoughts and feelings, I assure you."

"Anybody with any grudges against you?" asked Bernard.

"No, Bernard. Nobody has any grudges against me. I am, as you may have noticed, an extremely nice person. Nobody dislikes me. Everybody likes me. I go out of my way to make other people happy. Now, can we discuss something else, or am I going to be grilled on this all night? How's that carrot, Maya?"

"Fine. I feel better, thanks."

"Is your phone number listed?" asked Bernard.

Weezy nodded.

"Perhaps you should consider getting an unlisted number."

"Thank you, Bernard. That way nobody could get in touch with me—including gallery owners who want to show my work, or clients who want to commission a painting, or students who want to take my class. It wouldn't exactly be a boost to my career if nobody knew how to find me, would it? And now, enough about all this. If the phone rings again, don't answer it. I'll put the machine on. I have to put the machine on, otherwise my mother calls and thinks I'm dead. All right, now we can all rest easy. Would anyone like some more coffee or tea?"

"Weezy's worried," Maya told her husband later that night, as they got ready for bed.

"I know."

"I'm worried, too."

"I know you are."

"Are you worried?"

Bernard was brushing his teeth. "Yadonnowattoyink," he said indistinctly.

"Pardon me?"

Bernard spat into the sink. "I don't know what to think."

"It's strange, though, isn't it?"

"It could be nothing. It could be somebody who's playing around with phone numbers and likes the look of Weezy's."

"But you don't think it is, do you?"

Bernard stared into the bathroom mirror. His reflection stared back at him with tired eyes. "No," he said. "No, I don't."

Snooky knocked at Weezy's front door a few days later, then let himself in. Nobody in Ridgewood—nobody except Bernard, that is, and then only occasionally—ever locked their doors. He was carrying a small package under his arm. He walked, whistling, down the hallway toward the studio.

"Weezy? It's me."

The studio door opened and he was confronted by a stranger: a heavyset young woman with a round moon face and brown hair which hung in strings down to her shoulders. She looked at him in surprise. "Yes?"

"I'm Snooky Randolph. A friend of Weezy's. Is she around?"

"Oh . . . oh, yes. She's in the garden."

"Are you one of her students?"

She smiled shyly. "Yes. My name's Nikki. Nikki Cooper."

"Hi."

"Hi."

There was an awkward silence. She looked at him anxiously, as if begging him to say something.

"Do you come from around here?" asked Snooky at last.

"No . . . no. I live in New York City. I come up here for the classes, and sometimes in between to work with her on my own."

"I heard that she was giving classes. What kind of a teacher is she?"

The girl looked slightly scandalized. "Oh, she's wonderful," she began, when Weezy swept in, freshly cut daffodils filling her arms, her hair bright with sticks of grass and weeds.

"Gossiping about me, are you?" she said cheerfully.

"Oh, no—"

"Yes," said Snooky. "I was just asking what kind of teacher you are."

"I am a brilliant teacher," said Weezy. "Absolutely brilliant. My students are devoted to me. Aren't you all, Nikki?"

"Oh, yes, of course we are, Weezy," the girl said.

"Will one of you please find me a vase, so I can put these flowers down?"

Nikki vanished into the studio and came out with a widemouthed green glass jar. "Is this okay?"

"Perfect." Weezy began to arrange the flowers. "Gorgeous, aren't they? The first of the crop. King Alfred, large yellow trumpet. That's how they were described in the bulb catalogue I ordered them from last fall. And look, here they are, blooming out back. A host of yellow daffodils. What is that you're holding there, Snooky? It looks suspiciously like a present."

"You've guessed it. A gift from my sister."

Weezy was delighted. She took the package and began to tear at the paper. "A gift? How wonderful. But why?"

"She said it's to thank you for the baby's nursery."

"Oh, that's silly. But how wonderful of her. What is it? I love gifts, I can't wait. It's . . . it's . . ." She lifted a pair of ceramic candlesticks from the pink tissue paper. They were an antique Italian design, with red and blue flowers. She was ecstatic. "I love them. You must tell her how perfect they are. Maya knows my taste. She knows I have a thing for candlesticks. I can't get enough of them. I must have ten different pairs. Let me see now. How will these look here? . . . hmmmm . . . I can't wait to see how they look with candles in them. But right now, Nikki, back to work. How are you getting along with that drawing? All right? Good. I'll be back in the studio in a minute. As for you, Snooky, thank you so much. Now please get out of my house. I can't concentrate on work when there's visitors around. Give your sister a kiss for me. How's she feeling?"

"About the same."

"I'm sorry to hear it. Give her a kiss. Now shoo."

"Any more strange phone calls, Weezy?"

"No, thank God. Don't the three of you have anything better to think about? Tell Maya to stop fussing over me, it's ridiculous. Now shoo, I'll talk to you later."

"Okay."

On his way to the front door, Snooky nearly bumped into a young woman who was hurrying down the hall with a leather portfolio in her hand. She pulled back and drew herself up regally. She was almost as tall as he was, which put her at close to six feet. She had silky black hair which fell to her waist, and a proud face with strong features. Her dark eyes regarded him with distaste, as if he were some kind of strange insect which she had found devouring her rose bushes. "Who are *you?*"

Snooky felt vaguely miffed by her tone. "Who are you?" he responded.

"You're not a new student, are you?"

"No."

"Then who are you?"

"Don't you recognize me from TV?"

The contempt in her eyes slowly increased as she stared at him. "No," she said. "Should I?"

"No, I'm afraid not."

"This is pathetic," said Weezy, standing in the door of the studio with her arms crossed. "Pathetic. Two young people, supposedly adults, unable to manage the most basic introduction. Jennifer, may I present my friend Snooky Randolph. Snooky, this is a student of mine, Jennifer Zalinsky. You're late, Jennifer. Nikki's been here for half an hour already."

The young woman brushed past Snooky, her long dark hair flying. "I know, I know. I'm sorry. I read the train schedule wrong, and then I had to wait forever for a cab at the station. I'm sorry, Weezy, because there's all this stuff I have to discuss with you . . ."

The studio door closed behind them.

"Yes, I knew Weezy had some students," Maya said. "What about it? So one of them's six feet tall? So what? Were you threatened by that? Is she attractive?"

"Uh-huh. Like some kind of exotic model," said Snooky.

"I see." Maya chewed thoughtfully on a piece of frozen pita bread. "Do you absolutely have to get involved with various trashy women every time you visit us?"

"Oh, I wouldn't worry, she's not my type at all. And I'm willing to bet I'm not hers. She looked at me as if I were a rare mold. Maya, that bread isn't defrosted yet. Get a grip on yourself. I'll be serving it at dinner."

"I thought you were devoted to Weezy. I thought you promised her your life."

"I am devoted to Weezy, but it's an unrequited love. A twelfth-century Eleanor of Aquitaine and her chevalier kind of romance."

Maya pried off another hunk of frozen bread and inserted it into her mouth. "I wasn't aware of Eleanor of Aquitaine ever having an unrequited love. I thought she was married twice."

"Think of all those years shut up in the tower. What's the matter with you, Missy? Didn't you go to college?"

Maya rested her head on her hands. "I can't keep up this smart repartee anymore, Snooky. I feel too sick. My life is at an end. All I'm good for is sitting here eating this rock-hard piece of pita bread."

"Your life is just beginning, Missy."

"My whole consciousness is focused on my stomach." She took a piece of bread, swallowed and gagged slightly.

"So? Now you and Bernard have something in common."

"I'm tired of hearing you imply that Bernard lives for food. Bernard does not have a weight problem. He burns it off."

"That's right." Snooky expertly sliced an onion. He ladled some soup out of a steaming tureen, blew on it and tasted it. "He burns it off sitting in his study thinking about lobsters."

"It's true," Maya said miserably, "I don't think his work is going very well."

"His work never goes well, but he always gets it done on time. I wouldn't worry. You have other things to think about these days."

"He can't come up with a name for the lobster. You can't write a book about a character with no name."

Snooky lifted a lid and examined the contents of the pot. "Are you positive you're up for curry tonight?"

"As long as it's not greasy. I can eat spicy foods, I just can't stand anything that's the least bit greasy. I had some falafel the other day, I thought it was going to kill me. Rolling waves of nausea, like the ocean."

"How poetic. How about Henry?"

Maya was disconcerted. "Henry?"

"For the lobster."

"Why Henry?"

"I don't know. It always seemed to me like a good name for an invertebrate."

"I think Bernard is looking for something more . . . you know . . . more lobsterlike."

"How about Janie?"

Maya was irritated by this. "Janie? Snooky, what is wrong with your head? What in the world is lobsterlike about Janie?"

"Sophie?"

"I don't want to discuss it anymore. There is nothing in the least bit lobsterlike about Sophie. Sophie is a perfectly lovely name. In fact, it's one that we've considered for the baby."

"Oh, really? What else have you considered?"

Maya turned suddenly secretive and vague. "Oh, you know. Names. The usual names. We don't want anything too different. Too unusual."

"That's good. Pick something proud, Missy. Something to carry on the family tradition."

"Something like Snooky?"

"Nothing wrong with Snooky. It's better than the alternative."

"Arthur?"

"That's right."

"I've never understood why you always hated your name so much. It's a lovely name. Arthur. It resonates."

"I've never liked it. I never felt it was me. The true me. The me underneath. What do you think of this curry?"

She tasted it. "Delicious, Snooks. As always."

"Rolling waves of nausea?"

"None."

Bernard, when he heard about it over dinner, was pleased with the name Sophie. "That's perfect," he said with enthusiasm. "Sophie. It has all the right connotations."

Maya gazed at her husband in astonishment. "What connotations?"

"You know. Lobsters, and fins, and . . . you know."

"Lobsters don't have fins, Bernard," said Snooky, carrying the soup tureen in from the kitchen. "Back to the drawing board."

"Well, you know."

"I don't know," Maya said. "All I know is that we were considering it as a name for the baby. And now it's perfect for a lobster?"

"Sophie was never a first choice for the baby."

"I *liked* Sophie. Sophie Woodruff. It's a beautiful name."

"Too many *f* sounds," said Snooky. "Sophie Woodruff. No, no, Missy. Think again."

"Sophie Constance Woodruff," said Maya tearfully. Constance was their mother's name.

"Beautiful, and touching, but not quite right, if you ask me."

"I didn't ask you," said Maya, tears rolling down her cheeks, hormones thundering in her veins. "I never did ask you. You with your criticisms of the *f* sounds, and Bernard naming our baby after a lobster. I hate both of you."

"Fine," said Snooky, ladling soup into her bowl. "Try this soup. I guarantee it will bring calmness and peace to the household."

Maya wiped her face with her napkin. She grudgingly dipped her spoon into the bowl. An expression of beatific calm spread over her sharp, worry-worn features. "Delicious. And nutritious. It tastes—I don't know—like mother's soup. What is it?"

"Your favorite. Celery soup. I saw three tons of it in the refrigerator and decided I had to do something to correct the situation. Not bad, is it?"

"It's wonderful. What do you think, Bernard?"

But Bernard was far away, his lips moving slightly, his gaze focused out the dining room window.

"He's gone," Snooky said. "Far away in lobsterland. I told you Sophie was a perfect name. Have some bread, Maya, it's nice and warm now."

The next day Snooky picked up the phone after lunch and dialed Weezy's number.

"I'm tired of cooking and cleaning for this household," he told her. "Can I come over and drink some of your wine?"

"Of course, sweetie. Bring your sister and Bernard."

"Maya's upstairs lying down, digesting her lunch. Bernard's in his study planning the route of a lobster migration."

"What fascinating lives you all lead. All right, so it's just you?"

"Just me."

"Come on over. I have a couple of students here, but we're almost done."

When Snooky walked into the studio twenty minutes later, Weezy was conferring over a painting with a tall young man whose torn T-shirt did nothing to hide his well-muscled physique. In the corner, hunched over an easel, was a sweet-faced old lady with a cane.

Weezy was in the middle of a thought and did not like being interrupted. "Oh. It's you," she said ungraciously.

"It's me."

She waved her hand and performed perfunctory introductions. "Snooky Randolph. Elmo Oliveira. Snooky. Mrs. Castor."

The students nodded and turned back to their work. Snooky lounged around for a few moments; then, seeing that the lesson was not in fact coming to an end, he went out on the deck and sprawled in one of the lounge chairs, lifting his face to the unseasonably hot sun.

He slumbered for a few minutes; like a cat, he could fall asleep anywhere, at any time. When he opened his eyes, he felt disoriented. He looked at his watch. Twenty minutes had gone by. Stretching, he yawned hugely and then went inside to poke around in the refrigerator. He poured himself a glass of orange juice. Hearing voices from the studio, he wandered back in.

Weezy and the young bodybuilder known as Elmo were having a heated argument over a painting.

"No, no, *no,*" Weezy was saying, raking her hands through her hair until it stood out in a frizzy aureole around her face. "No, Elmo, that's all wrong. You can't do things at random, there has to be a vision before you start . . ."

"Who says, Weezy? Where's the room for creativity then? What's wrong with doing it that way?"

"Creativity comes from the moment, but there has to be a glimmer of purpose, surely you see that . . ."

The sweet-faced old lady was packing up her paints and brushes. She seemed to be unaffected by the sight of Weezy and Elmo shouting at each other.

"I'll be going on my way now," she said mildly.

Weezy raised her voice. "Haven't I taught you *anything?* You can't just toss paints at a canvas, that's not art—"

"That's not art?" the young man said incredulously. "Where have you been, Weezy, living with your head under a rock? Let me take you to a museum or gallery sometime—"

"Thank you so much for the lesson," the old lady said in bell-like tones. She took her leather portfolio and her cane and edged past Snooky. He held the door open for her. "Thank you, young man."

"I would get going while the going is good."

She smiled at him, her face wrinkling into a thousand

little fissures. "What, that? That's nothing. They do that every time. See you next week, Weezy."

"Good-bye, Mrs. Castor. Good work. Elmo here could learn something from you. See you next week."

Mrs. Castor crept away down the hall. Elmo, his huge arms crossed and the veins across his biceps bulging out monstrously, was towering over Weezy in a threatening manner. Weezy, uncowed, was shouting up at him, like a mouse threatening a skyscraper.

"You *never* learn! You are the most bullheaded, the most ignorant—"

"I don't have to listen to this—"

"You are driving me slowly crazy, trying to teach you a thing or two—"

"You don't have anything to teach me, I'm better than you are anyway—"

"I don't know why you came here in the first place—"

"Well, neither do I—"

"I feel like pounding your face in—"

"I could crush you," Elmo said, his face red, "flat as a pancake, and not even feel it."

Weezy was beside herself. "I dare you to do it! Go on, you big lug! I dare you!"

"This is ridiculous," said Elmo. He packed up in a huff and left. The front door closed with a loud bang. Snooky could imagine him, muscles bristling, striding off down the street.

Snooky and Weezy looked at each other.

"You've enrolled Grandma Moses and the Terminator as art students?" said Snooky.

Weezy patted her hair into place with a careful hand. She went into the kitchen, opened the refrigerator and poured herself a large glass of ice water, then went back into the studio and methodically began to clean up her paints and brushes.

She stacked Elmo's work against the wall along with Mrs. Castor's, put her supplies away in a large wooden cupboard, and hung up the light blue smock she always wore when she was working. Then she went into the living room, sat down on her white overstuffed couch, kicked off her shoes, put up her legs and sighed.

"He's so talented," she said admiringly. "He's going to be big. Very, very big."

"Elmo?"

"Yes, of course Elmo."

"I have news for you, Weezy. He's big already."

"Oh, he's going to be famous. Far more famous than I am. I don't have one-tenth his artistry, his vision. He's going to be huge. I should convince him to give me some of his paintings now, so I can sell them later and make my fortune. He's working on one called 'Girl in White' that's absolutely breathtaking. Did you see it? That's the one we were talking about in there. I should beg him for it right now, before he's even done." She sighed again, comfortably, and dabbled a finger in the ice water.

"So what was all the shouting about?"

Weezy looked at him vaguely. "Shouting?"

"Yes."

She waved a hand in the air. "Oh, that's nothing. That's how he and I communicate. I've known him for years. You know I have a thing for younger men. I keep telling him the only way I can get through to him is to shout as loud as I can. He's so stubborn, the big lunk. Looks are deceptive, though. Very deceptive. Inside, he's a sensitive person. And a wonderful painter."

"I'm jealous."

"Not as jealous as you're going to be when I tell you that he's Jennifer's boyfriend."

"This comes as no surprise to me. He's the only one tall enough for her. And they have the same sort of surly, misanthropic expression in their eyes."

Weezy smiled. "She's not for you, anyway. Take my word for it. Jennifer needs someone like Elmo who is as interested in art as she is. You don't know the first thing about art, do you?"

"Gouache."

"Pardon me?"

"Gouache. I know the word 'gouache.' "

"It's not enough," Weezy said regretfully. "I'm sorry, but it's not enough."

"Oh, well."

"You're young. You'll get over it. You didn't have time to fall in love with her yet, did you?"

"Weezy, I didn't even like her. I liked that other student, what's her name, Nikki, a lot more. At least she seemed like a decent human being."

"Oh, Nikki. That's her problem. She's too decent."

"Too decent?"

"Oh, she's always doing for everybody else, always putting herself last. She doesn't take care of herself at all. She's too damned nice, I can't stand it. You know, a real martyr type."

Snooky shrugged. "I don't understand what you and Maya have in mind, setting me up with everyone I meet. You know, I only have one plan right now."

"Yes? What's that?"

"It involves exerting all my considerable charm on you while I'm here."

She shook her head and laughed.

"Any more of those mysterious phone calls, Weezy?"

"Oh, no, no, no. I'm sure Bernard has frightened whoever

it was away. I'm so glad he answered the phone. Anyone else would have hung up immediately, when the caller didn't say anything."

"True."

They sat quietly together, in companionable silence.

"How's your sister?"

"I hate to say this, but sick as a dog. Sick as a dog, and cranky to boot. She seems to be appreciating my efforts less and less as the days go by. I feel undervalued."

Weezy laughed softly. "Undervalued. Yes, Snooky, that's your curse, to be undervalued. Like a piece of merchandise on sale. Marked down at K Mart. And Bernard? Does he appreciate you?"

"Bernard treats me like a slave, or a piece of furniture."

"Well, so what? He's always done that."

"Not as bad as this."

"Well, you can always crawl over here for a little appreciation, Snooky. I've always taken you at your full worth, whatever that may be. Stop whining about Maya. She's allowed to act however she wants. She has a full-time job, gestating that wonderful genius baby of hers."

Snooky looked at her, her intelligent horsey face, her wide smile, the way her hair tumbled into her eyes and down over her shoulders. She smiled at him and dabbled her finger in her water.

"You know, Weezy, I really do love you," he said.

"Oh, pooh."

"Really."

"Oh," said Weezy. She smiled at him. "Why couldn't you be ten years older and not my best friend's little brother?"

Snooky shrugged.

Weezy sighed. "Men," she said. "You're all so pigheaded. You and Elmo. Two of a kind."

"Except that he has the same name as one of the characters on Sesame Street. Oh, and he also happens to be a great artist."

"Well, I'm sure you have many gifts also, Snooky, although nobody has ever been able to figure out exactly what they are. Would you like some more orange juice?"

"I'll get it," he said, taking her glass and rising. "Orange juice and appreciation *chez* Weezy."

"That's what I'm here for," she said, turning her face to the sun that streamed in through the large bay window.

It was time for Maya's monthly visit to her obstetrician. Bernard, who hated doctors, hospitals, illness, and all things medical, sat unhappily cracking his knuckles in the waiting room as she was ushered into the inner recess, the sanctum sanctorum, of the rat maze which made up the doctor's offices and waiting rooms. On previous visits he had leafed nervously through the pile of magazines on the table, working his way unseeingly through *Child, Parents, Child and Parents, Working Mother, Mothering, Newsweek,* and *Vogue*. This time he did not have the mental energy even to pretend to be reading. He sat hunched miserably in his chair, his eyes fixed on a spot on the floor several inches in front of his feet.

A blond child of indeterminate age and sex, dressed in a turquoise and red jumpsuit, with a lollipop in its mouth, came up to him and put a hand confidingly on his knee.

"Mommy," it said. "Mommy. Look at the big man."

The child's mommy, busy reading *Parents,* put out a hand without looking and yanked the child away.

"Mommy," it said, like a wind-up doll, in a manner which Bernard found inexpressibly irritating. "Mommy. Look at the man."

"Shut up," its mother said kindly, patting it on the head. "Play with your toys."

"Mommy!"

Bernard shivered inwardly. Is this what was in store for him and Maya? Or would it be different if it were his own child, his flesh and blood, saying "Mommy" in that annoyingly high-pitched, nasal tone? The child sat down on the floor, took the lollipop out of its mouth, tossed it on the carpet, then picked it up and stuck it back in. Bernard shuddered.

"That's a good girl," the mother said, turning a page. "Play with your toys."

The child took the lollipop out again and grinned at him, revealing small white teeth spaced alarmingly widely apart. Bernard could foresee orthodonture in her future.

"Mommy. Look at the man."

"Shut up."

The child shut up. Bernard looked away in inward pain. The nurse came out, small, young, falsely cheerful. "Mr. Woodruff?"

He lumbered awkwardly to his feet. "Yes?"

"Please come with me."

He stepped over the little girl and was led through the maze into Waiting Room Three. His wife lay supine on the table, a white paper sheet covering most of her body.

"Hi," she said.

"Is everything all right?"

"Of course it's all right," said the doctor, a short dark middle-aged man with a beard and an Australian accent who resembled nothing more than a mountain troll. "Your wife wanted you to hear something."

He took out an instrument which looked like a large earphone, smeared it with jelly and placed it on Maya's stomach. He moved it around experimentally.

Suddenly, from a receiver in the doctor's hand, the room was filled with the sound of a loud, rapid thudding. It went on without pause, amplified like thunder. Maya and the doctor turned toward him, their faces open and expectant.

"It's the heartbeat," she said. "The baby's heartbeat, Bernard."

Bernard stood there, his own heart quickening in response. "So early . . . ?"

"You can hear the heartbeat at ten weeks," said the doctor.

The heartbeat thundered on, rapid as a bird's, strong and stable. Bernard tried to imagine it, that tiny being, the blood pumping, coursing through the arteries and veins, pulsing in and out like the sea. The doctor, bored, turned off the machine and put it away. Bernard reached under the sheet and took Maya's hand in his.

Snooky was stricken when he heard about the heartbeat.

"You heard the baby's heart, and you didn't record it for me?"

"Thoughtless of us," said his sister. "We didn't have a recording studio handy."

"A tape recorder, Maya. That's all it would have taken. A tape recorder. I'll give you one the next time you go."

She was picking at her potato salad. "Is this okay?"

"What do you mean, okay?"

"I mean, is it fresh?"

"I just made it this morning. Doesn't it taste right?"

"I don't know. Nothing tastes right anymore. I'm exhausted from seeing the doctor. He said that I'd be feeling better soon, but I don't think so. I don't think I'm ever going to feel better again. I'm going upstairs to lie down and stare at the willow tree."

"You do that. Do you mind if I finish your potato salad?"

"Go ahead."

"Where's Bernard?"

"He's upstairs in his study."

Snooky forked a potato cube into his mouth. "How did he react to hearing the heartbeat?"

"I think he was moved. Really moved. He hates my visits to the doctor, of course, but he couldn't get over this."

Bernard, when he came downstairs half an hour later to pour himself a cup of coffee, frowned slightly when asked about the heartbeat.

"It was interesting."

"Interesting?"

"Yes."

"Does it make the whole thing seem more real?"

"Yes."

"Does that frighten you?"

"No. Can I go now?"

"Maya said you were moved. Were you moved by the sound of your baby's heart beating?"

"Honestly, Snooky," Bernard said irritably. "Do I have to undergo the Spanish Inquisition every time I want a cup of coffee?"

"Just wondering. Just trying to be a little bit friendly."

Bernard stirred milk into his coffee. He headed for the door and safety.

"What's it going to take to make you open up to me, Bernard?" yelled Snooky.

There was no reply. He could hear Bernard's heavy footfall on the stairs.

"Apparently, the end of the universe as we know it," he said to himself, opening up the newspaper to the television page.

---

There was a small dispute later that afternoon about dinner.

"I'm going to serve lobster," said Snooky. "Fresh New England lobster."

Bernard shook his head. "I can't eat lobster. Not while I'm writing about Sophie."

"Come on. Don't be ridiculous. You mean you didn't eat lamb the whole time you were writing about Mrs. Woolly?"

"No, he didn't," said Maya, who was making herself a cup of tea. She wore an old ratty sweater with holes in it, one she had had since high school, which had once been white but was now a dirty gray. There were dark half-moons under her eyes where veins throbbed like underwater creatures. "He didn't, as a matter of fact. Not for years and years."

"Would you eat lamb now, Bernard?"

"No."

"Well, at least you have principles," said Snooky, scratching "lobster" off his shopping list. "Weird, ridiculous, nonsensical principles, but principles nevertheless. What's safe for me to cook, then? What won't offend you?"

"Anything else," said his sister. "You know Bernard will eat anything."

"I always thought he would, but I was wrong. He won't eat anything he's been writing about. And here I was going to make rat stew tomorrow night."

Bernard frowned. He had written two very successful books about a swashbuckling rat named Mr. Whiskers. "Is there anything you'd like, Maya?"

"No. All this talk about lobster and rat stew is making me sick. I'd just like a quiet cup of tea. Use your imagination, Snooky. You do have one, don't you? And listen, if you're going out shopping, will you drop this book off at Weezy's? She lent it to me ages ago and I just found it on the shelf. I'm not sure whether I read it or not. Tell her it was wonderful and I loved it, okay?"

"Okay."

"It was wonderful. Maya loved it," he told Weezy later, handing her the book.

Weezy tossed it aside. "She never read it, huh?"

"I don't think so. She said she couldn't remember."

"I knew when I gave it to her she wouldn't read it," she said cheerfully. "That's Maya. She asked to borrow it one day when she saw it in my apartment in New York, years ago. I told her she'd never read it."

"I don't think she did."

"Doesn't matter. At least she eventually returned it, unlike most of my friends. By the way, have you met Sao?"

Sao was a slender, dark-haired woman who at the moment was on her hands and knees scrubbing the kitchen floor.

"Sao helps me out around the house. I'm so disorganized. Aren't I, Sao? Sao is from Portugal. Isn't that wonderful? She came over here to live with her relatives. She speaks a minimum of English, and I speak absolutely no Portuguese. We get along marvelously. I can't stand people in my house, but with Sao I have total privacy. She understands not a single word I say. We communicate with gestures on a very primordial level, like apes."

Snooky glanced at Sao, who was wringing the cloth out in a pail of soapy water.

*"Boa tarde,"* he said.

The young woman flashed him a delighted smile. *"Boa tarde, senhor."*

*"Tenho muito prazer em conhecê-la."*

She laughed.

*"Compreende-me?"*

*"Sim, sim, senhor."*

*"Meu nome é Snooky Randolph. Sou um amigo da Weezy."*

*"Tenho muito prazer em conhecê-lo."*

*"À sua saúde,"* said Snooky. The woman's smile broadened. *"Qual é a especialidade da casa?"* he continued. *"Senhor, gostaria de beber um uísque com soda. Estão incluidos os impostos e o serviço?"*

Sao began to laugh helplessly. Weezy, nearby, was tapping her foot with impatience. "What's so funny?"

"Nothing. I'm just showing off some of the very useful Portuguese I picked up last time I was in Lisbon."

"What are you saying to poor Sao? You seem to be terrorizing her."

"I asked her what the specialty of the house was. Then I ordered a whiskey and soda from the bartender, and I inquired whether tax and service were included."

"How fascinating. I don't mean to be rude, but I must get to my studio. Elmo and Jennifer are coming, and Mrs. Castor will be along later. I'd like to get some work done before they arrive. Sao . . ."

"Yes?"

"I'm going to work now. Work now. In the studio." Exaggerated gestures accompanied this information. "No, no, don't translate for me, Snooky. You'll destroy my perfect peace here. Sao and I understand each other marvelously. Don't we? I'm going to work now. If you're gone when the lessons are over, I'll see you next week. All right? Good. You see, Snooky, you don't need to be such a show-off with languages. Sao understands everything. Good-bye now. Tell your sister I'm glad she enjoyed the book. It's so important that these illusions be maintained, even between the closest of friends. Good-bye now, good-bye."

*"Adeus,"* said Snooky to Sao, who waved her hand at him. *"Até logo."*

*"Até logo,"* she said, giggling, as Weezy ushered him to the door.

After that visit to Weezy's, it rained for an entire week. It was the end of April, and the rain poured down relentlessly day after day as if the floods were coming. Snooky, staring out the window, rivulets of water running down the clear glass past his face, began to feel that it had always rained and always would rain; that nothing had ever been different. He and Maya and Bernard, holed up in the great creaky Victorian, began to turn on each other, snarling and snapping like caged beasts. They forgot what the sun looked like. Gray day followed gray day in an endless, ominous progression. Maya, in particular, was miserable. She still felt weak and ill, contrary to her doctor's cheerful prognosis; she still felt vaguely queasy most of the time and sharply queasy part of the time; she still, if she did not eat several hundred small meals a day, had to take to her bed with a splitting headache, her body throbbing, her blood sugar dipping dangerously low. She cried in her husband's arms and snarled at her brother. She was sullen with her best friend when Weezy braved the storms and arrived, dripping, at their front door, decked out in a gaudy red raincoat and pink scarf.

"Cheerful, isn't she?" was Weezy's comment, later, sharing a comforting cup of coffee in the kitchen with Snooky.

"She's been biting my head off several times a day."

"Being pregnant doesn't seem to have improved her personality."

"I don't care if she is pregnant, one of these days I'm going to lose my temper. Especially if it keeps on raining like this."

"The weather's been terrible. I suppose it must be hard, being hormonal and everything, and having it so gray day after day."

"You're too kind to her."

"She needs a friend. You and Bernard look like you're going to murder someone. She needs a friend to recount later, at the trial, how you fingered a steak knife and talked about losing your temper."

Snooky guiltily put down the knife. "Everything's getting on my nerves. I'm not myself."

"It's the weather. Low barometric pressure does that to everybody. There are more murders and robberies on rainy days."

"Is that true?"

"I don't know. I just made it up. Probably."

"I don't know what I'm going to do if the weather doesn't change soon. I can't believe I left the Caribbean for this."

"It is incredible." Weezy drank her coffee. "Mmmm, you do make the best coffee. Just right. Heaven to my taste buds. Are you sure you won't marry Sao and become my second-in-help?"

Snooky looked bitter. "Why should I do that when I have such an enviable position, slaving away here for nothing?"

"If they're going to hire you, they could at least pay you."

"Sometimes Bernard forgets, and I have to spend my own money to buy stuff for dinner."

"Life is so terribly unfair."

"In St. Martin I didn't have to pay for anything. I didn't even have to cook or clean."

"You shouldn't have left."

"Apparently not."

"The weather's probably lovely there."

Snooky did not reply. He was sunk in gloom.

"I have an idea," said Weezy. "I have to go to New York

City the day after tomorrow. You know, about my show. The gallery owner and I have to talk over some details. Would you like to tag along? You could see friends, go to a museum, have a little time to yourself."

"That would be wonderful. I accept with gratitude. Thank you."

"Bernard and Maya might like to have some time to themselves also."

"I don't see why. All they do is snap at each other, and sometimes Maya cries."

"Oh, you're simply jealous, sweetie. Theirs is a great romance."

"I don't see what's so great about it. They don't seem to get along at all anymore."

"Which is why they need a day off, too," Weezy said wisely, patting him on the shoulder.

Maya was disturbed at the idea of Snooky going off for the day.

"Is it because you're tired of us?" she asked, clutching the bedspread to her thin body. Instead of getting rounder, she looked more emaciated than ever. "Is it because I've been mean to you? Is that why Weezy asked you?"

"Mean to me?" said Snooky. "Mean to me? You think calling me a pinheaded weaselnosed dwarf is being mean to me? You think gagging on my food and calling it simply inedible is being mean to me? You think saying I make too much noise when I'm walking around in my room upstairs is being mean to me? No, no, Maya, far from it. I'm enjoying myself so much I can barely tear myself away."

Maya lay back on the pillows. She looked very tired. "I'm in a bad mood these days."

"Really?"

"I'm pregnant. I'm allowed to be bad."

"Well, I'm not pregnant," said Snooky. "I'm allowed to go away for a day."

"I'm worried that you hate me," said Maya fretfully. Her eyes filled with tears. She plucked nervously at the bedspread. "I feel like you hate me, Snooks."

"I don't hate you. Why do you say that?"

"Because I've been so mean."

"You haven't been mean."

"I did call you a pinheaded weaselnosed dwarf. I remember that. I called you that the other day, didn't I?"

"I didn't take it personally, Missy."

"I don't know why I'm being so impossible," she said with a half-sob. Tears ran down her cheeks. "I never was before. I was always a nice person."

"Too nice," said Snooky, patting her hand. "Too nice. Underneath was all this meanness. Now you're letting it out, so it'll be gone before the baby is born."

Maya stared at him wildly. "Do you think so?"

"Yes, Missy. Yes. Now try to go back to sleep. You look tired."

"I feel like there's something terribly wrong with me, Snooks. I have no energy."

"You're just pregnant. People work in the fields while they're pregnant. Try to be brave."

"Bernard and I went for a walk the other day, and I had to come home and lie down. I used to be able to walk for miles and miles. Remember that, Snooks? I wouldn't be able to work in the fields. They would throw me out of the village. I'm no good for anything. I can't even get out of bed."

"You'll feel more like yourself again soon, Missy."

"Do you really think so?"

"Yes, I do."

She closed her eyes. "I hope so."

He waited until her frantic grip on his hand relaxed, then slipped out of the room. He met Bernard on the way downstairs.

"I don't know about you," he said, "but I don't think I'm going to make it through the first trimester."

Bernard laid a heavy paw on his shoulder and gazed into his eyes. "That bad?"

"Worse than bad. Terrible."

"Do you think she wants a cup of tea? I was bringing her one, just in case."

"No. She's asleep."

"Oh."

"I'm going to New York the day after tomorrow. You two are on your own. Good luck to you. Weezy says you need time alone, without me, for your great romance."

"Weezy says *what?*" said Bernard in horror, but Snooky had already gone past him, down the stairs and out of sight.

# THREE

WEEZY WAS nervous all the way into the city. She stared out the window of the train at the landscape of Connecticut and New York rolling by, she fiddled with her hat, which was a small thing with feathers that looked like a bird perched on top of her messy nest of hair, she refused to make conversation with Snooky, she looked anxiously inside her handbag. She applied lipstick several times and patted her hair in a futile attempt to cajole it into keeping its shape.

"Forget the hair," said Snooky at last. "It's hopeless."

"Thank you." She snapped open her handbag, took out a large pink plastic comb and began to drag it through her frizzy curls. "Thank you."

"I don't see what you're so nervous about."

"This is the first meeting I've had with this gallery owner in person, and you don't see what I'm so nervous about?"

"He's lucky to be able to represent you."

Weezy responded to this with a cynical snort. She finished struggling with her hair and put the comb away.

"You look beautiful."

"Please shut up."

"You do."

"I never have looked beautiful in my life, Snooky. The best I can hope for is neat and clean."

Weezy was conservatively dressed in a tweed jacket and skirt whose muted green shades showed off her flaming hair to advantage. She wore no jewelry except for a heavy turquoise and gold ring on the little finger of her left hand.

"Is that a beetle?"

She slipped off the ring and waved it in front of his face. "It's a scarab. You are so ignorant, it's amazing. It's Egyptian. It was my father's. When he died I had it sized so I could wear it."

"That's interesting. Odd, but interesting."

She turned to look out the window. "Are we there yet?"

"Weezy, we just passed the New York border. We're nowhere near there yet."

She sighed impatiently and swung one leg like a little girl.

Seeing that any further conversation was hopeless, Snooky opened up a magazine and buried himself in it until the train lurched to a halt in Grand Central Station. Weezy was already on her feet, prodding him with an impatient hand.

"Come on, come *on,* Snooky, we're going to get caught in the line."

She pushed him off the train and prodded him through the enormous vaulted lobby and out onto the street. It had finally stopped raining, and the sun spilled down onto the city, reflecting blindingly from glass office towers. An old man dressed in rags extended one filthy hand.

"Hey, mister . . . hey, mister . . ."

Snooky reached into his pocket and pulled out a five-dollar bill. The old man took it with a wintry smile. "Thanks." He turned away. "Hey, mister . . . hey, mister . . ."

"The gallery is in the East Forties," said Weezy, nervously checking a piece of paper. "It's not far. I thought we could walk."

"Still sure you want me to come?"

"Yes," she said, linking arms with him. "I need emotional support in this crisis. What if he hates me and decides to cancel the show?"

"That's a good thought."

"Or what if he comes on to me, but I hate him, so he decides to cancel the show?"

"Why don't you sleep with him in order to get your show put on?"

"I think I might," Weezy said, staring at the sidewalk and biting her lip. She seemed oblivious to the hordes of people surging around her. "I just might."

"If I promised to put on a show of yours, would you sleep with me?"

"Only if you had a really well known gallery."

"I've obviously chosen the wrong career," said Snooky, maneuvering her past a scaffolding which said DANGER.

"Oh, really? Being the black sheep of your family doesn't seem quite as attractive anymore?"

"I'm not really a black sheep. I'm just doing it to annoy William."

"Well, whatever. Look at that poor man there, give him some money, will you? God, every time I go away I forget, and every time I come back I'm so glad I went away. New York isn't what it used to be. Although I do love the way people dress. Look at that woman over there, in the purple outfit. I've only been away a year, and now when I come back I feel like a hick. I forgot how when rich people dress sloppy they can still look glamorous."

"Nobody in Ridgewood is particularly glamorous."

"Oh, I don't know. I think old Mrs. Castor is pretty glamorous. All that snowy-white hair and that little birdlike face and that red lipstick she wears. I hope I look that good when I'm her age. I won't, of course." She checked the slip of paper worriedly. "I think this is it. Yes, this is it, all right. Oh, my God. Here we go. Try to act sophisticated. Don't embarrass me."

"Weezy, I haven't embarrassed anyone since I was five years old."

As she pushed open the door, a man rose from a desk in the back and came towards them, his arms out in welcome.

"Ms. Kaplan . . . ?"

"Mr. Genuardi?"

"Call me Edward. This is a pleasure . . . a very great pleasure . . ."

"Oh, no, no, the pleasure is all mine. I was so thrilled when you called . . ."

The gallery owner was a short, slight man in his mid-thirties with large glasses and receding hair. He fixed Snooky with a pale, unanimated eye. "And this is . . . ?"

"Oh, this is Snooky, my friend Arthur Randolph, everyone calls him Snooky. And please call me Weezy."

"Weezy." He laughed. "How delightful. I thought there were a few details we should go over before the show . . ."

"Of course . . ."

They both turned to Snooky. Weezy was smiling as though she had never seen him before in her life.

"I'll look around a bit," he said. "Take a look at your fine collection here."

The gallery owner bustled away, Weezy in tow. Snooky strolled over to the paintings. The gallery was dark, with high ceilings and track lighting to offset the murky interior. There was a sculpture exhibit on at the moment, as well as a collection of large paintings. Snooky stopped to contemplate a brass object which appeared to be the stylized shape of a woman tied into some kind of knot. She was holding out a baby and her mouth was open in a soundless scream.

"Now there's the perfect shower present for Maya," he thought.

Next to it was another knotted metal shape that, after much reflection, he decided was probably an animal tied into a knot. He thought he could make out an antler and a hoof. After that were several free-form figures.

He was looking at one of the paintings when Weezy came out of the office fifteen minutes later. She was beaming.

"Thank you *so* much," she said to the owner, who shook her hand. There was a descending spiral of good-byes as they neared the door.

"Thank you for coming in today . . . we look forward so much to . . ."

"Oh, yes . . . you're very welcome . . . I look forward to seeing . . ."

"Yes, yes . . . talk to you soon . . ."

"Talk to you . . ."

"Good-bye, Edward."

"Good-bye, Weezy."

The gallery owner shut the door firmly behind them.

"Are you going to have to sleep with him?"

They were seated in a small diner on Lexington Avenue, near the gallery. Snooky was having a cup of coffee and Weezy was eating a tuna salad sandwich.

She brushed a lock of hair out of her eyes. "I don't think so. At least, he didn't mention it."

"But it went well?"

"Very well. He's enthusiastic. A nice man. Horrible eyes, of course, that pale color, like a frozen fish, but that's not his fault."

"He looks like he's already dead, Weezy."

She picked out some lettuce and ate it delicately. "Well, yes, he does, but fortunately that doesn't matter. Nothing matters except the show. He could be a zombie from outer space, and as long as he ran this wonderful gallery, it wouldn't matter. Do you see what I mean?"

"You have no morals at all, Weeze."

"Not when it comes to my work." She took a large bite of her sandwich. "Not when it comes to my work. Harold always said I was a monomaniac on the subject. Of course Harold was a complete moron when it came to art. A moron. He didn't have an artistic bone in his body."

"Go figure a doctor wouldn't be artistic."

"It doesn't necessarily follow. Look at Somerset Maugham. Look at the director Jonathan Miller. Look at Monty Python. I think one of them trained as a doctor. And you don't have to be an artist to appreciate art. You just have to be a joyous person. Art brings joy."

"Harold was not joyous?"

"No." She picked another piece of lettuce out of her sandwich and chewed on it reflectively. "No. He was not a joyous person. So few doctors are, don't you think? He was worried all the time."

"About his patients?"

Weezy snorted, a long horsey whinny. "His patients? No. How delightfully naive of you. No, he was worried about getting ahead, you know, in the medical hierarchy. Making money and making a name for himself. There's a whole structure there, a pecking order in the hospital, that we as civilians know so little about, but it's life and death to the people involved. I suppose that's true in any profession, but somehow with doctors I'd like to think . . ."

Her voice trailed away.

"Yes?" said Snooky.

"Oh, *God*."

"What?"

"Don't turn around."

Snooky instinctively lowered his voice, although the diner was so loud that he could barely hear himself. "Who is it?"

"Oh my God, it's Harold." Weezy sounded lost between laughter and tears. "It's Harold and his little chickadoo. What in the world do I do now?"

"Sit tight and ignore them."

"I can't do that. You know me, I can't avoid confrontations. Oh, God, I knew I shouldn't have been talking about Harold. It called him up, like some kind of demon from hell. Like a syllabus, or whatever that word is."

"I think you mean succubus."

"Whatever. It's bad luck even to talk about him, it summons him up, like the accursed spirit that he is. Well, never mind. Are you coming, for support?"

"Of course."

Harold and his girlfriend were eating at a small table nearby. Weezy stood up and strode over regally.

"Harold."

He looked up in surprise, flushing as he saw who it was. "Weezy. Weezy! How are you?"

"Fine, thank you. This is my friend, Arthur Randolph." Weezy took Snooky's arm.

"This is . . ." Harold cleared his throat, "this is Gabriela Loeser. Gaby, this is Weezy Kaplan."

There were murmured hellos. Harold's girlfriend's face was flushed scarlet. She glanced at Weezy, lowered her eyes, then looked back again, as if fascinated.

Snooky took advantage of the opportunity to put an arm around Weezy. "We have to go, darling."

"Yes, yes, I know. Stay just a minute. How are you, Harold?"

"Fine, thanks."

"The medicine business going okay?"

"Oh, yes, yes." He covered his mouth with a napkin and coughed violently into it, as if to expel all the stress from his body. "Yes, going fine. Very interesting, very busy, as always. You remember how it was, Weezy."

"I certainly do."

"And how are things going for you?"

"Just fine, thank you. I've moved out of the city, did you hear?"

"No . . . no, I didn't."

"The most charming little town. Ridgewood. Ridgewood, Connecticut. An hour and a half away, but it's another world. My blood pressure has dropped dramatically since I left."

"And your work? How's your work going?"

"Oh, not bad, thanks. That's why I'm here today, actually —I have an exhibit coming up."

"Oh, yes?"

"At a little place around the corner from here. You wouldn't have heard of it, but it's very exciting for me."

Harold, as if suddenly remembering his manners, got awkwardly to his feet. He was as tall as Snooky, more solidly built, with long dark hair and a European-looking face. He had a beaked nose and thin, sensitive lips. "That's nice. I'm happy for you, Weezy. I really am."

"Thank you."

Harold's girlfriend was looking at Weezy with great interest. She had thick straight blonde hair which fell to her shoulders, a fair complexion, huge dark eyes and a full mouth which was accented with bright red lipstick. Now she spoke.

"The Genuardi Gallery?"

"Why, yes. The Genuardi. You know of it?"

"Oh, yes, yes. I'm a big fan . . . really a big fan, Ms. Kaplan. I love your work."

Weezy paused. Her eyes flickered over her appraisingly. "That's good of you to say."

"It's true."

"Well, Harold, it's been a pleasure seeing you again. I'm sorry to bother you over lunch. Take care."

"You, too."

"Come on, Arthur. Good-bye," she said to Harold's girlfriend.

"Good-bye, Ms. Kaplan."

The last Snooky saw of Harold, he was getting back into his seat with a flustered, apologetic expression on his face.

"What's this 'Ms. Kaplan' deal?" Weezy said later, patting her hair. "Am I her second-grade teacher, or what?"

"I don't think you're being fair. That wasn't easy for her. Stop kicking me."

"I'm not kicking you, Snooky. It's the motion of the train."

"You are too kicking me."

They were on their way back to Ridgewood, seated opposite each other at the window of the train. Their legs were entwined familiarly, and Weezy was once again checking her reflection in her little pocket mirror. She sighed, put the mirror away and looked out the window at the countryside rushing past.

"I enjoyed being your boyfriend for thirty seconds," said Snooky.

"I thought you would."

"Do you think Harold was deceived?"

"Oh, no, no."

"What's the point, then?"

"Appearances." Weezy waved a hand vaguely in the air. "Appearances, Snooks. I needed a boyfriend, and there you were. It will leave a doubt in his mind, at the very least."

"I see."

Weezy propped her chin on her fist and leaned on the window. "So that's his little mouse. That's what he calls her, you know. His little mouse. Is that nauseating, or what?"

"Gabriela, huh?"

"Yes. She's very pretty. Exotic-looking."

"Not as pretty as you are," said Snooky loyally.

"Shut up, Snooky. She's much prettier than I am. She didn't seem like a bad person, either. I liked that trapped expression she got on her face. Another woman might have gotten bitchy. She actually tried to be nice."

"What does she do for a living, other than preying on other women's boyfriends?"

"She's a journalist. Works for some magazine. He met her at a news conference at the hospital." Weezy sighed deeply. "Did I make a fool of myself, going over to them?"

"No. You were brave."

"Brave, or stupid?"

"Brave."

"Did I look terrible?"

"You know you looked very nice. You were all dressed up for fish face at the gallery."

"I've always looked good in green."

"You look beautiful."

Weezy wet her finger and drew absentmindedly on the window pane. "She's much more attractive than I am, and she probably has a better disposition. I'm sure she doesn't throw tantrums or sulk for days, the way I did. It's hard to know why he left."

"Well, I wouldn't have."

"Are we talking about you?" Weezy drew a stick figure on the window, then absentmindedly drew a line through its neck, decapitating it. "This is the most horrible thing that's ever happened to me. Here I was having a wonderful day in New York, and a ghost from my past has to surface. Just when I was starting to get over the whole thing. Just when I was starting to build a new life for myself."

"Well, if it's any consolation, I think you ruined their entire day. I saw his face when he was sitting down again. I don't think his home life is going to be too serene for a while. You could be wrong about the tantrums. She looks to me like she could have a temper."

"Not like mine," Weezy said dourly. She did not say another word until the train pulled into the Ridgewood station.

When Snooky let himself in the house, he found Maya and Bernard sitting in the living room. Maya was propped up on cushions, her feet were on Bernard's lap and they were both absorbed in a TV show.

"Life in the fast lane," he said. "Did you miss me? Did absence make the heart grow fonder?"

"We did not miss you. Did we, Bernard?"

"No."

"You're looking a little better, Missy."

"So are you. Have a good time in the big city?"

"A weird time. I'll tell you all about it later. What's on?"

"Something called *Attack of the Killer Cucumbers*. It's very funny."

The three of them watched in silence. The dog wandered into the room. Snooky picked her up and fondled her silky ears. She settled down in his lap, giving a low grumble, her equivalent of a purr.

"There's the head cucumber destroying Manhattan," said Maya.

"Just lucky I escaped in time," said Snooky.

"How was it today?"

He briefly recounted the meeting with Harold.

"Oh, how weird. I'll have to call Weezy. How's she handling it? Is she okay?"

"Not bad. She was very courageous, going right over to them."

"Weezy never shirks from confrontation."

"No."

"Is Harold everything she said?"

"Frankly, I don't see the fascination she has with him. How did the two of you spend your day?"

"It was wonderful, Snooks. The sun was shining at last. I did some gardening and we took a long walk."

"You, Maya? You did some gardening?" Maya's garden was one of her great passions. "You must be feeling better."

"Somebody has to look after the garden. You and Bernard are hopeless at it. Remember the time I sent the two of you out to weed the patch near the sun room, and Bernard cut down the smoke tree?"

Bernard shifted his weight on the couch. "Not all of it."

"Enough of it, Bernard. Enough of it. It was mutilated. It was never the same afterwards."

"You weren't there," said Snooky. "The trunk looked dead. Bernard and I agreed it was dead before he cut it down."

"You could have looked up and seen the new branches. It's not hard, the whole tree isn't much taller than you are. I don't know what the two of you were doing near the smoke tree anyway. I sent you out to weed, not to rape and pillage."

"Pay attention," said Bernard, patting her foot. "The cucumbers are winning."

Maya paid attention for a while. Then she curled up on a pillow and went to sleep.

"What's for dinner?" asked Snooky, yawning. "Or should I just ask which cans you intend to open?"

Bernard, on Snooky's day off, had volunteered to cook. His eyes were glued to the screen, where the cucumbers were storming their way down First Avenue toward the United Nations Building. "Coq au vin."

"Come on."

"You heard me."

"Oh, right. From a frozen TV dinner?"

"No. Fresh. I made it myself."

"This I find hard to believe. Coq au vin takes time, and more importantly, talent."

"Nobody's asking you to believe it, Snooky. Or to eat it, for that matter."

"No, no, no, I can't wait. Coq au vin by Bernard. Have you ever heard of such a thing, Misty?" he asked the dog, slumbering in his lap. He lifted her so that her head and silky ears lolled downward into his face. "Have you ever heard of such a thing? I can't wait. Listen, Bernard, make sure to wake me up in plenty of time for dinner."

Then he, too, curled up in his chair and went to sleep. Bernard watched with a frown. He himself often had trouble falling asleep. He would toss and turn in bed, cursing silently, his brain nattering away at him. When he took a nap during the day, it was usually from exhaustion, and he would wake up feeling worse than before. Both his wife and Snooky, however, had the ability to fall asleep anywhere, at any time, and to awake refreshed from their catnaps. Now the two of them slept peacefully in the waning light of the afternoon. Even the dog was asleep. On the TV screen, tiny figures of people ran screaming before enormous cucumbers.

———

"What do you think of the coq au vin?" Maya asked later.

"I'm tactfully not saying anything, Missy."

"Why? What's wrong with it? I think it's delicious."

"I'm happy for you."

"You're going to hurt Bernard's feelings. He slaved over this all day long."

"With time out to watch one of the worst TV movies I've ever seen." Snooky leaned back and hooked his arms around the chair. "Besides, Bernard has no feelings to injure. His heart is made of steel."

Maya glanced at her husband, who was happily shoveling in his third helping of coq au vin. He did in fact seem oblivious to the conversation.

"So what's wrong with the chicken?"

"Well, first of all, Missy, coq au vin is (as you can tell from the name) supposed to be made with wine, not beer, which is apparently what Bernard used. Also, the chicken should be browned with minced salt pork, not what seems to be Bac-O-Bits. There are supposed to be spices other than salt in it. And I believe you should add about two tablespoons of flour to the sauce, not (as Bernard has so generously used) two cups. Other than that, it's just the way I would make it. If I were on drugs."

Maya glanced guiltily at her husband. "Bernard didn't put in a lot of spices because I've been so queasy up till now."

"How thoughtful of him."

"Would you like a bowl of cereal or something?"

"Yes, thank you, Missy. But I think I'll make it myself."

A few days later, the phone rang at the Woodruff household, and Snooky answered it.

"I want to talk to your sister," Weezy said. "Where is she?"

"She's out walking with Bernard."

"Out walking? She must be feeling better."

"She is. It's the second trimester, at long last. She says she's coming back to herself. She remembers what it's like to feel like a human being again."

"Oh, good, good, good. That's good."

"Can I give her a message?"

"The slimiest thing just happened, Snooky. You remember Edward Genuardi, the owner of the gallery that's putting on my show?"

"Dead fish eyes?"

"That's it. Well, he called up a few minutes ago and asked me out to dinner."

Snooky felt an unaccustomed surge of jealousy. "You're kidding."

"No. Pretty slimy, huh?"

"Yeah, pretty slimy, all right. What are you going to do?"

"Well, I don't want to endanger my show, so I'm going to sleep with him. Just kidding," she said when she heard the silence on the other end. "What's the matter with you? I told him I couldn't possibly mix my professional and personal life. Not to mention that his eyes turn me off completely. He doesn't even seem human, with eyes like that. I didn't tell him that, of course."

"Oh."

"You're no fun to tell this stuff to at all. What's the matter with you?"

"Well, I'm experiencing an increase in blood pressure and a small amount of tachycardia. Nothing to worry yourself about."

"Jealous?"

"Yes."

"You're jealous that some gallery owner from Manhattan asked me out on a date?"

"Yes. I guess I am."

Weezy gave her snorting, horsey laugh. "You are charming. You are charming, and good for my ego. Always stay the way you are. Never change."

"Do you think this is going to endanger your show?"

"What? He wouldn't dare. I could give him so much bad publicity, he'd never get out from under it. No, no, the show will be fine. And he and I will be lovely to each other and perfectly polite to all the guests at the opening reception. It'll be fine."

"That's good."

"You still sound a little worried. Are you that concerned about my career?"

"No, I'm that concerned about my heart. It seems to be jumping all around my chest right now. I'm getting irregular heartbeats, and then I feel like coughing. I feel a little short of breath. Will you call nine-one-one for me if I suddenly pass out?"

"I think you're spending too much time in that house discussing Maya's symptoms. You're all turning into terrible hypochondriacs. None of you is sick, and only one of you is pregnant, which is not an illness."

"Bernard's not turning into a hypochondriac."

"No, no, Bernard is a real man. Bernard never complains. Bernard is my dream man."

"That hurts me, you know. That really hurts."

"Give him and Maya my love, and come to see me sometime when your heart isn't acting up," said Weezy, and rang off.

---

When Maya and Bernard returned from their walk, Bernard escaped upstairs to his study and Maya came into the kitchen looking smug. Snooky was chopping vegetables for a wok dish.

"Hi, big sister." He pulled out a chair for her and returned to his work, his long-bladed knife flashing silver in the air.

"Hi."

"You seem content."

"I outwalked Bernard."

"Bernard doesn't walk. He only lumbers along, like a bear."

"I wanted to walk the last bit, the curve before you get to that big modern house, you know the one I mean, but he pooped out. He said he had to get back to his lobsters."

"How's the migration going?"

"I don't know. Okay, I guess."

Maya took some vegetables from the cutting board and began to nibble at them. She was smiling to herself.

"You seem happier than you've been."

"Thank you. I am."

"Feeling better?"

"Yes, I am."

"The queasiness and that low-blood-sugar thing are gone?"

"Yes, Snooks, you know, it's like a miracle. It didn't happen all at once, but over the last week or so, I've started to feel so much better. I'm coming back to myself, I think. I really am. I have some energy again."

"You have some joie de vivre."

"I do indeed."

"Have some cucumbers, in memory of the ones that overwhelmed Manhattan. Well, you look marvelous, Maya. I haven't said anything for fear that you'll bite my head off, but you look wonderful. You have that certain glow."

Maya blushed. "I do not. I certainly do not. That glow is a myth, my friends tell me. But at least I don't feel awful all the time."

"You have your strength back."

"I do."

"You could work in the fields."

"Yes, I could."

"Well, thank God you don't have to," Snooky said, handing her a plate of cucumbers and tomatoes.

The next day Snooky got a frantic call from Weezy.

"Come over here immediately. I need you right now."

"At last you've come to your senses. You've realized how much you care for me? How I've always been waiting in the wings, but now that I've grown up I'm absolutely the right man for you?"

"Don't be so stupid. Your face. I need your face, Snooky. Come over here at once."

"What about my face?" he asked, but she had already hung up.

When he showed up at her door ten minutes later, Weezy grabbed his face and pushed it about in the sunlight.

"Not too bad," she murmured. "I thought so. Aah! Yes. Those cheekbones. All right. Come with me."

"What's going on?"

"I have a class starting in exactly three minutes, and I need a model. Somebody with good bone structure. I thought of you at the last minute, and you'll have to do. Those great cheekbones that you and Maya have. I would ask her—her face is much finer than yours, of course—but I can't, not in her condition. You'll have to sit still for an hour. Can you do that?"

"No," said Snooky. She propelled him with a push down the hallway and into her studio. "I'm not taking my clothes off, either," he added.

"Oh, don't make me laugh. Sit there"—she indicated a chair at the front of the room—"and try not to fidget. Okay? Thanks very much."

"I thought you and your students only did abstracts. You know, things that don't look like anything. Blobs that look like people having sex with other species. That kind of stuff."

"Well, today we're doing faces. Yours, in particular. We'll see how it goes. Now, sit still and don't talk."

"I don't suppose I get paid for this or anything?"

Weezy snorted and walked away.

The first student to come into the room was old Mrs. Castor, who greeted Weezy and Snooky with a sweet "hello" and then opened her paintbox and went right to work. Weezy explained about Snooky's face, and Mrs. Castor nodded vigorously, staring at Snooky with a bright birdlike eye. "Yes, yes, I see. Yes. Oh, excellent bones. Very interesting. An excellent model."

"Thank you."

"Don't talk," snapped Weezy. "You're a model. A mannequin. Like one of those rubber ones in the store windows. Sit still, and don't breathe."

Snooky sat still.

Elmo and Jennifer came in next, hand in hand. They said hello to Weezy, set up their easels, opened their paints and pencils and began to work, laughing and talking together in whispered asides. Jennifer's long hair was pulled severely back into a thick braid, a style which accented her strong features. Snooky thought they could have used her cheekbones instead of his. He sneezed, and she glared at him. Elmo, on the other hand, did not acknowledge his presence at all. After working for a few minutes, he seemed to have forgotten where he was and who was with him. He ignored a suggestion from Weezy, and he merely frowned at a giggled whisper from Jennifer.

Nikki Cooper came in next, out of breath, her frowsy hair blown all around her face. "I'm so sorry, Weezy . . . hate being late . . . had to walk from the station . . . so sorry . . ." She looked at Weezy pleadingly.

"Goodness, Nikki, that's all right. Settle down. It doesn't matter."

"Oh, no, I feel terrible . . . hate being late . . ." Nikki rushed over to her place and set up her easel with a shaking hand. Her face was red and her breath came fast. She was obviously not used to any kind of exertion. Snooky eyed her with concern. She gave him a shaky smile. "Oh! Is that . . . is he the model for today?"

"Yes, yes," said Weezy in a disparaging tone. "We'll all have to limp along and try our best. I thought his face might be interesting."

"Oh, yes . . . oh my, yes . . ."

The last student to come in was another young woman. "Hello, Alice," said Weezy.

"Hi, Weezy. Sorry I'm late."

"Okay." Weezy tapped her foot impatiently. She explained the assignment, indicating Snooky with a wave of her hand. The girl stared at Snooky, fixing him with a pair of curiously expressionless green eyes, like pebbles at the bottom of a sea. She had long pale hair and an ugly, intelligent face with a great curved nose like a witch's. Snooky felt sorry for her. He turned his face toward her and held it immobile.

"Why is he looking at me?" she asked Weezy.

"I don't know. Because he's stupid. This is his first time modeling, and also, I would imagine, his last. Oh, I forgot to introduce you. Snooky Randolph, Alice Faber. Snooky, don't look at anyone in particular, it's unnerving. Look at the wall over there."

Snooky looked at the wall.

"Thank you. And try not to sneeze, it's upsetting for everybody. Pretend you're made out of rubber and you don't have a brain, that last bit shouldn't be so hard. Mrs. Castor, this is excellent. But don't you think that over here you could use a little bit of detailing, perhaps . . ."

After a quarter of an hour, Snooky's muscles were aching from the unaccustomed immobility. After twenty minutes, he was extremely uncomfortable. He began to move around on his chair, flexing his muscles surreptitiously, shaking his arms and legs.

"What's he doing?" Alice asked out loud. She had been drawing with fierce concentration, fixing him with a withering gaze. "Why's he doing that? I can't draw if he moves around."

"Snooky, what in the world do you think you're doing?"

Snooky stood up and stretched. "I'm stretching."

"Sit down and stay still."

"I can't. My muscles are aching. My blood circulation has stopped."

"Well, it is your first time, I suppose. Stand up and stretch again, then sit down for a while. I don't want your feet to fall off."

Ten minutes later Snooky stood up and walked in a rapid circle around his chair. There was a barely audible hiss from Elmo.

"I'm in the middle of something here," he said to Snooky. "Do you mind?"

"Try to remember what I look like. It shouldn't be that hard, you've been staring at me for half an hour. This is agony, by the way. Nobody in their right mind could do this for more than five minutes."

Weezy was wringing her hands. "Here Maya was always telling me you could sit in front of the television for hours. I thought you'd be a perfect subject."

"There's no TV here."

"Pretend we're the TV. We're an art show on TV. Now sit down again and let everyone finish, all right, sweetie?"

Snooky reluctantly acquiesced.

"I feel like Socrates after he took the hemlock," he announced twenty minutes later. "I have no feeling in my legs at all. Will somebody help me off the chair so I don't fall down?"

"That's all right, we're done with you." Weezy was standing behind Alice and conferring with her in a low voice. "That's all. Go into the kitchen and fix yourself something to eat."

Snooky stood up, stretched luxuriously, and left the room. He was rooting in the refrigerator a few minutes later when he heard several voices raised in argument. He straightened up and hobbled as quickly as he could toward the studio.

When he entered, Alice and Nikki were facing each other in the middle of the room.

"Stop *copying* my work!" Alice was shouting. Her pale skin was mottled red with emotion. "Stop copying me! I see you looking over while I'm working!"

There were tears rolling down Nikki's cheeks. "I'm *not* copying you . . ." she wavered.

"Yes, you are! Anyone can see! Look at this bit here, and *here!*"

"No . . . oh, no . . . you're wrong." Nikki turned to Weezy in mute appeal.

Weezy surveyed the two drawings impartially. Her hair had escaped from its clips and was frizzing around her face. She looked exhausted and frustrated. There was a long silence.

"I don't see it at all, Alice," she said at last.

Alice slammed the top of her paintbox down. "Fine! Just

like you didn't see it last time with Jennifer!" She gathered her stuff up with a clatter and headed for the door.

"Bitch," said Jennifer distinctly.

Alice swung around. "What did you call me?"

"I called you a bitch."

Alice stared, her mouth working.

"Alice, dear . . ." interposed Weezy.

Alice turned on her. "Don't you 'Alice, dear' me!" she hissed. "You always take everyone else's side, don't you? Well, don't you? And nobody here is half as talented as I am!"

"That's not true."

"It *is* true!"

"Good-bye, Alice." Weezy held the door open for her pointedly. "See you next week."

"No! I'm never coming back!"

The door slammed shut.

"Quite a scene in there," Snooky remarked later, over a glass of wine.

Weezy nodded. She had her feet up on her couch and a wineglass in her hand. Her head was pillowed on the cushions and she was staring out the big bay window.

"Does that happen often?"

"Oh, all the time. All the time. They're artists, you know. High-strung. Particularly Alice. A formidable talent, but high-strung. And she's so jealous, poor dear."

"Jealous?"

"Of Jennifer. Because of Elmo. All the girls are always in love with Elmo. I am myself, a little, you know. Nikki adores him from afar. And Mrs. Castor twinkles at him constantly. He and Jennifer have been together for years and she's always getting this kind of shit because of it."

"Do you think Nikki was copying off of Alice?"

"Not at all," Weezy said decidedly. "Alice is paranoid, that's all. Nothing's more important to her than her work. I couldn't agree with her in public, but she is more talented than anyone in the class except Elmo."

"She said you always take everybody else's side."

"Well, somebody has to. That's my role, I guess."

"She didn't seem too happy about it. Why was she giving Nikki such a hard time?"

Weezy sighed. "Because Nikki is there. Because she's meek and her entire personality irritates Alice. That's all. Alice doesn't mean anything by it."

"Really? She looked to me like she meant every word she said."

Weezy shrugged. "I'm not going to defend her, Snooky. She's a difficult case. Some students are easy to work with, and some are hard."

"They must all hate her guts."

"Oh, goodness, everyone knows she's difficult. They put up with her, that's all. Nobody's losing any sleep over it." Weezy stood up. "How would you like to see what you look like on paper?"

"On paper?"

"The work they did today. With your face bones. Would you like to see?"

"I'd be delighted."

They went into the studio, where canvases and drawings were neatly stacked against the walls. Weezy clipped five drawings up on a board.

"There. What do you think?"

Snooky surveyed them in silence. Only one looked like a human face. "I presume that's Mrs. Castor's?"

"Yes, that's right. How acute you are."

"It just seemed to me that she was more grounded in

reality than the others. Now this one here, Weezy, who did this thing?"

"That one is Elmo's."

"I hate to tell you this, but I don't think he was looking at me at all. I think he was looking at the wall behind me." The drawing in question was a series of brightly colored rectangles floating in space. "And who did *this?*"

"Guess."

"I have no idea." This drawing was a grouping of red circles shot through with different shades of white and purple. "Is that me? I'm offended. I really think I'm offended."

"It's Jennifer's. And this one is Nikki's."

Nikki had drawn two eyes, one much larger than the other, with a line for his nose and a circle for his ear. The bottom of the face trailed off in a series of zigzags.

"This is a strangely humbling experience. What's going on with my face down there?"

"Oh, nothing to worry about. This one over here is Alice's."

Alice had drawn a fanciful set of geometric shapes, squares and circles and rectangles, with forceful black lines joining them. Two of the ovals could have been eyes, or they could not have been, it was difficult to tell. Snooky thought it was mildly interesting, and said so.

"But it's not great."

"Oh, you have no eye, sweetie. A philistine, that's what you are. Alice is truly talented. She's one of the most talented students I've seen in years."

"Why bother to make me sit immobile for an hour if nobody is even going to try to draw anything resembling my face?"

"Inspiration," said Weezy. "You are providing inspiration for them. Those fine cheekbones of yours."

Snooky leaned towards her. "Admit it, you're attracted to me. My bone structure drives you wild."

"No, and please don't leer at me. It makes me nervous." Weezy did, in fact, seem to be uncharacteristically nervous. She patted her hair irritably.

"What is it?"

"What is what?"

"What's bothering you?"

"Besides your pathetic attempt to make a pass at me?" Weezy wrinkled her nose. "It's Alice, I suppose. I don't like it. It makes me unhappy when there's that kind of tension in class."

"It doesn't sound like she's coming back, so that should resolve the problem."

"Oh, she's coming back, all right. She's coming back. She tells me she's quitting every time something goes wrong, and then the next week, there she is. I can't get rid of her. But I don't like it, Snooky. Art class isn't supposed to involve warfare. I'm going to have to talk to her. Be more strict, lay down the rules." She sighed. "I hate doing that."

"You're already getting enough flak, Weezy. Maybe they'll work it out among themselves, without access to their mother superior."

Weezy gave a short laugh. "What, show some emotional maturity? No, no, I think not." She went over to the windowsill and fiddled with a hibiscus plant, then pulled a faded flower off with a sharp jerk of her hand.

At dinner that night, Bernard held up his fork and said, "What is this? Is this lobster?"

Snooky was amused. "No, Bernard. It is not lobster. Would I do that to you? Would I perform some kind of cannibalistic practical joke? No, that is a piece of fish. This is a fish stew, after all, you know. And a very excellent fish stew it is, if I say so myself."

"What kind of fish?"

"What kind? Well, there's some shark, you know, mahi-mahi, and some swordfish, and scallops and oysters and crab. That might not be fish you're holding there, that might be crab."

"Sophie has a friend who is an oyster."

"Sophie? Your lobster?"

"Yes."

"Sophie has a friend who is an oyster?"

"Yes."

Snooky threw his fork down onto the table. "Well, what is this now, Bernard? Am I responsible for the entire shellfish kingdom simply because you're writing a book about a lobster? If I had known that your dietary restrictions included *all* shellfish, and not just Sophies, I would not have dared to make this stew. But I've made it now, so please eat it."

"I can't eat lobster, and I can't eat oysters." Bernard put his fork down. "I'm sorry."

"Sweetheart—" said Maya, putting a hand on his arm.

"I can't. I'm sorry."

"This is ridiculous," Snooky said wrathfully, getting to his feet. "This fish stew took me three hours. It has my special cream sauce in it. It took me all afternoon to shop and cook. And now you won't eat it because of two fictional, may I remind you, *fictional* characters?"

"The oyster has a name."

"What is its name?"

"Sylvie."

"Sylvie?" Snooky paused. "Sylvie and Sophie?"

"That's right."

"Oh." Snooky sat down and played thoughtfully with his spoon. "Oh. Well, if it has a name already . . ."

"They've been friends since birth."

Snooky sighed. "All right, Bernard. Go into the kitchen and make yourself a peanut butter and jelly sandwich, or whatever else you can scrounge. While you're in there, write down on the pad a list of past and future book characters for me to study before I go shopping tomorrow. How can you stand being married to him, Maya? Doesn't he drive you crazy? Oh, and Bernard, one more thing. Pass over your bowl of stew before you go. I haven't tasted anything this good since St. Martin."

Weezy dropped by the next day with a bag of oranges for Maya and a smug look on her face.

"You have news," said Snooky, greeting her as she came into the kitchen.

"That's right. These are for Maya, by the way. They're not for you or Bernard. When we talked yesterday I told her she should eat a lot of foods rich in vitamin C. Very important for the baby."

"I can't have one?"

"Not even one. Where is she in this maze of a house? Upstairs? I have something I've got to tell her."

"You've won something."

"No, not exactly."

"Someone's giving you an award."

"No."

"Something involving money. Large, immense sums of money."

"No, you're not even close."

"A distant relative died and you've become an English peer and the sole owner of a vast estate and fortune."

"Where's Maya?"

"Upstairs in her room."

"Is she asleep? Will I be disturbing her?"

"I don't think she's asleep. She doesn't nap as much as she used to. She's doing whatever expectant mothers do when they're alone. Watching TV, most likely."

"See you later."

"Don't I get even one more guess?" Snooky called after her.

"No."

When Maya and Weezy came downstairs half an hour later, Maya's face was alight.

"You'll never guess," she said to Snooky.

"I've already tried at least three times."

"Weezy is going to be in *People* magazine."

Snooky stared. "Get out of here!"

"I'm serious. Look at her, doesn't she look famous already?"

Weezy glowed, hands clasped together in front of her. "It's a dream come true," she trilled. "A dream come true."

"*People* magazine?" said Snooky. "But . . . but . . . no offense, Weezy . . . but why?"

"Don't be insulting," said Maya. "Because she's a wonderful artist and the world should hear about her."

"I'm not going to be on the cover, Snooky. I'll be buried in the back, you know, where they have all the articles on real people that you've never heard of. That's me."

"Well, it's certainly wonderful. How did this happy event come to pass?"

"Oh, you'll never guess," said Weezy.

"I've already proven how little I can guess right today."

"It's all because of Harold. Harold and, more importantly, his girlfriend Gabriela."

Snooky raised an eyebrow. "Gabriela? The little mouse?"

"Yes, yes."

"The woman Harold left you for?"

Weezy waved a hand impatiently in the air. "What does that matter now, Snooky? That's ancient history. The point is, it turns out that Gabriela *works for* People *magazine.* You get my drift? She called me up today and asked me if she could come up here for an interview. She said they've been looking for an artist to profile for a while now, and she thought that I'd be perfect. If I didn't mind, that is. She said she'll bring a photographer and everything. Everything!" She closed her eyes in rapture.

"Isn't this the same woman who you were cursing a while back? The woman who stole Harold away? The little mouse with the sweet temper that he left you for? The leader in your personal pantheon of evil?"

Maya and Weezy regarded him pityingly, two sympathetic gazes.

"You don't understand, you idiot," said his sister. "This is *People* magazine."

*"People* magazine," echoed Weezy.

"He's a man. He doesn't understand."

"Apparently not."

"Men are so stupid."

"They don't understand anything, do they?"

"Let's go tell Bernard."

"He's a man, too, sweetie," Weezy reminded her.

"But he's got a strong feminine side. Let's go tell him, I'm sure he'll be thrilled for you."

"I'm thrilled for you," Snooky called, but the two of them had already left the room.

Bernard was asleep, his head cradled on a messy pile of manuscript pages, when they came into his study.

"It's good to see a man who loves his work," said Weezy.

"Poor Bernard. He's so upset over his new book and the baby and everything, he doesn't know what to do. He tosses and turns all night long."

"A lot of responsibility for one mere human."

"It is, it really is." Maya fondly surveyed the inert bulk of her husband. "It's a lot for him to deal with."

"Let's go downstairs, I don't want to wake him up. He seems so peaceful, doesn't he?"

"He always sleeps best up here, when he's supposed to be working."

Weezy leaned into the kitchen on her way out and said, "Well, at least one man in this household knows how to congratulate a person!"

Snooky looked stricken. "What did he say?"

"Well, he didn't fuss and moan about why they picked me from obscurity for an interview, I'll tell you that."

"I'm really sorry, Weezy. I really am. What did he say?"

"All the right things, sweetie. All the right things," said Weezy, and went on her way.

On a hot, sunny afternoon ten days later, the phone rang insistently at the Woodruff house. Bernard, true to his nature, did not even consider answering it. He was closeted in his study, pecking away at his typewriter. Snooky was outside getting the mail and did not hear it. At last Maya emerged from her study, a look of frustration on her face, and picked it up. "Hello?"

"Maya, something weird has happened again," said Weezy, her voice trembling. "Can you come over?"

"Right away. What is it? Are you okay?"

"Yes, yes, I'm fine. Please come."

When Weezy opened her front door ten minutes later, Maya and Snooky were standing there.

"I had to bring him," Maya said. "He whined and begged like a dog. What is it? What's happened?"

Weezy led them into the living room and pointed to the coffee table. "That."

On the table was a large bouquet of dead flowers. It was tied with a purple velvet ribbon. The faded roses, chrysanthemums and daisies drooped sadly over the edge. A withered spray of baby's breath stood up like a tiny skeleton dancing over the wreckage.

"It came in the mail just now," said Weezy.

The three of them stood and stared at it.

"Any card? Anything to identify where it came from?" asked Snooky.

Weezy shook her head. "Just the postmark." She picked up a long white box that was lying on the floor next to the table. "Manhattan."

"Sent three days ago," mused Snooky, taking the box from her. "Hmmm."

Weezy's name and address had been typed on a plain white label on the front.

"Word processor," said Snooky. "You can always tell. That computer look. There was no card inside? No message at all?"

"Nothing but the flowers," Weezy said. She was fiddling unhappily with her hair.

Maya brushed the dead flowers with her fingertip. A shower of petals came off and drifted to the floor. "Horrible," she murmured.

"Who has your address, Weezy?"

"I don't know. Everyone. I've never had any reason to keep it a secret."

"That article that came out in the *Times*," said Snooky. "Did it mention where you live?"

Weezy nodded tiredly. "Oh, yes. My move to idyllic Ridgewood, and so on."

"Who do you know who lives in Manhattan?" said Snooky.

"Everyone I know lives in Manhattan. Everyone except you and Maya and Bernard. Oh, and Mrs. Castor, she lives near here, too."

"Uh-huh. Remember all that excitement last time in class?"

Weezy chewed her lip, looking at the flowers. "Alice?"

Snooky nodded.

"I don't know. Maybe. She does have a paranoid streak. She always accuses me of taking everyone else's side against her. But still . . . this is so extreme. It doesn't seem like her."

Snooky was still looking at the box, turning it over and over in his hands. "You know, there's another possibility. I wonder . . ."

"What?"

"Have you told anyone else about the *People* magazine interview?"

Weezy looked surprised. "Just my students. Why?"

"You told them? When?"

"I don't know. Last week sometime. Five days ago, in class. Don't look at me that way, Snooky, I had to tell them about it. I wasn't bragging. I'm going to mention their names and maybe try to show some of their work in the article. You know, spread the largesse around. They deserve it . . . well, at least Alice and Elmo do. They could use the boost to their careers. It's not often that an artist gets mentioned in a big national magazine like that. They were really excited."

"Were they?" Snooky asked dryly.

"What's that supposed to mean?"

"Oh, come on, Weezy. Don't be obtuse. Those phone calls started after that first article came out. Now you have a chance for more publicity. I was wondering if maybe somebody doesn't like your career taking off."

"Maybe it's that gallery owner," said Maya. "Maybe he didn't like being turned down for dinner."

"Thank you," said Weezy. "Thank both of you. This is so extremely reassuring. I'm sure if we keep on thinking we can come up with two or three hundred other people who have a good reason to hate me."

Maya looked stricken. "I'm sorry."

"That's all right. Will one of you please throw that thing out?" Weezy sat down on the sofa. "I have to sit down. I feel exhausted all of a sudden. Thank you, Snooky," she said as he gathered up the bouquet and the white box and carried them into the kitchen. He came back with a paper bag and small broom and began to sweep up the petals.

"I'll put everything in your trash can outside. You won't have to look at it."

"Thanks."

"Shouldn't we save it to show to the police?" asked Maya.

"The police?" Weezy gave a snort. "What can they do? Say they're sorry I got dead flowers?"

"I'll save the box with the address and postmark," said Snooky.

"I hate the idea of you living here by yourself," Maya said with a worried frown. "Why don't you come and stay with us for a while?"

"No, no, no." Weezy brushed this suggestion away with a wave of her hand. "Thank you, sweetie, but no. No way. This is my home, after all. I'm not letting some phone calls and a stupid, trashy thing like those flowers chase me away. Anyway, I know how Bernard feels about visitors."

"Oh, Weezy, don't be silly. That doesn't include you. It includes—you know—Snooky, and everybody else, but not you. You're different. You could always come stay."

Weezy smiled at her affectionately. "Thank you, Maya, but again, no. I'll be fine. After all, nothing has actually happened, has it? Just some stupid flowers. Just some stupid flowers," she repeated, half to herself, gazing absently around the room.

"Do you have a security system?" asked Snooky.

"No. No, I don't."

"I think you should get one."

"I don't want to get one," Weezy said fiercely. "I thought I moved away from all of that when I left New York, for God's sake."

Snooky sat down on the couch and took her hands in his. "Listen to me. This isn't just a question of somebody dialing a long-distance number anymore. Whoever it is knows exactly who you are and where you live. I think you'd feel a lot safer with an alarm system. I know I'd feel better if you had one."

"All right, all right," Weezy said miserably. She looked around her living room as if she had never seen it before; as if the familiar furniture and rugs and paintings on the wall had suddenly become alien and frightening.

As soon as Maya got home she went upstairs to her husband's study and told him what had happened. When she was finished, Bernard thrummed on the desk with his fingers.

"Interesting."

Maya crossed her arms and stared at him angrily. "It is not interesting, Bernard. It's strange. It's menacing. It's creepy. It is not interesting."

"Oh. Yes. Yes, indeed."

"What are we going to do?"

"Will she come stay here?"

"No. She says she knows how you feel about guests."

Bernard was surprised by this. "I wouldn't feel that way about her."

"Yes, you would."

"Well, maybe, but under the circumstances it would be okay. What did you tell her?"

"I lied myself blue in the face and said that you wouldn't mind at all."

"And she still refused?"

"Yes."

"Well, we can't force her to move in with us."

"So that's it? We sit back and wait for something else to happen?"

"Maybe nothing else will happen," Bernard said soothingly. "Be calm. Think of the color blue. Think of the sky. It's probably somebody with some kind of grudge, and they've gotten it out of their system."

"You are a dreadful liar," Maya said, as she let herself be coaxed into sitting down on his lap and putting an arm around his neck.

"Be calm. Think of the baby."

"I am calm. I am perfectly calm. I'm visualizing the color blue. I don't know why I'm expected to be calm while all this stuff is happening to my best friend. I'd have to have a heart of stone."

Bernard was staring out the window.

"What are you thinking, sweetheart?"

"I'm thinking that the phone calls started after that other interview."

"Yes. That's what Snooky said, too."

"I suppose this is good for her career?"

"Well, of course it is, Bernard."

"I think you should tell her not to mention it to anybody else."

"She knows that already, Bernard."

"Still . . ."

"Still?"

"I think you should tell her to be very careful."

When Weezy called the next day, she made an effort to sound like her usual cheerful self. She brushed off Snooky's show of concern.

"Thank you, thank you so much, but I'm fine. Really, I am. Yes, yes, I'll get a security system, please stop nagging me. Are you my mother? Would you also call both the police and my seventy-five-year-old Aunt Meglet if I didn't answer the phone for a day or two? Just curious."

Snooky was disconcerted. "You have an aunt named Meglet?"

"Yes, yes. An accident of fate. Her real name is Margaret, and when she was little everyone called her Meglet. She simply never grew out of it, you know how it is. Sad, don't you think?"

"Poignant."

"Poignant, yes. *Le mot juste*. Now listen to me, sweetie, I have a favor I want to ask."

"Anything. You know that."

"Will you sit for my class again?"

"No. No way."

"Why not?"

"Because, Weezy, I practically had to consult an orthopedic specialist after the last time. It was an excruciating experience."

"Oh, come on. You know you loved it. You love being the center of attention."

"I don't know. It's not like they drew anything remotely resembling me, anyway. Why don't you just prop up a scarecrow or get yourself a store mannequin? A mannequin, now, that would really do the trick."

"Will you sit for my class again on Thursday?"

"Why don't you ask Bernard or somebody? Or are my cheekbones irreplaceable?"

"I can't ask Bernard, sweetie, he's all beard. You can't see his face at all. And can you imagine him sitting still for an hour with people staring at him? It would be torture, poor thing."

"But it's okay for me?"

"You're more sociable. You like being the focus of all eyes."

"Well . . . okay. If you insist."

On Thursday, Snooky stretched elaborately before sitting down in his chair. There was silence for nearly half an hour, broken only by Weezy's murmured comments to her students. Just when Snooky thought he would have to either move or scream, Alice let out an audible hiss.

"Stop looking at my work," she said to Jennifer.

"I'm not looking anywhere near you, you paranoid bitch."

"Yes, you are! Weezy!"

"What?"

"Jennifer's copying from me again!"

"Stop it, Alice," Weezy said dangerously. "Stop it right now."

"Stop it? It's not my fault, it's Jennifer's, she keeps looking over and distracting me—"

"Stop it, Alice."

Alice stared, scarlet flooding into her face. "I won't stop it, I won't! It's so unfair! That talentless hack keeps on stealing from me, copying my work, stealing my ideas, and you never do a damned thing about it—!"

"That's it," said Weezy. "I've had enough. I want to talk to you in private, young lady, right now."

She pushed Alice ahead of her out of the studio. Snooky let out his breath with an explosive sigh and stretched surreptitiously, flexing his muscles. He glanced around the room. Elmo had an arm protectively around Jennifer. Mrs. Castor was holding a paintbrush in the air, paint dripping, while she looked anxiously out the door. Nikki was staring at the floor, scuffling her feet like a child. But it was Jennifer who caught and held Snooky's interest. She was looking after Alice and Weezy with her dark eyes narrowed and an expression of the purest hatred on her face.

# FOUR

"WHAT HAPPENED with Alice?" Snooky asked later.

Weezy shrugged irritably. "I lectured her. She burst into tears. She said I never take her side. I said that was because she was always wrong. She said I was unfair. I told her if she caused a scene again, she was out of my class. Eventually she calmed down and agreed to try to be a little less difficult. I suggested that if she was so sure people were copying from her, she should work in the back of the room, where nobody could see what she was doing. She said that was a good idea."

"Why hadn't she thought of it before?"

Weezy gave him a pitying look. "Because she wants to be copied from. Because it feeds her ego, helps her feel like she's a big shot and everyone else is a hack. You see? Elementary psychology, my dear."

"She seems to be a big favorite with everybody by now. Jennifer gave her a look that could kill when you left the room with her. It was pretty scary. I assume it was meant for Alice and not for you?"

"Oh, no, no, that's for Alice, all right. That's Jennifer's stock in trade, looks that could kill. Unfortunately it hasn't worked so far." She gave him a weary smile.

"Takes a lot out of you, doesn't it?"

"Yeah."

"I'm sorry."

"That's all right. You're off the hook anyway, I can't use you as a model anymore. To be honest, the class is getting bored with you."

"This is the story of my life. Used for whatever I can give, and then tossed aside without a second thought."

"Sad, isn't it? But don't worry. You were never meant to work for a living, Snooky. You were meant to lie on a rock and soak in the sun, like a marmot."

His forehead was furrowed. "This is too bad. The class may be bored with me, but I'm not bored with them. There's a lot of odd stuff going on in there."

"Oh, yes, yes. A regular soap opera," she said lightly.

Weezy spent a week worrying over what she would wear for her interview in *People* magazine. She and Maya spent hours at a time closeted together in Weezy's bedroom, Maya cross-legged on the bed, watching with a critical eye as Weezy discarded one outfit after another.

"How about this?" Weezy asked, slipping a black dress over her head. "What do you think? Too plain?"

"Too somber."

"Do I want something livelier?"

"I think so."

A few outfits later, Maya shook her head. "I don't like that color blue on you. Too artisty. It looks like an artist's smock."

"Oh. How about this one? The heather-brown?"

"That's not bad."

A little while later Weezy said, "I hate to tell you this, but we've just gone through my entire wardrobe. I mean all of it.

Every single stitch of clothing I own. I'm panicking, Maya. My stress hormones are on red alert. What do I do now?"

"Don't panic. I thought the green suit was really nice."

Weezy took it out and looked at it, rubbing her chin thoughtfully. "I guess so. This is what I wore into the city to meet that gallery owner."

"It shows off your hair beautifully."

"Too businesslike?"

"No, no. Distinguished. 'I'm an artist, but I'm not flaky.' That kind of thing."

"Oh. Good. What color shirt should I wear with it?"

"You have to decide what kind of statement you want to make, Weezy."

"You mean like the flaky thing you just said?"

"You have to say to yourself, 'How do I want to present myself? What do I want to say?' Then match the shirt color to that."

"I see. Like, crimson for 'look at me'?"

"Right. Or red for 'I get angry easily.' "

"How about green for 'I hope they pay me a lot of money for doing this'?"

"No, no, green means 'I hope everyone who knows me just dies of jealousy when they see me in this magazine.' "

Weezy sighed. "How about blue for 'my lover just left me for this interviewer and I'm feeling kind of down about it'?"

Maya looked at her sympathetically. "It's not an easy situation, is it?"

"No. Not at all. You know, it still hurts about her and Harold, and I'm still mad as hell about it, but I'll be damned if I'm not going to give this interview. I mean, this is my one chance at fame; my five minutes of celebrity."

"You'll have more than five minutes, Weeze. You'll see. You're a great artist. I've always told you that."

"All I really want to say is, 'I'm thrilled to be in the pages of *People.*' "

"What color would that be, do you think?"

"Well, what color is their logo?"

Later, when Snooky asked what they had talked about, Maya looked mysterious. "Things."

"I assumed that. What kind of things?"

"Things."

He looked at her inquiringly.

"Women things. Things you wouldn't understand. It's not easy to choose what to wear to become famous in."

"I don't get it, Maya. Do you think my brain is constitutionally incapable of understanding women-type things?"

"That's right, little brother."

"Because I don't care what I wear?"

"That, and other things."

"You think a higher testosterone level renders me incapable of understanding what you and Weezy are giggling about for hours in her room?"

"Right," said Maya.

Gabriela Loeser smiled warmly. She was wearing a cream-colored suit which set off her blonde good looks. "Hello, Ms. Kaplan."

"Please call me Weezy."

"Weezy. This is Vince."

Vince was short, with a receding hairline and a face as wrinkled as a prune. He was looking around the living room appraisingly.

"Vince is our photographer."

"Hello, Vince." Weezy shook hands. She was wearing her moss-green suit and a black silk blouse which she and Maya had decided at the last minute showed off her pale skin to advantage. She adjusted the silk bow at her throat with trembling fingers. "This way, please. I think you wanted to see my studio?"

"Yes, the photos would be best in there, I think," said Gabriela.

Weezy led the way down the hall, exchanging casual banter with the two of them. She was thinking, *This is Harold's girlfriend. His* girlfriend. *The little mouse that he left me for.* That fact, which had seemed so unimportant a few days before, now played itself mindlessly over and over in her brain. *Harold's girlfriend . . . Harold's girlfriend . . . Harold's girlfriend . . . Harold's girlfriend in my house . . . oh my God, Harold's girlfriend in my studio . . .*

These thoughts droned on in her head while on the outside she was saying brightly, "Oh, yes, lots of light, and I love plants so much, so it really works out nicely."

Gabriela seemed nervous, too. Her smile was apologetic, as if she were sorry now for trapping the two of them in such an awkward situation. But she seemed genuinely interested in the studio and in Weezy's work. "These paintings are yours? They're beautiful!"

"Thank you, yes, these are mine. I keep my students' over there. These are my latest, the ones I'll be showing at the gallery."

"Gallery Genuardi," said Gabriela. She snapped open her briefcase with a sharp *click*, took out a tape recorder, slipped in a cassette and pressed a button. "Gallery Genuardi," she repeated, a little more loudly.

"That's right."

Gabriela turned off the recorder. "Can we get a shot of you next to the paintings? Vince?"

"Stand over here," said Vince. He had taken out his equipment and was setting up lights. "I'll arrange the paintings behind her."

"Okay," said Weezy. She pressed her hands together nervously. She stood in front of her paintings and smiled when Vince told her to. She was quite sure it was an idiotic smile. She was quite sure this whole thing was a terrible mistake. There was Harold's girlfriend, doubtless despising her, pitying her . . . pitying her willingness to prostitute herself for a fleeting moment of fame. Gabriela was standing behind Vince, murmuring occasionally in his ear, pointing to one or the other of the paintings.

"Turn your head this way and smile," said Vince.

Weezy turned and smiled. She felt hot under the lights. She was sweating, and her black silk shirt clung to her under the suit. This was the stupidest thing she had ever done in her entire life. She sighed and passed a hand over her face, then touched one of her paintings protectively.

"Don't move, please," said Vince. "Thanks. Actually, move that way. Turn a bit—that's right—then look straight at me. Good. Good."

It was like having your children examined by a particularly strict headmistress, thought Weezy. Examined, and not passing muster. She remembered a moment from her childhood when the young Weezy, overweight, with unfashionably frizzy hair (why oh why did I have to grow up when the Morticia Addams look was so popular, she moaned to herself), her nose sticking out and her complexion in the throes of early adolescence, was shoved by her parents into a bunk at her new summer camp to be met by the hostile gazes of five or six sleek-haired, smooth-skinned girls her own age. It was a riding camp, and Weezy had enthusiastically gone out and bought riding boots and a Western hat, which she was wearing at the time. After a dumbstruck pause, the other girls had simply laughed.

"That's good," said Vince.

"What?" asked Weezy. She had flushed deeply at the recollection.

"That look. You look far away."

Far away in the Land of Humiliation, thought Weezy, turning and posing as instructed. Mercifully, it was soon over. Vince nodded and began to put away his camera. "Thanks a lot."

"I wonder if I could show some of my students' work as well?" Weezy asked timidly.

Vince glanced over at Gabriela, who shook her head. "No pictures, if you don't mind, Weezy," she said. "The article's about you. You can talk about them later, if you want."

They went back into the living room and sat down on the sofas. Gabriela took out her tape recorder again. Weezy regarded it fearfully. She always felt so inhibited when she knew she was being taped. Her voice took on a funny singsong cadence and, on playback, she always sounded like a stranger to herself: a distant relative, with an entirely different sort of voice. Someone she did not know at all.

"When did you first begin to paint?"

Weezy talked about her childhood, painting in her room when she was young; then, gaining confidence (it really is so easy to talk about yourself, she thought) she spoke about her recent career, her gallery shows, her students. She mentioned all of them by name. She made it clear that this was a master class of her best students, artists who were nearly ready to go out on their own. Then, under Gabriela's prodding, she talked about her move to Ridgewood (by silent mutual consent, boyfriends past and present were never mentioned; Weezy talked about the hubbub of New York and the peace and quiet of Connecticut, nothing more) and her life there. She spoke enthusiastically about her new exhibit and her hopes for the future. When Gabriela turned off her recorder and packed it away, Weezy felt perversely disappointed. But I have more to say about myself, she felt like shouting; much, much more!

"Thank you very much," said Gabriela.

"Oh, you're welcome. My pleasure. Thank you for calling me."

"Well, as I told you, I'm a big fan. I, ummm, I always tell Harold that." She glanced sideways at Weezy.

"Oh. Yes."

Weezy showed them to the door and shook hands with both of them. Vince ambled out to the car. Gabriela turned to go, then turned back suddenly.

"Weezy . . ."

"Yes?"

"I guess you think it's crazy, my calling you like this."

"No. No, I don't at all. I was . . . flattered."

"I'm sorry everything's so awkward because of Harold."

"Harold has a genius for making things awkward," Weezy said dryly, and for a moment they laughed quietly together, two women in silent accord.

"Well, I think the article's going to turn out great. I'll let you know when it's coming out."

"I'd appreciate that."

"Good-bye," said Gabriela. "Thanks very much for your time."

"Good-bye."

Afterward, Weezy felt despondent. She went into the kitchen, poured herself a glass of white wine and picked up the phone.

"I think I made a fool out of myself," she said to Maya. "Oh, yes, I did. No, it didn't go well. How could I have let Harold's girlfriend into my house? Into my life? How could I have let her come here and interview me? Snooky was right after all. I was blinded by greed. Would you put him on? Do you mind?"

She waited, thrumming listlessly with her fingers against the countertop.

"Hello, Snooky. You were right. It was ridiculous. Why did I let her come here? Why do you think she wanted to come? Just to see the harridan Harold used to live with? What?"

A pause.

"No, I don't think she and Harold are admirers of my work. Harold never cared for my work one way or another. I could have painted my face blue and my nose green and stood on my head for all he cared."

She sniffled.

"Yes, I'd love some company. You don't mind coming over? Good, I'm sure Maya and Bernard are sick to death of you. How long have you been here, anyway? Aren't you leaving soon? You're staying until the baby's born? Have you told Bernard that yet? No? Good idea. Okay, we'll throw something together here for dinner. I'm not hungry."

She hung up and sat down at the kitchen table, playing idly with her wineglass. Outside, the day continued sunny and warm, undisturbed by her turbulent state of mind. She hated the weather. She hated herself. She sighed and sipped her wine. As always when she was upset or moved by something, she saw her emotions in her mind's eye painted in vivid colors: dark red, the color of blood. Purple. A swirl of deep cerulean blue.

When Snooky rang the doorbell and let himself in, she went straight up to him and threw her arms around him. He leaned down to give her a hug. His heart skipped a beat.

"I'm so upset," she said, drawing away and wiping her eyes.

"If you made love with me, maybe it would make you feel better about Harold."

"I'm not that upset. Is Maya mad that I asked you to come over instead of her?"

"She didn't seem to be. Her last words when I left were, 'Thank God you're getting out of here at last.' Why did you ask me, by the way?"

"I don't know. I don't know. I needed a man around. Besides, you're a wonderful cook and I know you'll take care of me."

He followed her into the living room. "Fame isn't all it's cracked up to be, is that the problem?"

"Yes. Why did I let her in here? I feel so violated."

"You kept telling me that the only important thing was that she worked for a certain magazine."

"That's what I thought, but I was wrong. I was terribly, terribly wrong. I hated her, and I hated myself. I had no dignity."

"I'm sure that's not true. You have innate dignity."

Weezy poured him a glass of wine. "No, no, no. I was ridiculous. I groveled at the altar of instant fame. When the interview was over, I wanted to talk longer, Snooky. I *loved* talking about myself. And she saw it all, and she must have thought I was ridiculous. Who in their right mind would let their lover's new girlfriend into their house the way I did? Oh, I feel so . . . so *low.*"

"Did she talk about him at all?"

"Just a little, at the end."

"Maybe she called you because she's always wondered about you and she couldn't help herself when an opportunity came up. Maybe Harold talks about you all the time and it makes her crazy. Maybe she feels just as insecure as you do."

Weezy gave him a withering look. "Maybe little green

men are going to come down from the planet Vor and take me away to live in luxury on the moon."

"You don't have to be snide. I'm just trying to help."

"You don't understand anything."

"Well, I'll tell you one thing I don't understand. If they're from the planet Vor, why would they carry you away to our moon? Wouldn't they have a moon of their own? Why wouldn't they take you back to Vor itself?"

There was a silence.

"Deadly gases in the Vorian atmosphere, perhaps," mused Snooky. "Inhospitable to human life."

"Would you like some more wine? Not that you need any, the way you're babbling on."

"I'd love some."

Later, he made her dinner (chicken breasts cooked with peaches; frozen broccoli, which he steamed and then lathered with butter; a spinach salad with olive oil, balsamic vinegar and garlic dressing). Weezy dug a cherry cobbler out of the back of the fridge, and they shared it for dessert. They ate in the dining room, under a skylight which Weezy had had installed at the same time that her studio was being remodeled. Overhead, the moon winked solemnly, a yellow orb floating in the dark blue sky.

"It's like a primitive astronomical observatory here." Snooky tilted his head back.

"My plants love all the light. Oh, God, that's something I blathered in the interview today. But it's true."

"Your kitchen is a lot better stocked than Bernard's. You understand how to live, Weezy. Bernard would rather be consumed by ants than buy balsamic vinegar."

Weezy smiled faintly. "We are alike there, Snooks. You and I. We both like to live well."

"Nothing but the best."

"That's right."

Snooky leaned forward and grabbed her hand. "Then why not be together?"

Weezy flushed a deep red. "Don't ask me that," she whispered.

"Why not?"

"Don't pester me today. Pester me tomorrow."

"Why not today?"

"I'm weak today." She withdrew her hand.

Snooky regarded her thoughtfully over his wineglass. "All right."

"Really?"

"Uh-huh."

"That's very gentlemanly of you."

"Thank you."

"Some more wine?"

"No, thanks." He tilted back his head again. "Look at that moon. It's like being at Stonehenge, having dinner here."

"You mean cold, dark and unwelcoming?"

He smiled at her and took her hand, in a friendly way this time. "No. Don't take everything so personally. Just a little chitchat about the moon. Have you ever been to Stonehenge?"

"No. I'm sure you have. You've been everywhere."

"I don't know about everywhere, but I've been to Stonehenge all right."

"Tell me about it," said Weezy, and settled back in her seat.

When Snooky let himself into his sister's house later that evening, he found Maya and Bernard cuddling together in front of the TV set.

"This is all you do while I'm out?" he said, coming in and throwing his jacket down on the armchair. "This is the best you can do?"

"Shut up, Snooky," they said simultaneously.

"What's this?"

The TV screen was filled with what looked like blood vessels stretched over a filmy membrane.

"*Nova,*" said Maya. "The development of a human fetus. They're up to two months. Shut up now, Snooky, I'm trying to see what my baby looks like."

"Did you ever wonder how they take these pictures?"

"Be quiet, Snooky. There, Bernard, where are they now? What's that, around ten weeks?"

Maya and Bernard leaned forward, their mouths open, drinking in the sight of the fetus floating in space. Its gigantic head nodded at them familiarly. It turned and rotated in its blurry red world.

"Hard to believe," said Snooky. "Looks like a mutated shrimp. Looks like one of those giant Frisian Island shrimps I thought Bernard was cooking the day I arrived."

"Go to your room," said Maya. "Leave us alone."

"I'm in love with your best friend."

"What?"

Snooky repeated himself. Maya stared at him blankly.

"You've always had a thing about Weezy. It's nothing serious. You're always attaching yourself leechlike to somebody or other."

"I'm in love with her, Missy."

Maya waved him away irritably. "Go to your room. Clean it up or something."

"I'm not eight years old anymore, Missy. You can't order me to my room. Anyway, it's not my room, it's your room. Your spare guest room."

"It could be your room for all the time you've spent in it," rumbled Bernard.

"Thank you, Bernard. And thank you, Maya, for that heart-to-heart talk."

---

"I'm sorry," Maya said later. She came into Snooky's room and sat down cross-legged on his bed.

"About what?" Snooky put down the paperback he had been reading.

"For not listening to you before. We really wanted to see what the baby looks like."

"Did you find out?"

"Yes."

"How does it look?"

"Like nothing human," said Maya, shuddering slightly. "Like something from outer space. What's that you're reading?"

"*Crime and Punishment* by Dostoevsky."

Maya looked closer at the cover. "In French?"

"I picked it up the last time I was in Paris. It's not bad."

"Why not read it in English?"

Snooky shrugged and tossed the book aside. The one thing he had excelled at in college had been his language courses. It had made his older brother William very happy, until he realized that Snooky's language ability simply made it easier for him to wander the globe as he pleased.

"You've always been good at languages."

"Ah, well. *Merci.*"

"Listen, about Weezy . . ."

Maya's voice trailed away. There was a heavy silence.

"Yes?"

"I don't know what to say. You've always had a thing for her."

"Yes."

"Ever since you were little, you used to tag after her and look at her funny."

"Thank you."

"I don't think she's really open to a new relationship right now, Snooks. Not after what happened with Harold. She's been pretty badly burned, you know. She's throwing herself into her work instead."

"I know."

"Plus, I don't like it. I mean, she's my best friend and everything, and you're my younger brother. It doesn't seem right. It makes me feel uncomfortable."

"Gee, that's too bad, isn't it, Missy? I would hate to disturb your perfect life in any way or make you feel uncomfortable."

Maya flushed. "What do you mean?"

"I mean, you have a relationship, maybe with someone who's very strange, but a relationship anyway. You're happy. I would hate to disturb you by seeking a little happiness of my own."

"That's not what I meant."

"Really? Then what did you mean?"

"I have news for you, Snooks, Weezy's not interested in you anyway. She's known you her whole life, it would be incestuous. She's like your other big sister. She's told me again and again she's not interested."

Snooky reddened. "You don't know that. You don't know what she really feels, you just know what she tells you. Did it ever occur to you that maybe she didn't want to disturb you or mess up your friendship?"

"That's stupid. You're just being stupid."

"Oh, yeah?"

"I would never stand in the way of anybody else being happy. That's not the point."

"What's the point, then, big sister?"

"The point is that even if the two of you go out for a while, then you'll break up, just as you have with countless other women, and it'll be awkward the rest of our lives! It's a situation we'll have to live with forever!" Maya was shouting, her face red.

"You mean a situation *you'll* have to live with forever."

"Yes, that's what I mean!"

"Well, I'm sorry if my feelings make you so damned uncomfortable, Maya. I'm sorry if my feelings are disturbing you. Far be it from me to set up a bad situation for *you* by how I feel about your best friend! God knows the only thing Weezy and I should be thinking about in this situation is you, you and you!"

"That's not what I meant—" began Maya, but her brother was gone. The old rickety door slammed shut, and then bounced open and swung slowly to and fro on its hinges.

"Didn't you leave here a couple of hours ago, or have you been standing on my porch this entire time?" asked Weezy, opening her front door.

"Can I stay here, just for tonight?" Snooky looked at her forlornly.

"Why? What's wrong?"

"I had a big fight with Maya."

"With Maya? The sweetest-tempered person in the world? Over what?"

Snooky shrugged. She looked at his face for a long moment. "Come on in."

She settled him on the sofa and brought them both cups of tea with honey. "Now tell me all about it, there's a dear boy. Spill out your heart to your old Aunt Weezy."

"I can't."

"Why in the world not?"

He looked at her woodenly. "It's too . . . personal."

Weezy drank her tea thoughtfully. She had changed from her green interview suit with the black shirt to a pair of worn blue jeans that were so faded they were nearly white, and a yellow T-shirt that said CORNELL.

"Where'd you get that shirt?"

"Old boyfriend."

"Oh." Snooky felt more dispirited than ever.

Weezy dabbled her finger in her tea and seemed about to say something, when the phone shrilled outside in the greenhouse. Weezy went into the kitchen and Snooky could hear her talking in a low voice. When she came back, she said cheerfully, "That was Maya."

"Oh."

"She figured you'd run over here like the squeaking rat you are, she said."

"Uh-huh."

"I told her you wouldn't talk about it, and she acted all mysterious and strange and said she couldn't talk about it either, but could I please tell you that she thinks she was wrong. That she thinks you had a point. That she wants you to know she's sorry."

"Oh. Okay."

"What's this all about, Snooky?"

"Nothing."

"Yeah. It sounds like nothing." She sat down next to him again and picked up her mug of tea. "You're all upset and won't talk about it, and Maya's nearly in tears, and she's with child, may I remind you. I'm sure Bernard is happy as a clam right now, too. What's going on over there with the three of you?"

"I have to go," said Snooky, standing up abruptly.

"You what?"

"I have to go. Thanks for the tea."

"Why am I always one step behind in this?" asked Weezy,

following him to the door. "Didn't you just arrive? I thought you wanted a place to stay?"

"I should get back. I shouldn't stay here. Maya needs me. Thanks anyway."

"You're welcome," said Weezy, and stood at the door watching with her arms folded as he got in his car and, gunning it, drove away.

Maya enveloped him in a hug as he came in the door.

"I'm sorry, Snooks," she said in a muffled voice into his shoulder. "I'm sorry. You're right. It's none of my business. It's up to you and Weezy what you want to do."

"You were right, too, Maya. I couldn't stay there, it was so uncomfortable to be fighting about it in front of her. I have to get things sorted out about this."

"Do you forgive me?"

He took her by the shoulders and tilted her chin up. "I don't blame you for how you feel. I'd feel the same way, I guess. How's the baby? We shouldn't be fighting in front of the baby."

"Will you still stay here and cook for us?"

"Of course."

They hugged each other again.

"How touching," said a voice from the top of the stairs. Bernard descended, his face like thunder. "You mean you're back already? How long did you stay away after upsetting Maya so much? Twenty minutes?"

"I just said I was sorry."

"Don't nag at him, Bernard, it wasn't his fault."

"I don't care whose fault it was, I don't want him upsetting you. I don't want anything upsetting you right now. I went upstairs and found her crying in your room," he said to Snooky.

"I really am sorry."

Bernard came up and put his face very close to Snooky's. "I don't care if you are her brother, any more fights and you're out of here."

Snooky winced slightly. "I understand."

Maya was patting her husband's arm in a vain attempt to get his attention. "Stop it, Bernard. You don't have to act so protective of me, for God's sake. He didn't mean anything. He was right and I was wrong."

"I won't have her upset," said Bernard, breathing heavily into Snooky's face.

"I understand. Did you by any chance have liver and onions for dinner?"

"I won't have anyone fighting with her."

"Bernard, you and I fight all the time," Maya said crossly.

"That's different."

"It is? Why?"

They went off into the other room, still arguing heatedly, while Snooky took the opportunity to vanish upstairs.

After this, things settled bumpily back into their usual routine, with Snooky running the house and Maya and Bernard busy at their jobs. Nothing more about Weezy was said. She came over frequently, to sit at their kitchen table and complain about her art students; but she did not ask Snooky over to her house again. Occasionally he would look up to find her gazing at him, her green eyes narrow and inquiring, like a cat's. She would give Maya the same curious look; but she never asked about it again. She came and drank their excellent coffee and complained freely about her students.

"It's driving me crazy, it really is," she said one day. "I'm going to have to check myself into a spa for a rest cure soon."

"What's going on now?" said Maya. "I thought Alice promised to be good."

"Oh, she did, she did, but she still has her charming little ways of letting people know what she thinks of them. She doesn't actually say anything, but she gives people looks, and sets up her easel noisily at the back of the room, and so on. The other day she accused Nikki and Jennifer—she wasn't sure which, she said—of using one of her brushes when she wasn't there. As if her brush had some magic quality, you know. As if they could paint better with it because it was hers. Really, the sheer, hideous egotism of it, it's enough to make one despair of the entire human race. I told you I hate artists."

"That's awful," Snooky said. "More coffee?"

"Thanks."

"No wonder you need a spa vacation."

"I do, I need to get away. Mud baths and facials and steam rooms and someone serving me three meals a day, that's what I need. Not all this aggravation from a roomful of overaged children. I don't include Mrs. Castor in that, Mrs. Castor is a living doll."

"Hmmmm," said Maya. "Any more weird things happening? Phone calls or flowers or—you know—anything?"

"No, no, thank God. Not a peep. I don't want you worrying yourself, Maya."

"I'm not, I'm not. By the way, do you think I'm beginning to show?"

Weezy regarded her friend's angular frame dubiously. "I don't know, sweetie. Maybe a little."

"I wish I would show, it doesn't seem real otherwise."

"At least your appetite has returned."

"With a vengeance," said Snooky. "I shudder to think what's going to happen as this goes on. She's already eating enough for two full-sized adults."

"It's good for her to eat. Remember how worried we all were when she wouldn't eat anything the first trimester."

"You don't have to worry anymore," said Maya with a groan. "My doctor told me I'd better slow down, or I'll have put on sixty pounds by the time the baby comes. I'm serious."

"You shouldn't worry about what you eat," said Snooky. "It's ridiculous. Eat whatever you want."

"That's not what the doctor says."

"You're so skinny, you need to catch up a bit," said Weezy. "Here, have another one of these low-sodium pretzels. They're not bad."

"I found them at the health food store," said Snooky. "I do a lot of shopping there now that Maya is pregnant. I only want the best for my nephew or niece."

"That's nice," said Weezy, crinkling her nose at him. Snooky felt his heart turn over. He smiled back at her. Maya rested her chin on her hand and looked back and forth between them with an expression of resignation and dread on her face.

Bernard, unexpectedly, stuck up for Snooky.

"Weezy could do worse," he told his wife as they were getting ready for bed that night.

Maya lowered her toothbrush and stared at her reflection in the mirror. "Pardon me?"

"I've been thinking it over. Weezy could do a whole hell of a lot worse."

"You've got to be kidding."

Bernard shook his head.

"But I *hate* this."

"I know. I know. I hate it too. I hate watching him prey on your friend, and I hate having him moon around here like a lovesick antelope. But it might not be so terrible. I just wish he'd move in with her and get it over with."

"Oh, God."

"At least then he'd be out of here."

"But I don't want him to be out of here." Maya gripped the sink with both hands, feeling tears well up in her eyes. "I don't want him out of here. I like having him here. And I like having Weezy as my friend. It seems now that they both like each other more than they like me."

"Oh." Bernard gave her a gentle hug. "Come on."

"I know."

"Hormones."

"Yes." Maya accepted the Kleenex and made a loud honking sound into it. "Thanks."

"Snooky's nothing but trouble. I'm going to talk to him tomorrow."

"About what?"

"I don't know," Bernard said, getting into bed. "But I'm going to talk to him."

"Well, that'll be a first," said Maya, her good humor restored.

Snooky was chopping vegetables in the kitchen when Bernard came downstairs the next afternoon.

"Hi, Bernard. Have a seat. Emerged from your lair, have you? We don't usually see much of you before dinner is served."

Bernard grunted and sat down.

"I told Maya we shouldn't even call you for dinner, we should just open the study door and fling in some raw meat, but she didn't agree with me."

"Mmmm-hmmm."

"Hand me that cleaver, would you? Thanks. What is it?"

"I wanted to talk to you."

"Well, here I am. Let's talk. Hand me that green pepper, will you? Thanks. Go ahead."

Bernard opened his mouth, but what he was about to say was lost forever. The phone shrilled.

"Hold on a minute," said Snooky. He picked it up. "Hello?"

Bernard could hear a woman's voice sobbing on the other end. Snooky's cheerful expression dissolved.

"Weezy? What's wrong?"

He listened for a moment, then said, "Coming right over," and slammed the phone down. He turned to Bernard.

"Someone broke into Weezy's studio. All her paintings have been slashed." The two of them stared at each other for a moment. Then Snooky stirred himself into action.

"I have to go."

"I'll come with you."

"No. Stay with Maya."

"Maya's at the library," Bernard said irritably. "She'll be there all day. I'm coming with you."

"All right."

Weezy met them at the door, her eyes wild, her face streaked with tears. She flung herself into Snooky's arms.

"Oh, God," she said, and broke down again.

Bernard pushed past them, feeling awkward and out of place. He lumbered down the hallway into her studio. He looked around grimly. Paints and brushes were scattered everywhere. Canvases were lying on the floor, their surfaces ripped open and gaping. Easels had been knocked over. It looked like an unimaginable force of destruction had hit the room. Even the plants had been thrown violently on the floor. They lay among the torn canvases, clay pots broken, soil mingling with paint.

Bernard was leaning over one of the paintings when Snooky and Weezy came into the room.

"Oh, Jesus," he heard Snooky murmur.

"They got everything," said Weezy. "Everything."

"Take her into the living room and pour her a drink," Bernard said sharply, straightening up. "Have you called the police?" he asked her.

"Yes, right after I called you."

"Good."

Snooky led her away. Bernard walked gingerly around, trying not to disturb anything. He examined another canvas, then walked over to a pile stacked in one corner. A short while later he went into the living room.

"I'm sorry, Weezy, but I wonder if you'd come back in there with me for a minute? Something I want you to look at."

Weezy was sitting curled up on the sofa with Snooky next to her. "Okay."

"Did you get her something to drink?" Bernard asked.

"I don't want anything," Weezy said shortly. She followed him into the studio.

"These paintings over here, in the corner. Whose are they?"

She glanced at them, chewing her lip. "They're Alice's."

"Oh."

"Why?"

"They're the only ones left untouched."

"Oh," said Weezy. Her eyes met Bernard's. "But they were off by themselves in this corner here. Whoever it was might just not have seen them."

"Who do you think did this, Weezy?"

"I don't know. I don't have the faintest idea."

"One of your students?"

"I don't know."

"Was anything else in the house messed up or taken?"

"Not that I can see."

"So they just came in here," mused Bernard. "How did they get in?"

Weezy flushed guiltily. "Well . . . the front door was open."

"What?"

"This is Ridgewood. I never lock my door. It was such a luxury after New York, not to have to worry." Her eyes filled with tears. "You can imagine. I locked my door for a while after those flowers came, but then . . . well, then I forgot."

"Yes, we never lock our door either," Bernard said reluctantly. "Where were you?"

"Out shopping for dinner."

He nodded. "Are any of your knives missing?"

"My knives?"

"I can't find a knife in here that seems sharp enough to have done this. I wondered if one of your kitchen knives might have been used."

"I don't know. Let me go check."

She was back in a few minutes. "Not that I can tell, Bernard. I have a drawer full of knives, it's hard to remember how many there are supposed to be." She leaned over one of the slashed canvases and examined it closely. "This wouldn't necessarily have to be that sharp a knife. Canvas isn't that hard to cut."

"Okay. Listen, I'm going to call a security alarm company for you. I want to see an alarm installed in here as soon as possible."

"I should have done it right after the flowers came." She looked at Snooky. "I don't know why I didn't. I feel terrible about it now."

"And I think you should come stay at our house for a while," said Bernard.

"Oh, thank you, but Snooky's already offered to stay here with me."

Bernard's gaze flickered over his brother-in-law. "Yes, well," he said dryly, "I'm sure that would be very nice, but I know Maya, and she's going to want to make sure you're safe. Come stay with us."

Weezy looked around her studio, at the ruined canvases and the toppled easels, at the plants lying broken on the floor. "Thank you," she said in a low voice. "I think I will."

"Trust your brother to try to use this whole thing in the service of his libido," Bernard told Maya later.

"I'm sure that's not what he meant."

"Really? Why?"

Maya was fiddling with a pencil. "This whole thing with Weezy is so . . . so unreal. I can't believe it happened. I'm glad she's coming to stay with us. I've been nervous for months about her."

"Yes."

"Did the police find anything?"

"Just one of my footprints."

"What?"

"There was some dust in the corner, and they managed to find one of my footprints there. Everyone was all excited until I matched my shoe to it."

"They didn't just haul you away to the local jail?"

"No, Weezy stuck up for me. She didn't think I had done it."

"Well, you see," said Maya. "So friendship counts for something after all."

---

Weezy was quiet at dinner that night. Maya watched her anxiously. Snooky danced attendance, running back and forth from the kitchen to serve her every whim.

"I feel like a princess," Weezy said at last, smiling.

"We're all royalty here," said Snooky. "Bernard, for instance, eats like a king."

Bernard was eating as quickly as he could, forking huge mouthfuls in, his mind elsewhere.

"I feel bad leaving my house all by itself," Weezy said.

"Don't worry. I set up a timer for the lights. Nobody will know you're not home," said Snooky.

"They will, though. Can't they just tell? Doesn't an empty house look different?"

"No."

"This was a delicious dinner, Snooky."

"Nothing but the best for you."

Later that evening, when Maya showed her up to her room, Weezy put her bag down and gave her a quick hug.

"Thanks for letting me stay."

"Don't be silly."

"This is a lovely room."

Maya had shown her to a tiny room under the eaves on the second floor, down the hall from Maya and Bernard's room and the nursery. It had pink and white floral wallpaper and a thick cream-colored rug on the floor.

"Why didn't you use this for the baby?" asked Weezy, surveying the walls. "It could have saved Bernard a hell of a lot of trouble."

"Too far away from our room."

"Oh. Of course."

"Weeze . . . are you all right?"

"Yes."

"You sure?"

"Yes, I'm okay."

"How are you . . . how are you feeling?"

Weezy sat down on the bed. "You want to know the stupidest thing? I keep thinking about that gallery owner, and how I jinxed everything by not going out to dinner with him. Maybe if I had done that, it all would have worked out all right."

"Oh, come on."

"I know it's ridiculous. I just feel like I must have done something wrong, to have this happen to me. I mean, it'll be a year before I can put a show together again. Or longer. Everything I had was in my studio."

"I know." Maya sat down and put an arm around her.

"It's not fair, My. Everything I had." Weezy's voice choked.

"I know."

"Not fair." Weezy leaned her frizzy head against her friend's smooth one. "Not fair." Tears ran down her cheeks.

Maya hugged her gently. "I know. I know, sweetie. It's awful."

They sat together while Weezy cried. Then she straightened up and dragged a hand across her face.

"Okay," she said, sniffling. Maya gave her a Kleenex. "Thanks."

"Anything I can do? Get you some hot chocolate, or something?"

"No. You shouldn't have to take care of me while you're pregnant. You're gestating, after all."

"A full-time job," said Maya, and they laughed together.

Half an hour later Snooky came upstairs, holding a heavy ceramic mug in his hand, and knocked on Weezy's door.

"Come in."

"I brought you some hot chocolate."

"Oh, thanks."

She was sitting in a white wicker seat in front of the vanity in the corner, brushing her hair. She was wearing a long nightgown of thick white cotton which rustled when she moved.

Snooky leaned against the doorjamb.

"Do women really brush their hair at night? That Victorian thing? Silver hairbrushes with your initials on it and so on?"

"I don't know about most women. I have to tame my hair every night, otherwise it grows onto the bedposts while I'm sleeping and I can't get it untangled in the morning."

"Like ivy."

"Exactly. Thank you for the hot chocolate."

"That's okay. How are you doing?"

Weezy laughed softly. "Everyone in this family is so solicitous, I don't know how to handle it. Everyone except Bernard, thank God. He hasn't asked me once how I'm feeling."

"Bernard is not aware that other people have feelings. He has demonstrated that to me on numerous occasions."

"Well, I'm all right, Snooky. I'm all right. Just put the hot chocolate down on that table and go away now, there's a good boy."

He sighed and went away.

The next morning Weezy woke up early. She got up, changed and went downstairs to find Bernard already sitting at the kitchen table drinking coffee and reading the paper.

"Good morning," he said politely.

"Good morning, sweetie. Can I help myself to some coffee?"

"Right there."

She poured herself a cup and stirred milk into it. "Anyone else up?"

Bernard shook his head. He absentmindedly felt around the table, underneath the newspaper, for his coffee cup. "No."

"Then you'll have to say good-bye and thanks for me. I'm going home."

He lowered the paper. "Are you sure?"

"I'm sure."

"The men from the security alarm company should be there in a few hours. They said they'd come before noon."

"Thank you."

"Be careful."

"I will."

"And Weezy, one more thing before you go."

"Yes?"

"Were you planning to clean up your studio today?"

"Yes, of course. I can't leave it looking like that. I have students coming later."

"How would you feel about letting them see it the way it is?"

"Why, Bernard? To see if one of them looks guilty and screams out, 'It was me, I did it'?"

Bernard shrugged. "It might be useful, that's all. To see how they react."

Weezy toyed with her cup. "Well . . . I want to get it cleaned up, but I guess they could help me. After I spring it on them, I mean. All right, I guess, if you say so."

"You could bring Snooky along."

"Snooky? Why?"

Bernard shrugged and lifted the paper again. "He's good at stuff like that. How people react. What they're feeling. That kind of thing. It's the only thing that seems to stick in that tiny reptile brain of his."

"Snooky is a creature of emotion and instinct," agreed Weezy. She pulled part of the newspaper towards her. "Oh, my, look at all the terrible things going on in the world. This puts my own personal traumas into perspective."

"Does it?"

"No. Not really."

Bernard, in an unaccustomed spasm of sympathy, said, "Can I make you some breakfast?"

"Thank you, my dear, that's the nicest thing you ever said to me, but no thank you. I'm going home now. Give Maya a kiss for me and tell her thanks very much. I'll call her later. Oh, and tell Snooky if he wants to be present at the unveiling to be at my house by one o'clock. That's when the class arrives."

"Okay."

"Oh, my God," Alice said. Her eyes widened and her hands went up to her face. "What . . . what is this?"

"This happened yesterday," said Weezy, watching her steadily. "Yesterday afternoon."

"Oh, my God," said Alice feebly, her eyes scanning the destruction. All at once she gave a little scream. "Oh, no, *no!* Not the 'Girl'!"

She went over to one of the slashed canvases and touched it with trembling fingertips.

"The girl?" said Snooky in an undertone.

" 'Girl in White,' " said Weezy, still watching Alice. "The painting I told you about. Elmo's best. Something he's been working on for a while, here and at home. Unfortunately it was here yesterday."

Snooky nodded.

There was a wide and interesting range of reactions among the students. Mrs. Castor, who was the next to arrive, simply tightened her lips and nodded grimly as Weezy explained to her. She lowered her head over her torn paintings as if they were children. Jennifer, who came in soon after with Elmo, was horrified and teary; Elmo was enraged. He looked as if he wanted to put his fist through the wall.

"Calm down," snapped Weezy. "You're not making it any easier for the rest of us."

"But Weezy, who would do this?"

"I don't know."

When he saw "Girl in White," he shook his head in pain and turned away.

Nikki, who came in last, gasped and turned pale when she saw the room. She stood wringing her hands as Weezy spoke to her, murmuring under her breath, "No . . . oh, no . . . how awful . . . who in their right mind would . . . oh, my goodness . . . not Elmo's 'Girl in White,' how *awful* . . . I can't think how . . . you mean, some of my paintings, too?"

She went to where her slashed canvases lay on the floor, and stood over them, wringing her hands, muttering to herself.

"Is she okay?" Snooky asked.

"I don't know. I guess so." Weezy was wound as tight as a spring. She had her arms crossed, as if to protect herself.

"How are you doing?"

"Not good. I don't like playing tricks on my students. I feel very low. I should have called the class off and cleaned up on my own."

"You could use the help cleaning up."

"No. I would have done better by myself. I should have called Sao, she and I could have done it. I should never have listened to Bernard."

"Well, that's true in general."

"It's not funny. I feel terrible. What a trick to play on them."

"Somebody," he reminded her, "played this trick on you first."

"Yes, but it's not one of them. Don't you think so? I'm sure it's not one of them. They all seemed really surprised."

"Ye-es," he said slowly.

"I hate not knowing who did it. I hate not trusting anybody."

"You can trust me."

She looked at him tiredly. "Don't you ever lose an opportunity to insinuate yourself?"

"Well, actually," began Snooky, when suddenly a voice was raised from the other side of the room. It was Jennifer.

"Look at this," she said, sounding surprised. She lifted up a painting. "This hasn't been touched. And neither have the rest of these."

There was a stirring and a mumbling among the other students, like the roaring of a distant, angry ocean.

Alice was looking through the unharmed paintings. Her face was very white.

"They're all yours," Elmo said at last. "They're all yours, Alice."

"All right. So they're all mine." Alice swayed from foot to foot like an angry child. "What of it?"

Jennifer hesitated and seemed about to say something; then she put the painting down. "Nothing."

"What of it?" repeated Alice, into the silence.

"Nothing."

"They were in a corner by themselves," Mrs. Castor pointed out reasonably. "You know, out of the way."

This was greeted by silence. The atmosphere suddenly seemed very thick, filled with waves of anger and hatred. Snooky could almost see them, vibrating with one lone figure at their center.

"I didn't do this," said Alice. Her voice sounded oddly calm. "You can't think I was the one who did this."

"No," said Jennifer. She backed away from Alice, as if to get away from the lines of force converging in her direction. "No."

"If I had, I wouldn't be stupid enough to leave my own paintings. Now would I?"

"No."

"I wouldn't be that stupid," said Alice. She turned to Weezy in entreaty. "I didn't do it! How can you all think—"

They were silent, staring at her. Weezy started to move towards her. Alice sobbed once, a deep guttural sound in her throat, then ran out of the room. They could hear the front door open and slam shut.

# FIVE

"WHAT A VERY good idea you had, Bernard," Snooky said when he returned home. He sat down in a chair in Bernard's study and stretched out his long legs.

Bernard looked up from his desk hopefully. "Did you find out anything?"

"Why yes, yes I did, Bernard. I found out that your little idea traumatized one of the students and totally disrupted the class. Weezy hates your guts and probably mine, too, through association."

Bernard was silent, toying with a pencil. "What happened?"

Snooky recounted the events of the afternoon. When he was finished, Bernard hunkered back into his leather chair, leaned back to look at the ceiling, and scribbled absently on a notepad. He stood up and went to look out the window.

"I feel bad," he said.

"Who doesn't?"

There was a pause.

"It's interesting, though, about the girl Alice. Interesting."

"Weezy didn't think so. She chewed me out afterwards, and told me to tell you she's coming over later to chew you out."

"Oh, good," Bernard said heavily. "Good, good, good, good, good."

"She said that Alice would probably never come back again. She said Alice's trust had been violated. She said her students couldn't create in an atmosphere of violence and betrayal."

"Did she say that, really, 'violence and betrayal'?"

"Uh-huh."

"Hmmmm." Bernard turned back to the window.

"She's very articulate usually, and that's nothing to her command of the language once she really gets going. Believe me. I was awed by her grasp of the subtleties of the English vocabulary and syntax."

"Yes."

"Plus, I read an article recently saying that only seven percent of communication is through words, and the overwhelming majority of meaning is communicated through tone of voice and body language. Well, it turns out she handles that very effectively also."

"I can imagine," Bernard said in sympathy. He came back to his chair and sat down.

"Very effectively," Snooky repeated. He gave his brother-in-law an icy stare.

"Well," said Bernard.

"Well."

"Yes. Well."

"Any more bright ideas?"

"Let me just point out that the class would have learned sooner or later that Alice's paintings were the only ones left untouched."

"That's true."

"And it's interesting that there's so much hatred towards her."

"I could almost see it," Snooky mused. "Lines of force

coming towards her. The air seemed thick where she was standing."

"Oh, I'm sure."

"No, really. I mean it."

"The air seemed thick?"

"Yes."

"What else, Snooky? What other New Age claptrap are you going to give me? Are you seeing auras now? Why didn't you just read their palms to find out who did it? Which reminds me, how did they all look when they came in and saw the place?"

"Distressed. Every single one of them. They all reacted differently, but they all seemed really upset."

"And surprised?"

"Yes. And surprised."

"That's too bad. I was hoping—"

"We all know what you were hoping, Bernard. That somebody would drop to their knees and cry out, 'I did it! Lock me up, I'm the guilty one!' Right?"

"No," he said sullenly. "Not at all."

"Well, something more subtle, but along those lines. The guilty look, the furtive glance, the obviously fake reaction. Something like that?"

"Tell me more about how they reacted."

Snooky obligingly told him in detail. His memory for conversation and body language was uncannily accurate. He detailed what had happened from beginning to end, to the final slam of the front door behind Alice.

"It sounds like they were all surprised," said Bernard.

"Yes."

"Damn."

"Yes, too bad."

"We need to know more about these people. Why don't you sit in on her class for a while?"

"Well, I can think of a couple reasons why not. First, because I don't know anything at all about art. I don't think I could pass as a serious student. I already flunked being a model. Secondly, because Weezy isn't speaking to me right now. I don't think she's going to let me sit in on her class."

Bernard sighed. "All right. Who else might have done it besides one of the students? How about the interviewer from *People* magazine?"

"How about the gallery owner who was going to put on her show?"

Bernard shrugged irritably. "What do you think, Snooky, the gallery owner wrecked her studio because she turned him down for a date?"

"How do you know about the date?"

"Maya told me."

"I didn't think Maya bothered you with that kind of stuff. You know, interpersonal relationships and so on."

"Maya tells me everything," Bernard said smugly. "So what do you think?"

"Well, it doesn't seem likely."

"He'd have to be crazy. Did he seem crazy?"

"No, not really. He has very pale eyes, but I guess that's not his fault. Heredity, you know. He seemed as normal as anybody."

"So we're left with the journalist. What's her motive?"

"Jealousy?"

"Of her boyfriend's ex-lover?"

"Maybe she's a frustrated artist herself, and Harold always holds Weezy up to her about it."

"Maybe the sky is green and the moon is blue," Bernard said kindly.

"I agree, it doesn't seem likely. The only thing that seems likely right now is that you're going to get a very angry phone call from Weezy in the next half hour or so. What do you plan to do about it?"

"Lay low," said Bernard, turning back to his typewriter. "Lay very low."

Weezy, however, did not call. Snooky grew worried towards evening and dialed her number.

"Oh, hi, Snooky."

"Hi. I thought you were going to call and chew Bernard out?"

"Oh, I can't do that. It's not his fault he knows more about lobsters than about people, poor thing. And anyway, when I thought about it afterwards I realized that he's not responsible for what happened with Alice and the others. That's been brewing for a long time."

"How very rational of you. What a shame all these kind thoughts didn't occur to you when you were screaming your head off at me."

"I'm sorry."

"Oh, that's okay."

"No, I'm really sorry. It's not your fault."

"I think I was trying to point that out to you at the time."

"I just needed somebody to yell at, and there you were," said Weezy.

"Ah well, there I am, whipping boy to the universe."

"Yes, your life is hard. Time to jet back to St. Martin, perhaps? Or the Côte d'Azur? Or wherever else you seem to spend most of your time?"

"I've never been to the Côte d'Azur. What a good idea."

"Time to go, perhaps?"

"Only if you go with me."

In reply, she slammed down the phone.

---

When Snooky dropped by the next day, he found Weezy sitting in her kitchen, staring out the window thoughtfully. "Hi," she greeted him.

"Hi. Thought I'd come by and see how you're doing. You're not still mad at me, are you?"

"No, no. Listen, I just called Edward Genuardi. You know, the gallery owner."

"Yes?"

"Well, he told me the strangest thing, Snooky. I was struggling to spit out the words to tell him that there wouldn't be a show—I know it's not the end of the world, but it's taken me this long to get my courage up to call him—when he told me that he knew already."

*"What?"*

"He said somebody—a woman, he said—had called up this morning and told him that my paintings were destroyed and the show was off. Can you believe that?"

"A woman," Snooky said.

"She hung up before he could ask any questions. He called and left this cryptic message on my machine—he was sure it was a sick kind of practical joke, and he didn't want to upset me by repeating something some loony said. He just left a message asking me to call him, there was something he had to ask me about. When I spoke to him, he said she didn't even sound serious, she laughed as she hung up."

"She laughed as she hung up," repeated Snooky. He sat down and took Weezy's hands in his.

"Yeah. Creepy, isn't it?"

"Yeah, it is. Do you believe him?"

Weezy stared. "Believe him?"

"Uh-huh."

"Yes, I believe him. Why would he lie?"

"He would lie if he came up here and slashed your paintings himself."

"Oh, come on. Why? Because I turned him down for dinner? Don't be ridiculous."

"I'm sorry."

"No, no. I don't mean to snap at you. It's just that . . . it's so sick. Who would do that to me? Who do I know who would do that to me? She laughed as she hung up, he said."

"That is sick."

"He couldn't believe it when I said it was true. He thought for sure it was some kind of prank."

"How did he react then?"

"Oh, well, he said he was sorry and so on. You know. What's he going to say, for goodness sake? He said he was terribly sorry and he certainly hoped they could put on another show of mine very soon, etcetera, etcetera." She shook her head. "The usual bullshit."

"I'm sure he means it."

"Oh, come on. It just makes me so angry. I want to find out who did this, Snooky. I want to grab whoever it is and slap them and shake them till their eyeballs fall out."

"Don't you have any . . . any hint at all? Any intuition about it?"

She considered this, tracing with her finger the pattern of the tiles on her countertop. "No. I don't. I wish I did. It seems incredible to me. Nobody dislikes me. I'm such a friendly person. I can't understand it."

"Does any of your students seem likely to you?"

She shook her head. "If I was going to pick one, I'd say Alice, of course—she's the most temperamental, and she certainly holds grudges. But it seems incredible that she'd go this far."

"Maybe it's nothing against you. Maybe it's something between the students that doesn't include you."

She nodded. "That's possible. That's certainly possible.

There's all kinds of things going on in that class. They're one of the most volatile mixes I've ever seen. It could be that. But then why wreck *my* paintings?"

"Because they were there. Because whoever did it couldn't just pick out one person's stuff to destroy, it'd be too obvious."

"But then why call the Genuardi Gallery? And what about those phone calls and the dead flowers?"

"That's true," said Snooky. "But maybe . . ."

"What?"

"Maybe somebody is trying to make somebody else look bad. You know, get someone else into trouble."

"I don't know," she said wearily. "I just don't know. As far as I'm concerned, they're all in trouble. I'm this far from saying to hell with it and canceling the class."

"A good idea," said Snooky. "Why don't you?"

"I'm thinking about it."

There was a silence.

"You know another thing I've been thinking about," she said at last. "Since this whole thing happened. I've been wondering which one of them could have slashed those paintings. What I mean is, which one of them would be physically capable of slashing paintings. I mean, I don't think I could slash somebody else's paintings unless I really, really hated them. I know what goes into someone else's work and I would find it hard to deface that. The same for Elmo, for instance. He has a lot of respect for the work itself. Alice, too. The others . . . I don't know. Jennifer. Nikki. Nikki's so mild, it's hard to imagine . . . and of course there's Mrs. Castor, evil incarnate. I hate to even suspect her. Can you see that sweet old lady ripping at my paintings with a knife? But you see what I'm talking about."

"Yes. But even you could do it if you hated somebody enough."

"That's right."

"Well, maybe somebody feels that strongly."

They stared at each other morosely.

"I'll tell you one thing," said Snooky. "I'm not letting you stay here by yourself alone. No, I'm not," he said over her protests. "I'm getting my stuff and moving in here for a while. This is not a proposition, just a statement of fact."

"Getting your stuff," she said with a faint smile. "What does that consist of? Putting your toothbrush in a brown paper bag? Stealing Bernard's clothes?"

"And I'll tell you another thing. You're going to have one more student in your class from now on."

"Oh, no."

"Yes. It was Bernard's idea, and while I thought at the time it was idiotic, now I think it's a good one. I'll sit in the back and not make any trouble. You can tell them I've always been interested in art."

"What are you planning to do, exactly? Sit in the back and fingerpaint? Paint by numbers? Use a coloring book? This is a serious class, these people are for real, it's not a hobby for them. You're going to look ridiculous."

"I'm used to that," said Snooky, and leaning over, he gave her a kiss.

She stared at him owlishly. "That wasn't bad."

"I can do it again," he said, and did.

"I'm leaving, and I'm not sure when I'm coming back," Snooky announced.

Bernard glanced up from his desk. "Fine."

"You'll have to fend for yourselves from now on."

"Okay."

"I'm moving in with Weezy. Something strange happened."

"You mean, something strange besides you moving in with her?"

Snooky briefly recounted the phone call to the gallery owner.

"Okay."

"I'm worried about her being alone. Why are you alone, by the way? Where's Maya?"

"She's out taking a walk."

"Oh. Tell her I'll call her later."

Bernard nodded.

"I've decided to follow your suggestion about sitting in on her classes. I'll keep in touch if I find out anything interesting."

"Thanks."

"I'm taking some of your clothes with me."

Bernard shrugged irritably.

"Anything I can do for you before I go? Cook a meal or something?"

"Have you forced your presence on Weezy, or is this voluntary on her part?"

"Well, I'd say a little bit of both, to be honest."

"That's what I figured."

"You'll take good care of Maya for me? You won't let her and the baby starve?"

"Good-bye, Snooky."

"There are some cans of food in the pantry. Remember to open them when you feel hungry."

"Good-bye."

"So long, Bernard."

When Snooky had left, Bernard sat tapping idly on his typewriter keys. The dog, a pile of fluffy red hair, was curled under his desk, snoring gently. Bernard leaned down to pat her head; then he typed

IIIIJJJKKKKLLSDMGJJSLDSLSLDKLSLSM

His mind was elsewhere. He had been hard at work on the tale of Sophie the lobster when Snooky had come into the study, but once interrupted it was difficult to get back into the flow. He cleared his throat, spaced down a few lines and then wrote,

RT STDNTS???

This, in Bernard's special shorthand, translated as "Art students???" He had learned long ago that by eliminating all vowels it was possible to take notes that nearly always could be deciphered later.

GLLRY WNR? ("Gallery owner?")

NTRVWR? ("Interviewer?")

followed in quick succession. Bernard stared somberly at the page for a while.

HRLD? ("Harold?")

From what Maya had said, Harold had left Weezy. It was difficult to see his motive for harassing her and wrecking her studio now, but perhaps there was one.

Underneath that he typed one letter, followed by a question mark.

Y?

He knew Weezy. Weezy had been a part of his life since his marriage. Everyone loved Weezy, with her friendly nature and her outgoing ways. Everyone, apparently, except one person. What could she have done to make someone hate her so much?

The first night Snooky slept on Weezy's couch. The next night, without ceremony, he moved into her room. Weezy seemed perplexed by this course of events. He would catch her looking at him from the corner of her cat-eyes, with a puzzled, vulnerable expression on her face. She acted as though a gigantic whale had somehow landed in her bed, despite her best efforts to persuade it to swim elsewhere. She seemed to find it difficult to get around the house without bumping into him and apologizing. They were awkward with each other and overly polite.

"We have to stop this," Snooky said at last. "I can't say 'oh, excuse me' one more time. Is this your piece of toast I'm eating, by the way?"

"Yes, it is. Mine's the one with marmalade, yours has blueberry jam." She switched them neatly.

"I love you, I'm allowed to be in your kitchen for breakfast. I'm tired of apologizing for being here."

"Oh, geez." Weezy was playing with her napkin, folding it this way and that, into tinier and tinier squares. She was wearing a ratty pink bathrobe whose hems were frayed. Her hair was curling loose on her shoulders. She brushed back an errant strand impatiently. "Yeah. Okay."

"What's the matter?"

"I don't know. I keep wondering what Maya will say."

"It's not exactly going to be a devastating surprise, if that's what you mean."

"Oh, I know. I know. I just . . . I don't know." She shrugged unhappily.

Snooky took her face in his hands. "Listen. Maya's married, she's having a baby, remember? She doesn't need to live her life through us. We're something separate."

"We're something separate, all right. You never spoke a truer word, Snooky. We're something separate from the entire human race."

"I don't see why you say that," he said cheerfully, buttering another piece of bread. "More toast?"

"Yes, thanks."

"Admit it, you like me better every day."

"I liked you fine in the beginning," she said, almost under

her breath, and gave him another one of her strange, absorbed, puzzled looks.

Maya took the news with equanimity. "I'm happy for you," she told Weezy. "I really am."

Weezy regarded her doubtfully. "You are?"

"Yes."

"Don't lie to me, Maya, you know I hate it when you're polite."

"I'm not lying. I really am happy for you. Bernard and I were talking about it the other day. He said Snooky's not so bad, you could do a lot worse."

Weezy was struck by this. "Bernard said that?"

"Uh-huh."

"From Bernard, that's a rave review."

"Yes."

"Snooky will be touched. I'll have to tell him."

Maya gave her a quick hug. "And as for Snooky, you're the best thing that could possibly have happened to him. He should lie down and thank his lucky stars he met you again."

Weezy laughed and shook her head. "He's protecting me, you know. He's enrolling in my class to keep the students from killing me."

"It's the silliest idea I've ever heard."

"I know. Has he ever shown the slightest sign of any artistic talent? Other than the creative way he spends his life?"

"He's very good at origami. You could have him make unicorns or boats or hats or whatever."

"That'll go over big. Especially with Elmo, he's such a stickler. I'm dreading class this week."

Maya gave her a sympathetic glance. "Any word from Alice?"

"None. And not likely to be. I give her at least two weeks before she gets in touch."

"You've been calling her?"

"Over and over again. I just get her machine. And I'm sorry, but Manhattan is too damned far away for me to go chasing her down and trying to deal with her. Honestly, Maya, she's such a little prima donna, sometimes I think I'd be glad if she never came back. Although of course I wouldn't want her to leave this way." She fell silent, brooding.

"You've always said how good she is at her work."

"Well, she is, damn it, but sometimes I wish she'd pick somebody else to take classes from. She's just so difficult. They all are, in their own ways. Goddamn individualists."

"Are you frightened?" Maya asked bluntly. "Of what's happening?"

Weezy laughed and shook her head. "I would be, except for your brother. It's incredibly comforting, Maya, it's like living with a great big basset hound. You just know if anybody broke into the house he would bay his head off."

"And then lie down and let them pet him," said Maya cynically.

Snooky had thought that there would be some protests when he joined the class, but very little was said. Weezy remarked offhandedly, "I think you all know Snooky—well, he'll be here with us for a while," and they stared at him curiously, but the only comment came from Elmo, who grunted in contempt before turning back to his easel. Jennifer tossed her black hair over her shoulders, glanced at Elmo and then set to work. Mrs. Castor gave him a gentle smile, and Nikki came up and whispered, "How nice . . . really, how nice . . . it'll be nice to have an extra person . . . this class was a little too small, if you know what I . . . oh, dear, well . . ." She retired, covered in confusion.

Snooky had taken a position, as promised, in the back of the room, and now he stared dubiously at the blank canvas in front of him. The last artistic endeavor he distinctly remembered being involved in was the creation of a knobbly ashtray from clay in second grade. On the other hand, sometimes he thought anybody could create modern art; so often it seemed to him to be a case of the emperor's new clothes. He had been to a museum once where he had managed to walk across an actual exhibit, unaware that the newspapers strewn across the floor were not a precursor to the display but the display itself. He sighed and dipped a brush into the paint.

When Weezy wandered by later, she found him hard at work painting the entire canvas red.

"Interesting," she said.

"Thank you. I call it 'Study in Red, Number One.' Like it?"

"It's been done."

"In that case, I'll call it 'Animals Copulating, Series Four.' What do you think?"

"I think you think you're awfully funny."

He smiled and went back to work.

Alice had not shown up, as Weezy had predicted; and in her absence the class seemed somehow subdued, their voices lower, without any of the emotional sparks Alice usually sent flying. Elmo was giving Jennifer some pointers; they were arguing over something, but quietly, whispering to each other. Nikki and Weezy were conferring, their voices murmuring back and forth. Mrs. Castor was hard at work; when she painted, her face looked years younger, serene and youthful, Snooky noted. He was stationed behind her and could see that her painting consisted of colorful figures dancing across the canvas, marching along the frame and jumping into what looked like a blue lake. It was a happy, childlike scene in vivid colors, and Mrs. Castor smiled as she worked on it.

"Oh, good," said Weezy when she saw it. "Oh, my goodness, it's wonderful, Mrs. Castor. This is your best yet."

The old lady glowed. "Thank you."

"Oh, yes, you'll be ready for an exhibit of your own soon."

This remark was ill-timed, following on the destruction of her own paintings. Mrs. Castor looked at her in sympathy; Weezy winced and murmured, "Sorry," then moved away.

The class without Alice, Snooky noted, seemed to be missing its emotional center, the force that made it move. Whatever you could say about Alice, she was a personality, he mused.

"Oh, she's a personality, all right," Weezy agreed when he told her this later. "Yes, the room seems empty without her, but who cares? It's so peaceful. Mrs. Castor did her best work in months."

"You care," Snooky said pointedly.

"Yes, I do, damn her, but I'm still going to wait. I know Alice, she'll show up when she feels like it. She knows she still needs me and the class."

And true to form, the next week when class assembled Alice walked in, set up her easel in the back and went to work as if nothing had happened. There was a stir as she entered, and Snooky glanced around expectantly, but no one said anything, not even hello. Jennifer and Elmo looked at each other, but said nothing. Nikki seemed disappointed. Her shoulders were hunched and her head lowered, like a turtle withdrawing into its shell. And Mrs. Castor, far away in a land of happy dancing figures, did not even seem to notice the stir. She hummed to herself as she worked, a happy tuneless sound.

"I told you she'd come back," Weezy said that night, smugly.

"So you did."

"Did she say anything to you?"

"No," said Snooky. "She looked up at one point and stared at me as if I had come from Mars, but she didn't say anything."

"Artists," sighed Weezy. "So temperamental. I loathe them all."

"Then it's just lucky that I'm not one," said Snooky, giving her a kiss.

As the weeks went on, Maya began to show. Her abdomen puffed out and she found it impossible to get into her old jeans. She was thrilled with this. She and Weezy rushed out to buy maternity tops and pants. As with everything, Weezy had strong opinions on what Maya should wear during her pregnancy.

"Not the fifties look, sweetie," she said in the dressing room. "Not the Laura Petrie look. Don't they have any maternity overalls? You could wear them with a flowered blouse. No, take that off immediately. Oh, here's a long sweater, I love those. Try that on. Where's that saleslady? Don't they have any creative ways to dress pregnant people?"

Maya came home clutching several shopping bags, her eyes sparkling. She felt as if she were in a movie starring herself, pregnant. "A movie about me," she told Weezy.

"Fulfilling all your fantasies," Weezy said, laughing.

"I feel like I'm a movie star and somebody is recording my every move on film."

"Well, why not? It's a special time."

"I had no energy before, and I have so much energy now. Bernard and I are going shopping soon for baby furniture."

"Oh, don't go with him. He has no idea about anything. Go with me. I can see the cradle already, white with a white lace bumper . . . or maybe pale yellow, to go with the walls . . ."

"I have to go with him. He'd be so hurt if I didn't include him."

"All right, but just remember the color he painted the walls of the nursery. Attack of Fuchsia, if I remember correctly."

"Bile Green."

"Lots O' Liver, like a cat food."

"Smog Gray."

"I can't think of any more, but it was vile, remember? You can go with him, but kindly keep in mind that he has no aesthetic or color sense whatsoever. No offense, dear."

Maya did not care. She had laid the new clothes out on her bed and was surveying them with satisfaction. "I love the overalls."

"And they'll expand as you do. See these clever pleats here on the sides?"

"I love the jeans."

"Try them on again. That's right. Oh, yes, you look wonderful." Weezy looked her over with a nod of approval. "Wonderful."

"Bernard will have a hemorrhage when he finds out how much I spent."

"He doesn't care how much money you spend as long as you're happy. Bernard is the perfect husband. And you needed something, my goodness, you couldn't wear your old clothes any longer now that you're really showing."

"I am, aren't I?"

"You certainly are." Weezy smiled at her old friend. Maya looked at her thoughtfully.

"Weeze . . ."

"Uh-huh?"

"Do you ever . . . I mean, don't you . . . ummm . . ."

"Want to have kids?"

Maya nodded.

Weezy flopped back on the bed. "I don't know. I really don't know. Do you remember when Snooky was born?"

"Not really. A little. Why?"

"Well, I remember when Janey was born." Janey was Weezy's youngest sister in a family of four girls. "I was ten. I remember it well. It was horrible. Horrible! My mom was exhausted all the time. Of course, she had the other three of us to worry about. But I was old enough to help her, and I helped a lot with Janey, even more than I had with the others. Well, I'll never forget it. Janey was this whiny little blob of a thing that cried nonstop for months and nursed my mother's breasts off and never, ever slept. It was a nightmare. Oh, not to discourage you, sweetie, I'm sure yours will be an angel. But sometimes I think having to help with my younger sisters turned me off of babies entirely. It's not the way they tell you it's going to be."

Maya sat down next to her on the bed. "I know. At least . . . I think I do. I remember a bit with Snooky. I was only five when he was born, but I remember him when he was little, and he was a real pain. Of course, Snooky's always been a real pain. Oh, no offense."

"And it would be hard for me to get any work done with a baby. They don't need you just occasionally, you know, it's all the time."

"I know."

"And the diapers. I've never forgiven Janey for the diapers. That was my job when she was little. I can still barely talk about it, it was a nightmare. It ruined my relationship with her forever."

"You had to do too much," Maya protested.

"Well, maybe, but at least I got a glimpse of what it's like. Think of all the people who have babies and have never even held one before. At least you helped raise Snooky, you know what it's all about."

"I know, but . . . Bernard is afraid it's going to change everything. We have so much freedom now. We're not tied down at all."

"Well, I'm sure it does change everything. The only thing is, there must be some rewards, or nobody would have more than one kid. Look at my parents, they had four, even though it was so hard."

"And are they glad?"

"Well, no," Weezy said. "I don't think so. I mean, Janey's a real pill—even my mom can't stand her—and Mattie's so wild, they're constantly fretting over her. It's only recently that I've been able to make any money from my work, so they were bailing me out financially for years. Only Rose has a real job and a real husband and family and everything. Of course she always did suck up to them, even when she was little, that little do-gooder." She subsided, brooding. "Not to discourage you from having a large family."

"Well, do you think I don't know? Snooky and William have always been at each other's throats. They're complete opposites. Family get-togethers are ordeals from hell, as Bernard calls them."

"This isn't the right conversation to be having while you're pregnant. Bad vibes for the baby. Remember that Snooky and I are dying to baby-sit, so you'll get out sometimes. Think of us as extended family. Well, I guess Snooky already is."

"And so are you," said Maya, giving her an affectionate hug.

---

Alice let out a gasp of horror. "Oh, no . . . Weezy . . . look . . . look at this!"

She had opened up the wooden case in which she kept her paints and her brushes. Now she stood staring into it, her eyes wide with shock.

Weezy came to stand at her side. She nodded grimly. The tubes of paint had been opened and their contents squeezed all over the inside of the case. Colorful swirls of blue and gold and pink and green lay intertwined like snakes. The brushes had been taken out and smeared in the paint. The bottle of thinner had been emptied over everything. A rank smell arose from the soaked wood.

Alice's lips were trembling. "I don't believe this."

Weezy turned to look at her face. She felt some pity stir in her as she saw the shock and disbelief. "I'm sorry, Alice."

"I don't believe this."

"This is supposed to be an art class," said Weezy, raising her voice for the benefit of the other students, who were watching them silently. "Not an invitation to destruction and mayhem. When's the last time you saw your case, Alice?"

"Last week. I left it here. I always leave it here. I have another one at home."

Weezy calculated rapidly in her head. Last week . . . but nobody had come in, as they so often did, during the week. Nobody, that is, except Mrs. Castor, who had dropped by a few days ago to ask for some help with a drawing she was struggling with. And she was damned if it was Mrs. Castor who had done this. It must have been one of the others, at the end of last week's class. She tried to remember who had lingered behind, but it was impossible; one class blurred into the next, week after week after week. She rubbed her cheek wearily. She had been doing this too long already.

"All right," she said. "There's one thing I'd like all of you to know. Any more episodes like this, and the class is over—for good. I can't teach under these circumstances, and you sure as hell can't learn. Is that understood?"

Everyone nodded. Snooky, in the back of the room, stood with his arms folded, watching their faces closely.

"Alice, let's get this mess cleaned up. I'll help you. Everyone else, back to work."

Alice sullenly began to clean the inside of the paintbox with a cloth. The other four turned back to their work. Mrs. Castor, Snooky noted, looked very upset. She stood silently in front of the easel, her hands clasped together, her brushes lying unused on a chair by her side. Elmo resumed work as if nothing at all had happened, and soon was painting furiously. Nikki looked anxious, but then Nikki always did look anxious. She was fiddling with her paints and making tiny, nervous strokes on the paper. Jennifer, when she turned to steal a glance at Alice, had a wooden, immobile expression on her face. Her gaze met Snooky's, faintly mocking him, challenging him to know what she was thinking behind the dark curtain of her eyes.

"More destruction," he said to Weezy later, as they were preparing dinner together.

"Yes."

"Not a coincidence, perhaps?"

"No." She sounded dispirited.

"Somebody has a penchant for wrecking things."

"Yes. What have you done with my olive oil?"

He indicated with a knife. "Over there. On the counter."

"Oh. Thanks."

"None of them seemed terribly upset by what happened, except for Mrs. Castor."

"Oh, Mrs. Castor's an angel. I love Mrs. Castor. I'm going to ask her to come live with us. Do you think Mr. Castor would mind?" She poured some olive oil into a frying pan.

"Is there a Mr. Castor?"

"Oh, my goodness, yes. They've been married for about a million years. He drops her off in the car and picks her up at the end of class. When she gets in the car he opens the door and hands her in like she's a treasure. Which she is, if you ask me."

"So who do you think did it? I assume you're not including Mrs. Castor, after those paeans to her character."

She turned the burner on and rolled the pan from side to side. She was frowning. "I honestly don't know. It could have been any of the other three. God knows they hate Alice enough. And after the stink she made about her brush being used, well . . ."

"She deserved it."

"Oh, nobody deserves that, Snooky. It's so spiteful, so childish. God, they can't even think of mature ways of taking revenge on somebody. It's like running a nursery school."

"How long have they all known each other?"

She shrugged. "For a couple of years now, I guess. I taught them in New York before I came here. All except Mrs. Castor. She joined the class when I moved."

"What do you know about them personally? What about Elmo and Jennifer?"

She poured a bowlful of chopped vegetables into the pan and stirred them with a wooden spoon. "They've lived together for maybe three years now, and known each other much longer. She's not as good an artist as he is, and she knows it. I think it bothers her sometimes, but she loves him. He likes his work better than he likes her, but at least she's second best."

"How do they support themselves? I assume they're not making a living from their artwork?"

"Don't be ridiculous. I was just telling your sister how I leeched off my parents for years. No, Elmo's rich. His father's an international businessman or something like that. You know the type. He hates what Elmo's doing, but he supports him anyway. And Elmo supports Jennifer."

"How about Nikki?"

"Nikki tries hard," Weezy said briefly. "I don't know much about her. She lives by herself in some dump that she's been in for years. She has dreams of making it in the art world."

"And will she?"

"I don't think so. She's not as talented as the others. Of course, you never know. It's hard to tell what's going to catch on. Meanwhile, she works as a waitress to support herself and does her painting in her off hours."

"And Alice?"

"Alice does set design for the theater. And makes a pretty penny off it, too. Sometimes she works for the movies or TV and makes an absolute fortune."

"Do you think she'll try to take revenge on the class for what happened today?"

She spooned the cooked vegetables into a serving bowl and carried it out to the dining room table. "I don't know. I wouldn't put it past her. She's a vindictive person, certainly. But she also likes to play the poor injured victim, poor Alice who's always being ripped off and misunderstood, so she may simply enjoy sulking for a while. It's hard to tell."

"Does she enjoy playing the victim enough to do it to herself?"

"What do you mean? Mess up her paints like that herself? Why?"

"I'm just saying that the person with the easiest access to that paintbox was Alice."

"What a mind you have," she said, amused. "I don't know. It hadn't occurred to me. She seemed so upset by what happened."

Snooky opened the oven door to check on the roast chicken. "It's done." He put it on a platter, carried it to the table and began to carve it. "White meat? Dark meat?"

"Both."

Over dinner they chatted about other things, carefully avoiding any discussion about art, paintings, or Weezy's class. They argued over the merit of an action-adventure movie they had seen on TV the night before ("Did everybody have to die except Schwarzenegger and his girlfriend? I mean, everybody?" asked Weezy), and gossiped about Maya and Bernard.

"I think she's getting really nervous," said Weezy.

"Oh, yes. When I went over there the other day she held onto me and asked with tears in her eyes whether I thought it would change everything once the baby's born."

"Really? What did you say?"

"I said I thought so, yes. Well, what did you want me to say?" he said, seeing the disapproval on her face. "Obviously the baby's going to change their lifestyle. No more leisurely Sunday brunches, no more picking up and going whenever they feel like it. I told her that Bernard could use more responsibility, he's too lighthearted as it is."

"And what did she say to that?"

"She said I wouldn't know about responsibility since I've never had any. She said she didn't want to talk about it any more."

"Well, at least you made her feel better."

"There's no use cushioning the blow, Weezy. She'll find out soon enough. What have you been telling her?"

"Oh, the same sort of thing, but in a much nicer way. I'm a kinder person than you are, you know."

"Absolutely."

"And the two of them are dying to have this baby, you know that, they've been talking about it for years."

"Really? No, I didn't know that. Nobody talked to me about it."

"They were probably too busy trying to figure out how to ask you to leave," said Weezy, patting his hand.

Snooky did not take offense. "Oh, they love my visits. Well, Maya does, anyway. Bernard is a misanthrope, he can't be expected to enjoy company."

"Bernard is a wonderful, decent, kind, warmhearted human being. I won't hear him maligned like that."

"He may be decent," said Snooky. "He is not kind. I do not find him wonderful, and he is not warmhearted in the least. You are seriously deluded about him, believe me. I speak as someone who knows."

She shook her head and laughed.

At that moment, Bernard was sitting in his study, staring at a page in the typewriter. Sophie and Sylvie were going off together to find the path of the lobster migration. Since Sophie could travel faster, she was carrying her friend in one large claw. Every so often Sylvie would open her shell and hiss instructions at her.

*"This way!"*

*"That way!"*

*"Over here!"*

*"Over there!"*

Sophie was weary. She had been traveling for a long time, and she doubted that she could find her friends. She had been lost for so very long. Bernard rested his chin on one fist. He was weary, too. It was difficult, moving around on the bottom of the sea. It required a great deal of concentration. Right now he had just eaten dinner, and his digestive system was signaling for more blood from his brain. He closed his eyes as his brain complied and his thoughts shut down.

As he sat there, eyes closed, in a state of dreamy lassitude, Weezy's face swam into his mind's eye. She had called Maya after class with the latest news, and Maya had told him. So somebody had wrecked Alice's paintbox now. Served her right, thought Bernard. She was practically begging for trouble, that girl. Like Snooky, he was wondering if she had done it herself, to keep herself in the limelight. Maybe things had gotten too boring in class for her taste. There was no telling what people would do. Bernard, who preferred the safe and familiar, preferred not to meet any new people, since they were inherently unpredictable. However, he thought . . . he just thought that it was time to find out more about these art students. Not him, of course—no, no, he shuddered at the idea. Snooky would do it. Somebody had a taste for violence, and Bernard felt it was important to find out who that was. Snooky would do it, he thought. That was Snooky's kind of thing.

He put his head down on the desk and began to snore.

The next time Snooky dropped by the house to bring Maya some food ("I just want to make sure you're not starving, Missy, trapped here alone with Bernard"), Bernard cornered him in the kitchen.

"I want you to find out more about Weezy's students."

"I'm already spying on them as much as I possibly can. What more do you want?"

"You have to talk to them more. You haven't talked to them enough."

Snooky stared at him. "This from the man who never talks to anybody if he can help it?"

"Be more sociable," urged Bernard. "Turn on your charm. According to Maya, you have some. Use it. Be chatty. Hang around after class and talk to them."

"And what should I talk about, exactly?"

"I don't know. You'll have to see as you go along. Be inventive. You're good at that type of thing. You do want to help Weezy, don't you?"

"What do you think?"

"So there you are," said Bernard. "This'll never stop until we find out who's doing it."

"Whoever it is has covered their tracks pretty damn well."

"But a pattern is emerging, don't you think? The same kind of thing. The same rather childish way of getting back at somebody."

"I guess so."

"A pattern," said Bernard, his eyes glowing. "A pattern of destruction. Somebody who's been taking every opportunity they can find. Maybe that girl Alice, except . . . except that it's too obvious. Maybe somebody who's doing everything they can to make it *look* like it's her."

Snooky regarded him doubtfully. "Do you get any work at all done up there in your study? Or do you spend your whole time thinking about Weezy's problems? I'm not judging you, you understand, I'm just asking."

"Try to find out more," said Bernard, moving away. "We need to know more." He left the room.

"Easy for you to say!" Snooky yelled after him.

"What's easy?" Maya said, coming into the kitchen with an empty teacup in her hand.

"Oh, nothing, Missy. Nothing, nothing, nothing, nothing, nothing. Just Bernard being himself."

His sister looked at him inquiringly, but said no more.

---

After the next class, Snooky put down his paintbrush and edged up to Elmo.

"Hi," he said.

Elmo did not respond. His arms were crossed and he was staring at the canvas in front of him.

"Good work," said Snooky. He kept his voice low, so as not to be overheard.

"Do you mind?" Elmo said irritably. "I'm working here." He picked up his brush and made a small stroke at the edge of the painting.

"I was wondering if you had any idea who messed up Alice's stuff last week. It's really upsetting Weezy, and I was wondering if you knew anything about it."

Elmo turned away from the painting and looked at him for a long, seemingly endless moment. Snooky tried an affable smile, but was frozen by that look until the smile slipped away and he was sure he resembled nothing more than a deer trapped in the headlights.

Then Elmo surprised him. "I have a very good idea who did it."

"You do?"

"Uh-huh."

"Are you going to tell me?"

Elmo shook his head.

"Would you tell Weezy if she asked you nicely?"

"No."

"Why not?"

"Look, stop pestering me, okay? I don't know what Weezy thinks she's doing, planting you like a spy in the back of the room, but we're not idiots here. We know what's going on. And if you don't know who's causing all the trouble here, then you're the only one. I can't believe Weezy doesn't know who slashed her paintings. I sure as hell do." Elmo's face was flushed. He clamped his lips firmly together, as if he had said too much, and turned away. "Leave me alone," he said fiercely.

Snooky backed away.

When he tried to talk to Jennifer, she leveled a glance on him that, like Elmo's, froze his blood. With her height and her dark good looks, she was a formidable personality. He tried the affable smile again. "Hi."

She was cleaning her paintbrushes and putting them neatly away in a case. "I heard what you and Elmo were talking about. Leave me alone."

"If you know who's doing all this, why don't you tell Weezy? Maybe she could put a stop to it. It seems like you almost don't want it to stop."

She did not reply. Her beautiful face was set in a frown.

"Just answer one question. Why won't you tell her?"

She finished putting her brushes and tubes of paint away, and closed the case with a snap. "Why doesn't she know?"

"What?"

She straightened up and put her hands on her hips. "Why doesn't she know? Isn't it obvious? Who's the one nutcase in this class?"

"You mean Alice."

"If I were Weezy, I'd have gotten rid of her a long time ago," Jennifer said with venom. She picked up her case and stalked away.

Nikki, in contrast, was thrilled to talk to him. She showed him what she had done that day, and blushed happily when he complimented her on it.

"It's very nice. Not that I know anything about modern art, but I like this, I really do."

"Oh, you don't have to know anything," she said seriously. "There's such a mystique about it, but I don't understand why, myself. It's just things you like and things you don't like. Don't you think so?"

"Yes, in fact, I do," said Snooky, a little surprised. "But Weezy doesn't. She says I'm a philistine."

This threw her into confusion. "Oh, well . . . I don't want to . . . I didn't *mean* to contradict what . . . oh, my goodness, well, you understand what I . . ."

"Don't worry. Weezy doesn't care whether we agree with her or not. She's perfectly happy with her own opinion."

This made her laugh, a nervous little giggle.

"Listen," he said, watching her closely. "You know that Weezy's very upset over what's been happening in here. Do you have any ideas about it?"

Her eyes widened. "Me? Any ideas? Oh, no, I couldn't . . . I wouldn't be able to . . . I haven't even thought . . ."

"Don't tell me you haven't thought about it. And I bet you have a pretty good idea who's behind it, too."

Then Nikki, like Elmo earlier, surprised him very much. She put her chin up, and an unaccustomed steely look came into her eyes.

"Well, yes, I do," she said. "I do have an idea. And I have been thinking about it, quite a lot. I think I know who's been doing everything. And I'm quite sure I know who wrecked Alice's paintbox, because, you see, I saw it happen."

Snooky stared. "You saw it?"

"Yes. Yes, I did. And I'm glad."

"Glad it happened?"

"Yes. Because, you see, the person was only doing it to get back at—at *her.*" Her glance flickered over to where Alice stood, talking to Weezy.

"At Alice?"

"Yes. And—" her chin went up even higher, "and I'm glad!"

"You hate her that much, then?"

Her gaze went back to Alice, as if drawn there by a magnet. A shadow passed over her face. She put up her hand and rubbed her eyes. "I hate her," she said in a low voice. "She's so mean all the time, I . . . I hate her."

"I can't say I blame you," Snooky said, also in an undertone. "But if you know who's doing all this—"

"Oh, Weezy can't do anything," she said dismissively.

"Why not?"

"What can she do?"

"She can get rid of whoever's messing things up."

Nikki stared at him, her eyes dilating wildly. "But that's just what I don't want!" she cried. "I don't want that—that other person to go! I just want Alice to go! So does everybody else! It's all her fault that this is happening, anyway. It's all her fault!"

Snooky looked into her round moon face and her wide, angry eyes. For some reason he felt compassion stir in him. "I'm sorry," he said.

"Sorry for what?"

"I don't know. I'm just . . . sorry."

She stared at him for a moment, then rushed out of the room.

On his way over to Alice, Weezy stopped him and hissed, "What do you think you're doing?"

"Just talking. Just chatting to people."

"Well, stop it. You're making me nervous. You look like a spy."

"That's what Elmo said."

"Well, he's right. Leave my students alone. I don't think you should come to class anymore, it's making everybody crazy."

"I don't think it's me that's making people crazy."

She pushed back a curl of hair irritably. "Well, maybe not. But leave my students alone. Nobody likes to talk to a spy. Did Bernard put you up to this?"

"Oh, no, it was my own brilliant idea."

"So he did, did he? Well, he'll pay. He'll pay."

"What are you going to do?"

"I'll think of something," she said darkly.

Alice had already left by the time Snooky looked around for her. He managed to trap Mrs. Castor on her way out the front door by sidling up to her and offering her his arm.

"Thank you, young man," she said, smiling at him.

He helped her down the steps, where an elderly white-haired man was waiting. "This is my husband," said Mrs. Castor. "Tom, this is Snooky Randolph. He's in my class."

"How do you do," said Mr. Castor, and shook hands cordially. He turned to his wife and gave her a peck on the cheek. "Ready to go, Lizzy?"

"Yes, sweetheart."

After Mrs. Castor was safely installed in the car, Snooky leaned in the window. "Do you mind if I ask you one question before you go?"

She eyed him curiously. "No, not at all."

"Who do you think is causing all the trouble in the class? Is it one person, or is it two? You've been there for a while, do you have any feeling for what's going on?"

She sat very still, looking straight ahead of her. When her husband started to turn the key in the ignition, she patted his arm and said, "One minute, Tom."

Snooky waited patiently. Finally she stirred and said, "I don't know who's doing it. I can't answer your questions. But I do feel one thing very strongly."

"What's that?"

"I think that Alice is a genius. Well, I do. And there's a lot of jealousy around. Artists are so insecure, it's hard for them to believe in their own work. They hate anyone who they think is better. Yes, they do, Tom, I've told you that many times," she said into the car. She turned back to Snooky. "You know what La Rochefoucauld said."

"No . . . no, I don't."

*"Nous avons tous assez de force pour supporter les maux d'autrui,"* she quoted in her soft voice. "We all have enough strength to bear the misfortunes of others."

Snooky laughed.

"Yes, but it's true," she said earnestly. "I see in their faces that they're *enjoying* what's happening. They're enjoying Alice's misfortune, and they don't care what happens to everyone else's work."

"Who? Who is 'they'? All of them?"

She sat quietly, fiddling with her cane. "I shouldn't say," she said at last. "It's not for me to point someone out. But there's a lot of hatred there . . . a lot of hatred."

"Yes," Snooky said heavily.

"Can I give you some advice, young man?"

"Certainly."

"I think you should convince Weezy to take a vacation. Whatever's going on in there is unhealthy. She should take a break. The students will survive without her."

He nodded. "I've been thinking about that myself. I think it's a good idea. It would give everything a chance to settle down while she's away."

"Yes, indeed."

"Thank you, Mrs. Castor. You're very kind. Weezy always sings your praises, and I can see why."

This made her smile. "Oh, it's my pleasure. I've been meaning to mention it to her ever since this whole thing started. Oh, well, would you like to hear something else that clever man La Rochefoucauld said?"

"Yes, by all means."

"He said, 'Old people like to give good advice, as solace for no longer being able to provide bad examples.' "

Her husband chuckled and started up the car. Mrs. Castor waved as they pulled away.

A few days later, sorting through her mail over morning coffee, Weezy said suddenly, "What's this?"

She held up a white envelope. Her name and address had been painstakingly lettered on the front with shiny stick-on gold letters. There was no return address.

"Let me open it," said Snooky.

"Oh, come on. What do you think it is, a letter bomb?" She turned it over and ripped it open.

The thin sheet of paper inside had no handwriting on it, just the same metallic gold letters that were on the envelope. Weezy unfolded it and smoothed it out.

**I DESTROYED YOUR PAINTINGS BECAUSE YOU DONT DESERVE TO HAVE AN EXHIBIT YOU HAVE NO TALENT YOU ARE NO GOOD DO YOU HEAR ME YOU ARE NO GOOD**

# SIX

WEEZY COULD not even speak. She felt physically ill. She felt the gold letters rise up before her dazed eyes and claw at her. She turned her head away.

Snooky read the letter impassively. He folded it and stuck it back into the envelope. Then he turned to her and took her in his arms.

They stood that way, clinging to each other like limpets under the water, for a long time. Finally Weezy said,

"I'm scared, Snooky. I'm really scared."

He nodded, pressing her to him. "Yes."

"What . . . what are we going to do?"

"I don't know, but we'll think of something. I don't want you to worry."

She gave a gulping laugh. "Oh no, I'm not worried. I'm not worried."

He nodded and held on to her tightly.

They decided, after some deliberation, to show the letter to the police, and to Maya and Bernard. Snooky insisted on the police; Weezy insisted on Maya and Bernard.

"I have to show her," she said stubbornly. "I *want*

to show her. If something else happens, I want her to know what was going on. I don't want to disappear without a trace."

"Maya maybe, but why Bernard?"

"Well, first of all, because she'll tell Bernard right away. Of course she will, Snooky, there are no secrets between them. And also, I want Bernard's opinion. He has a very clear mind."

"What about my mind? My mind isn't clear?"

"You're right about the police," she said mutinously, "and I'm right about Maya and Bernard. Let's not argue about this."

"Okay. I'm sorry." Snooky turned the letter over in his hands. According to the postmark, it had been mailed two days earlier in Manhattan. "Just like the flowers," he said, staring at it.

Weezy, huddled in her chair, suddenly began to cry. "I don't understand," she said, rocking back and forth. "What have I done? What have I done? I feel like I'm being punished, and I don't even know why."

"Now, now. It has nothing to do with you. It's some nut out there."

"Some nut who knows all about my exhibit. Some nut who slashed my paintings!"

Snooky pulled her onto the sofa and stroked her hair. "Now, now."

"Why me, Snooky? Why me?"

"I don't know," he said soberly.

"I've never done anything—*anything!*—to anyone. I'm always so careful about hurting other people's feelings. I'll bend over backwards not to hurt anyone. I'll go out of my way. I spend all my time feeling resentful because people aren't as nice to me as I am to them. And now, this."

"I don't see how you could have made such an enemy," Snooky said. "It doesn't seem possible."

She took a Kleenex from him and blew her nose noisily. "An enemy," she whispered. "That's what it is. An enemy. I have an enemy. Why? Why do I have an enemy? I haven't done anything!"

"Apparently, you're too talented."

She shook her head wearily.

"You were going to have an exhibit. Maybe the person who sent this to you thinks he or she deserves one instead."

She was silent.

"That's what it said, you know, that you don't 'deserve' one."

She nodded. "Yes."

"Somebody with a chip on their shoulder."

"Yes."

"Now who in the world could that be? Who has a chip on their shoulder about their talent? Who thinks everybody else isn't as deserving?"

Her fingers clenched on his arm. "It's not Alice. I'm telling you, it couldn't be. She wouldn't have done that to those paintings, she just wouldn't. She wouldn't do this to me."

"Are you positive, sweetheart?"

She shook her head dumbly.

A little while later, Snooky kissed the top of her curly head and picked up the phone.

"Who are you calling?"

"The police."

"Fat lot of good that will do us. They were useless about the studio. Remember how they found one of Bernard's footprints and got all excited?"

"I haven't completely ruled Bernard out as a suspect yet.

Hello, Ridgewood Police? Who do I talk to about a threatening letter?"

Bernard read the letter slowly and carefully, as if he were searching for something to eat on a particularly interesting menu. When he was finished, he placed it on the coffee table in front of him.

Maya, Snooky and Weezy looked at him expectantly, three pairs of anxious gazes.

"Well?" said Snooky.

"Well, what?"

"Don't you have anything to say?"

"It's a disgusting piece of trash. What else do you want me to say, Snooky?"

"I don't know. Something else. Something we don't already know."

"Well," said Bernard, "apparently they don't sell punctuation marks along with those gold lettering sets. Either that, or the writer was in a hurry. I feel there's never any excuse for poor punctuation."

"Sweetheart," said Maya icily, "I don't think you understand. This isn't a joke. This letter is . . . well, it's frightening. It's an outright threat."

"So it is."

"What are we going to do about it?"

"What did the police say?"

Weezy shrugged. "Nothing much. Took down the information, made a photocopy of the letter, said they'd get back to us. What can they do, after all? They said if I was worried I should hire a bodyguard."

"I'm her bodyguard," said Snooky.

Bernard looked at him sadly. "I think they were referring to somebody competent, Snooky."

"I am competent."

"Maybe Weezy should come live with us for a while. Get out of the line of fire."

"I suggested that," said Maya eagerly, "but she says no. Tell her to stay with us, Bernard, she's crazy not to."

Weezy was shaking her head. "I don't want to get the two of you involved in this. It's not like my whereabouts would be a secret, anyway. My God, it's impossible to keep a secret in a little town like this. Besides, you don't have a security system and I do. I'll be okay."

Bernard unfolded the letter and looked at it again. *"You are no good,"* he mused. "Said it twice, in fact. *You have no talent.* Somebody who really needs to tear you down, Weeze. Who could it be?"

"Don't know. I just don't know."

"Where can you get these gold stick-on letters?"

"Any art supply store in Manhattan, any stationery store. They're everywhere, you've seen them."

He nodded. "Any of your students spring to mind?"

She lifted her hands in a gesture of bewilderment. "I don't know. I mean, there's been all these weird things happening in there, but . . . what do they have against me, Bernard?"

"Your talent, my dear."

She gave a shaky laugh. "I'm not that talented, believe me. Not talented enough to deserve this kind of treatment."

Bernard folded the letter up and put it away in the envelope. He held it out to Snooky. "Do you want to keep this?"

Snooky regarded it with distaste. "No. Do you think we should throw it out or burn it?"

"Neither," said Bernard. "I'll keep it. You may need it later, as evidence."

"Evidence?"

"Yes." Bernard turned and bent a kindly gaze on his wife's best friend.

"Come stay with us for a couple of days," he said. "Just long enough to get your feet back on the ground. Leave your security system on and come let us take care of you. Snooky can cook for everybody and I think both Maya and I would like to have you around where we can make sure you're okay."

This, for Bernard, was a long speech. Two tears rolled down Weezy's pale cheeks.

"Okay," she snuffled, "if . . . if you're sure."

"We're sure," said Maya, patting her arm. "Come stay here, and Snooky can dance attendance on all of us."

"Thank you," said Weezy, and, with a trembling sigh, she put her head down on Maya's shoulder.

"Did you notice how both my sister and Bernard emphasized the part about my cooking and dancing attendance on everybody?" Snooky remarked later. "Am I wrong, am I overly sensitive, or did you notice that too?"

"Oh, Snooky." Weezy folded a sweater and put it neatly into a suitcase. "They were being kind."

"Oh, yes, tremendously kind. Maya gave me some pointers afterwards, a list of things they'd like to eat. That's kind, too, don't you think? Does the phrase *bloodsucking parasites* spring to mind?"

"You never mind cooking for me." She folded a blouse and put it on top of the sweater.

"That's because you're you. You're not my sister or Bernard."

"I thought it was very nice of them," said Weezy. "I'd *like* to get out of this house."

Snooky caught a glimpse of the mulish expression on her face as she bent over the suitcase. "Oh. I see. Okay. Do you think they'd like lasagna tonight, or shepherd's pie?"

---

Bernard had thought that it would be nauseating to see Snooky and Weezy together under his roof, but since they acted just as they always had, with no sign of their changed relationship except a few shared jokes and the fact that they retired to one bedroom at night instead of two, he gradually began to relax. This was easy to do in the happy postprandial haze induced by Snooky's cooking. After a few days, it was as if the four of them had been together always.

"It's not so bad, is it?" asked Maya one night, when she and Bernard were reading in bed.

"Weezy and Snooky?"

"Uh-huh."

"No." Bernard turned a page.

"I mean, we hate having company, but if you're going to have company, they're the best around."

Bernard grunted.

"I'm going downstairs to get something to eat. I'll be right back," said Maya, throwing off the covers.

"Didn't you just have a snack?"

"Yes, I did, Bernard. Why? Do you have some kind of problem with that?"

"No."

"I'm pregnant. I'm supposed to eat as much as I want."

"Good, good."

"I'm feeding your precious offspring, okay?"

"Yes, yes, okay."

"Want anything from the kitchen?"

Bernard was always in the mood for a snack. "Bring me some of those whole-wheat crackers Snooky bought the other day."

"Okay."

"And some peanut butter."

"Uh-huh."

"And a little bit of jelly."

"Blackberry or cherry?"

"Blackberry."

"Okay."

"And don't forget the cream cheese!" he bellowed after her as she went down the stairs.

Maya returned ten minutes later with a laden tray of goodies.

"Bernard, you should talk about what I eat. Look at you," she said, watching him shovel it down. "You're going to gain as much as I am."

"Mhmmmhmmm," said Bernard, his mouth full of crackers.

"I mean, this is ridiculous. How dare you say anything about my food consumption?" She spread a cracker thickly with peanut butter and cream cheese, and stuck it in her mouth. "How dare you?"

"Mmmhmhmxmhxmmjm," explained Bernard, gesturing.

"What? Well, I don't care. You have no right to talk to me that way." Maya rubbed her abdomen fretfully. "I'm starving all the time."

"I know."

"It's an uncomfortable feeling."

"I know." Bernard was normally hungry all the time. He gave her a sympathetic glance.

"I feel bloated."

"Mmm-hmmmm."

"Weird things are happening all over my body. I feel out of control, Bernard. I feel like I've been taken over by an alien organism." Maya was near tears. She crammed a cracker angrily into her mouth. "It doesn't seem right."

"Mmmm-hmmm."

"And now I can't even fit into my jeans. I have to wear those stupid maternity pants." Maya had taken to wearing black stretch pants and enormously oversized sweaters, culled from Bernard's wardrobe. Bernard thought she looked very nice in them, and said so.

"You know I think you look terrific."

"Oh, I know, I know," said Maya, in a tone which clearly conveyed to him that she didn't care. She fiddled absently with her peanut butter knife. "I just feel so . . . I don't know . . . so *helpless,* somehow. I feel like I don't live in my own body anymore, somebody else does. It's so busy building somebody else's body that it doesn't have time for me anymore." She burst into tears. "It's a horrible feeling."

"Now, now." Bernard hugged her awkwardly over the crumb-filled tray. "Now, now, sweetheart. I know it's hard. Everybody says it's hard."

"Who, Bernard? Who says it's hard? Nobody does, everybody just idealizes it into this perfect experience. Nobody talks about this sense I have of being taken over by an alien being. Do they? No, they don't. Am I the only one? Am I the only person who's ever felt this way? Am I all alone in the universe?"

Bernard regarded her lovingly. "Now, you know the answer to that."

"Oh, I guess so." Maya raked her fingers through her hair and moved over to snuggle against his shoulder. "I guess so. I'm sorry I'm so horrible already, and it's only the second trimester. Can you imagine where I'll be by the seventh or eighth month?"

Bernard couldn't imagine. He kissed the top of her head and offered her a cracker with cream cheese and jelly.

Upstairs, in Snooky's tiny third-floor bedroom under the eaves, another conversation was taking place.

"Beautiful view you have here," Weezy said. She was sit-

ting up in bed, wearing a long pink nightgown and leaning her elbows on the windowsill. The window was open to the warm May night and the moon shone bright yellow overhead. The light streamed in, making the edges and planes of her face look mysterious, illuminating her wild hair in an aureole. "Look at that moon."

"Something, isn't it?" Snooky propped the pillows up behind him. "Full tonight."

"When I was younger," Weezy said dreamily, "much younger, about your age, let's say, I used to open all the windows on a night like this and paint by the light of the moon. The moon changes all the colors, it's wonderful, you can't tell what the hell you're doing. Everything looks completely different. I used to go crazy and paint and paint and paint. In the morning my roommates would find me asleep with the paintbrush in my hand, surrounded by all these crazy drawings."

"And how would they look by daylight?"

"Oh." Weezy gave a low laugh. "Psychotic, really. Not much sense to them. But sometimes the colors would be wonderful. And I could never get over the difference between day and night, looking at them."

Snooky shook his head, his eyes riveted on the pale orb floating overhead. "That's something, Weezy."

"Oh, I don't know. It was pretentious, really. I was convinced it showed how wild and creative I was."

"When I was younger and there was a full moon, I used to stand in front of William's door and howl. I was convinced that showed how wild and creative I was. Used to drive him nuts. And when I was in college, I would get into a car with a bunch of other guys and go around trying to pick up women. Our theory was that since people go crazy at the time of the full moon, maybe they would go out with us."

"I see. The biorhythmically-deranged dating theory?"

"Exactly." He slipped an arm around her waist. "Do you feel like flinging open all the windows—well, there's only two in this room—and painting till dawn?"

"No." Her voice went curiously flat. "I don't feel like painting at all anymore. With everything that's going on . . . I don't feel like it."

He nodded. "I was wondering if you were working these days."

"No. Not a bit. The only time I pick up a brush is in class."

He looked at her face, beautiful and serene in profile, like a Renaissance goddess with fiery hair burning on her shoulders and curling over her arms. Weezy turned to him, her face a pattern of light and dark, lovely and mysterious.

"I keep waiting for the other shoe to drop," she said.

"What do you mean?"

"I keep waiting for the next letter," she said patiently, as if explaining something to an idiot child. "The next one. You don't seriously think whoever it is is going to stop now, do you? Now that they're on a roll?"

"There doesn't have to be another one, Weezy."

She shrugged again, lightly. "I don't know. I don't have a good feeling about it, that's all." She drew with her fingertip on the windowsill. "I don't have a good feeling about it."

Snooky nodded. He tightened his grip around her waist. Weezy smiled at him faintly, then propped her elbows on the windowsill again and gazed out at the moondrenched night.

The second letter came three days later.

Weezy had gone home to check on the house, water her plants and pick up the mail. She came back looking wan and frightened, and handed Snooky the letter.

"Oh, God," he said, pulling out a kitchen chair and sitting down.

"I couldn't open it," she said. "I saw the gold letters and thought I was going to throw up."

He nodded. The outside looked exactly the same as before: the Manhattan postmark, the shiny golden letters spelling out Weezy's name and address. Snooky tore it open.

**YOU THINK YOU ARE SUCH A BIG DEAL YOU THINK YOU ARE SUCH A GREAT ARTIST IM JUST AS GOOD AS YOU IM BETTER I DONT KNOW WHO YOU THINK YOU ARE TRYING TO IMPRESS EVERYBODY**

The color drained out of Weezy's face as she read it. "I want it to stop, Snooky. I just want it to stop."

He was reading it over again, grimly. "I know."

"Somebody hates me, and I don't know who or even *why!*" Her voice ended on a long wail.

" 'I'm just as good as you,' " Snooky read out loud. His eyes met hers. "Now who could possibly think that?"

She shrugged miserably. At that moment Bernard came into the kitchen with his coffee cup in his hand. He paused when he saw their faces.

"Should I go away?"

In reply, Snooky held out the letter.

Bernard took it and read it through impassively. When he was done, he folded it and handed it back.

"Well?" demanded Snooky.

"Well, what?"

"Any thoughts?"

"Yes," said Bernard, going to the stove and pouring himself a cup of coffee. "Whoever did it must have bought a lot of those alphabet sets. There aren't that many letters in just one set, if I'm not mistaken."

Weezy leaned her head in one hand. She laughed shakily. "Thank you, Bernard. Always the unique point of view."

"Childlike," said Bernard.

"What? Your reaction?"

"No, no. The letters. Childlike, and spiteful. Like a jealous kid. Part of the same pattern as all the others."

"Yes," said Snooky, much struck by this. "That's true. That's certainly true."

Bernard added cream and three sugars to his coffee and stirred it thoughtfully, looking out the kitchen window to the woods behind the house.

"Who thinks you're trying to impress everybody, Weezy?"

She spread her hands in a gesture of bewilderment. "I have no idea. I told my students about the magazine interview because I thought it could help them. I never talked about my exhibit or anything else in front of them. Never!"

"But they knew you were going to have a show."

"Yes," she said reluctantly. "Yes, but beyond that we never discussed it. Frankly, they weren't that interested. Even Elmo, if it doesn't concern him directly he doesn't give a damn."

"Which of them thinks they're better than you?"

"Well . . . Alice, I guess," she said slowly. "But to be honest, she *is*. I don't need a letter to tell me that. The same for Elmo, he's a genius. Not the others, unless they've totally flipped out. I mean . . . well, that didn't come out right, but you know what I mean. They're not all puffed up about themselves." She fell silent, wringing her hands together.

"Are you sure?"

"I'm not sure about anything anymore. All I know is that

I want it to stop. I want to get on with my life and my work and not have to be looking over my shoulder, scared to death that somebody will trash my paintings or send me this kind of letter or hurt me."

Bernard nodded, gazing out the window. Snooky took the letter gingerly, as if he were handling a scorpion, and stuffed it back into the envelope. There was a long, heavy silence.

"I'm going to disband the class," said Weezy, with decision. "I can't stand it any longer. I don't have to tell them about these letters. I'll just say that it's getting too volatile in there, too frightening, and it's hurting everyone's work. I'll say I'm going to wait and get a few more students, maybe dilute the mix a little bit, make everybody happier."

"That's a good idea," said Bernard.

"And if you don't mind, I'll stay here a few more days. I feel safe here, somehow."

"Absolutely. As long as you want."

"Don't tell Maya about this new letter, it'll upset her too much," said Weezy. "She shouldn't see it, with the baby and all."

"That's nice of you, Weezy, but it's not necessary. Maya can handle it."

"Oh, no, no, men don't understand. Maya is like a finely tuned racehorse coming down the home stretch with this pregnancy, I don't want anything to get in her way."

"I wouldn't call the second trimester exactly coming down the home stretch," said Bernard.

"Well, whatever. Now, remember what I said, both of you. Nobody breathes a word of this to Maya."

They promised.

Weezy's resolve lasted until Maya came home from shopping, a few hours later.

"Hi," she said, hanging up her coat. "How're you doing?"

Weezy burst into tears. "Look at this!" She held up the letter, waving it in front of Maya's face. "I got another one, Maya! Another one!"

"What?"

"Another one!" cried Weezy, and fell into her best friend's arms.

"Don't feel bad," Snooky said later. "You held out until she actually asked how you were doing. Never mind that it was a rhetorical question."

Weezy was picking disconsolately at the cherry pie left over from dessert. They were seated alone at the great mahogany dining room table, Maya and Bernard having excused themselves after a late dinner and gone up to bed. "Oh, I'm disgusted with myself. But what can you do, it's Maya's fault, really. She's so sympathetic. Just the way she said, 'Hi, how are you?' totally unhinged me."

"Listen, I have an idea." Snooky leaned forward and gathered her hands in his. "Why don't we go away together? Don't say no immediately," he said when he saw the doubt in her face. "You don't have anything keeping you here any longer. You're going to stop teaching for a while, and God knows you could use getting away. I thought we could go to the islands together. You haven't lived until you've seen my friends' place on St. Martin."

"Go away? I don't know, Snooky . . . gee, I haven't even thought . . ."

"Big modern place, painted pink, with floor-to-ceiling windows everywhere. Kind of glows at sunset. You can walk from the living room down to their private beach. I spent most of my time drinking rum and swimming."

"Sounds nice," she said wistfully.

"They'd love to have you. They have about a zillion guest rooms, the place is so big they can never fill it up. And they're isolated there, really, it's an act of charity to go visit them and give them some company. Peter and Nancy, you'll love them, they're old friends of mine."

"Oh, I'm sure they're dying for company. Out in this paradise of theirs."

"They are, they are, they're bored to tears. They're perfect hosts—I mean, not to say a word against Maya and Bernard, but you don't have to lift a finger while you're there, they provide food and drinks and then leave you alone. It's great."

She twiddled a curl of hair between her fingers. "I don't know. Maybe. It . . . it sounds nice. Relaxing."

"Relaxing. Relaxing is the word, sweetheart. Relaxing, and far, far away from here."

She nodded. Her face had a tired, anxious expression on it. "Well . . ." she said doubtfully.

"Say yes."

She lifted her chin decisively. "Yes. Why not?"

"Good. I'll call Peter and Nancy and get the tickets. We'll leave tomorrow."

"Tomorrow? Are you crazy? I can't get away, I have a class tomorrow. I can't tell them I'm stopping class over the phone," she said in response to his look. "Don't be stupid. I thought I would tell them tomorrow."

"All right. We leave the next day, then."

She laughed, shaking her head. "The next day? Get a grip on yourself, sweetie. We can't invite ourselves that soon."

"Watch me," he said, and picked up the phone.

"You can't stop teaching!" cried Alice, distressed, when Weezy broke the news.

"Not forever, Alice, just for a little while."

"Well, how long?"

"I don't know," Weezy said truthfully. "I need a break. I . . . I have some things going on in my personal life that are upsetting me, and I need some time to myself."

She hadn't planned to tell the truth, but confronted with their shocked faces she had felt it impossible to do anything else. Now she twisted her hands unhappily. This was harder than she had anticipated. "I'm sorry. I'm really sorry. I can give you the names of some people in New York you can study with for a while." She gave a faint smile. "It might do you good to study with somebody else, you know. All of you. A different point of view."

"Some things in your personal life?" Alice repeated, as if she had not heard beyond that point.

"Yes, that's right."

Snooky suddenly found himself the focus of four hostile gazes. Mrs. Castor was the only one smiling. He swallowed and looked away.

"Hmmm," said Alice sourly. She turned back to Weezy. "Will you—will you call us when you're ready to teach again?"

"Of course I will." Weezy was delighted with this apparent capitulation, just where she had expected the most resistance. She looked around the class. "Of course I will."

Elmo had crossed his arms, his biceps bulging, and was staring at her with a frown on his face. "You don't have to leave, Weezy. You could get rid of what's bothering you easily." He shot a look towards the back of the room, at Alice. "Easily!"

"That's not fair," said Alice, her voice rising. "How dare you imply—"

"Well, it's clear what's going on, isn't it?" Elmo pounded his fist into his other palm. He was red with rage. "Weezy's running away because she can't handle what's happening in here. She's so fragile she could break. A few things get messed up, and she drops us all."

Weezy looked at him icily. "I wouldn't call my exhibit just a few things, Elmo. I wouldn't say the same to you about 'Girl in White.' "

"Well, it's damned unfair, Weezy. We're all being punished for what one person is doing. One person!" he added, with another furious glance towards the back of the room. There was a wail from Alice.

"I didn't do it—"

"Oh, the hell you didn't—!"

"I didn't do anything, I tell you—"

"Go to hell," Elmo said crisply. "You're screwing up everything for us here. Everything! Now you've driven Weezy out, are you happy? Are you finally happy?"

"That's quite enough," said Weezy. Elmo turned away, his shoulders rigid. Alice's wails trailed off into silence.

Weezy turned to Mrs. Castor. "I'm so sorry about leaving you in the lurch right now, with the work you've been doing and all. It's some of your best work ever, you know that as well as I do. And you don't live in Manhattan like the others, so I don't know who to refer you to."

"That's all right," Mrs. Castor said, smiling at her. "You take care of yourself first, dear. The classes can wait." She shot a reproving glance at Elmo and Alice. "Despite what some people may think."

Alice pursed her lips, but she seemed too stunned by Weezy's announcement to say anything more. She seemed deflated, like a large balloon with a tiny hole in it, slowly spiraling towards the floor.

Nikki was wringing her hands. "Oh, Weezy . . ." she fluttered mindlessly. "Oh, Weezy, I'm *so* sorry that . . . oh, Weezy . . ."

Elmo's face was set in a cold, unforgiving expression. He packed up his paints and brushes neatly, picked up his canvases and left the room without a backward glance.

Jennifer, in his wake, looked at Weezy with an odd, faintly amused expression in her eyes. "I'm sorry. You know how he is."

"Oh, yes, I know," said Weezy, raising her voice. She bellowed down the hallway after him, "I KNOW HOW HE IS! HE HAS ALL THE EMOTIONAL MATURITY OF A TWO-YEAR-OLD!"

"Go to hell, Weezy!" he shouted.

"You go to hell!"

"You go to hell!"

"You go to hell!"

The front door banged shut.

"You're going away?" Maya said incredulously, when they broke the news over dinner. "You're going away—*tomorrow?*"

"Yes, Missy," said Snooky. "Is that okay with you? Can the two of you get by without us?"

"You're going away? Where?"

"I told you, Missy. St. Martin. To my friends' place on the beach. Sun, sand and surf. I figured Weezy and I could use a vacation."

"Oh." Maya digested this. She speared some of Snooky's perfectly cooked asparagus and forked it down. "Okay. I think . . . well, it sounds like a good idea."

"You don't mind, do you?" asked Weezy. "I was sure you'd be glad to get rid of us. I know how much Bernard hates company. I feel we've been straining him to the limit."

Bernard did not contradict this. He continued to eat in silence.

"No, no, you haven't been straining us," Maya said distractedly. "No, it's been fun. It really has. How long did you say you'd be away?"

"We don't know, Missy. Maybe three or four weeks. It depends how much we like it."

"Oh."

Snooky eyed her, puzzled. "I didn't mean to totally unhinge you, Maya. What's the matter?"

"I don't know, it just seems so . . . so *sudden.* I mean, we just got used to both of you being here, and now you're going away? It seems so sudden."

Bernard put an arm around her. "Change," he explained. "The nesting instinct. Pregnant women don't like change. It disturbs them."

"Well, don't worry, Missy, we'll be back well before the baby's born. I mean, it's not due until October, right? October twentieth? And here it is, not even summer yet. There's plenty of time. I wouldn't get all ruffled up about it."

Maya nodded.

"If the leaves start turning and we're not back, give us a call."

"Oh, stop tormenting her," snapped Weezy. "I think the two of you should get away. You won't be able to once the baby's born, you know. And the second trimester is a perfect time to travel."

"I guess so," Maya said. She picked at her food dispiritedly. "What's this stuff here, Snooks?"

"Shallots. You going to be okay while we're away? Bernard will cook for you?"

"I'll be glad to cook."

"Wonderful," said Maya. "Baked beans every night." She got up and left the table.

---

"I'm sorry," she said later, when Bernard came upstairs in search of her. He found her sprawled on the bed, watching TV, Misty curled up on the pillow next to her.

He sat down on the edge of the bed. "You okay?"

"Uh-huh. I'm really sorry. I don't know what came over me."

"I understand."

"No, you don't." Her lower lip was sticking out. "You don't understand. All I could think of was that the two of them can pick up and leave whenever they want, and we can't. In a few months we won't ever be able to take a real vacation again. Don't look at me that way, with pity in your eyes. I don't need your pity. I remember what it was like when my parents used to take us on vacations together. It was a nightmare. Snooky would drive William crazy, and William would drive everybody else crazy, and my parents would say they were never taking us along again, but then they would, and it would be just the same. I think everybody kept hoping it would be different, somehow."

"We'll get away, just the two of us."

"Oh, yes," she said scornfully. "And while we're away, what will we do with the baby, Bernard? Put it in a kennel? We don't even do that now, with Misty."

He sighed and shifted his attention to the TV screen. "What're you watching?"

"I don't know. Something called *Invasion from Venus*. You know, aliens disguised as humans. It's pretty creepy."

The two of them watched in silence for a few minutes.

"Hey," said Bernard. "This is a good movie."

"Yeah."

"I'll go downstairs and make some popcorn."

"Okay."

They were sitting on the bed, happily eating popcorn,

sharing some with Misty, when there was a soft knock on the door.

"Come in," called Maya.

Weezy opened the door a crack. "You okay, sweetie?"

"Yeah, I'm all right. Just my hormones. Come on in."

Weezy came in and jumped on the bed between them. She was wearing a yellow nightgown and an old pink bathrobe. Snooky followed, wearing a ratty blue bathrobe.

"This is cozy," he said, sprawling on the bed. "Pass the popcorn, Bernard."

"No," said Bernard. "Make your own."

There was a chorus of protest, but in the end Snooky went downstairs ("I'm just doing this to keep peace in the household and because I don't want to see you upset, you understand, Missy") and made three large bowls of popcorn. "One for each of us," he said, passing them around. "Since Bernard—and I'm not saying the word *selfish,* you understand —won't share his."

"This is a great movie," said Weezy, deeply absorbed.

"Isn't it?" said Maya.

"I mean, the bit where the little girl's dog warns her that her father's an alien, I love that kind of stuff. Why do dogs always know? I mean, his own wife didn't pick up on it, did she?"

"Dogs are very finely attuned to whoever's going to give them dinner," said Snooky. "It enables them to sense when their owner's body has been taken over by someone from outer space. It means their food supply is endangered."

"Oh."

"Ask Misty, she'll tell you." He prodded the sleeping dog. "Wake up, Misty. Wake up, little Misty. Oh, well, she'll tell you later. Is Misty getting old? Does she do anything other than sleep?"

"Misty is not getting old," said Bernard.

"Really? How old is she?"

"She's only eight."

"Isn't that fifty-six in dog years? She's middle-aged, then."

"Dog years are only an approximation," said Bernard. "It depends on the size of the dog and their general condition. Misty is still a young dog."

"Bernard has a theory about dog years," said Maya. "He feels that he ages a week for every day that you stay with us, Snooky. He told me the other day that he's already aged over two years during the few months you've been here."

"Thank you, Bernard," said Snooky. "I understand. Most people find it difficult to have a free, full-time live-in servant."

The four of them watched the entire movie, and agreed to watch whatever came on after that without changing channels. It turned out to be a compilation of old silent Buster Keaton clips. Maya laughed until her eyes watered and her stomach hurt.

"I can't laugh anymore, turn it off, it's dangerous," she gasped. "It's bad for the baby."

"Don't be silly, laughter is good for the baby," said Weezy.

Bernard was looking at his popcorn bowl sadly. "No more."

"All gone, sweetheart?" said Maya.

"All gone."

"Want some more?"

"Yes."

The three of them looked at Snooky expectantly.

"Hey, I don't think so. Fend for yourselves, will you?"

"Make me some, too, when you go downstairs," said his sister. "Mine is almost gone."

"Gee, I'm sorry, Missy, but my shift was over at midnight. I'm not on again as your combination butler and cook until nine o'clock tomorrow morning."

"I'll go with you," said Weezy, giving him a shove which pushed him off the bed, "and we'll do it together."

The party broke up at three A.M. Snooky and Weezy were leaving early that morning, so they kissed Maya and Bernard good-bye.

"Have a wonderful time," said Maya, suddenly tearful again.

"We will, Missy. Take care of yourself."

"Okay."

"You have our address and phone number there, so don't panic. We'll call you every other day or so to see how things are going."

"You don't have to do that, Snooks."

"I want to. Remember to keep eating a lot for the baby."

"I don't think you have to worry about that," Maya said, regarding her swollen waistline with mingled pride and despair.

"Good. Call if you need us for anything."

"I will. Have a wonderful time. Don't worry about us, we'll get along fine. I'll miss you, but you know Bernard won't. He hates company. And, Snooks—"

"Yes?"

"Take good care of her," Maya whispered.

He bent down and kissed his sister lightly on the cheek. "What do you think this is all about?"

The first three nights in St. Martin, Weezy woke up sobbing and drenched in sweat in the early hours of the morning. Snooky held her and talked to her, telling her little stories, using funny voices to make her laugh, singing her stupid little songs until she dropped off in his arms. The nightmares were all the same: something evil was creeping after her in the darkness.

"I'm so scared," she sobbed. "I'm so scared!"

He told her little stories and enacted all the parts in different voices until at last she smiled and slipped off to sleep. One night she whispered, "When I lie down to go to sleep, this little film of everything I've ever done wrong in my life unwinds in my brain. Every embarrassing moment, every misstep, every person I've ever hurt, every person who's ever hurt me, every action I've ever regretted."

"Sounds charming."

"It's awful. Completely, totally awful. A living nightmare."

As the days went on, however, Weezy slowly began to unwind. She spent her days curled up in a beach chair under a palm tree, reading voraciously. Their hosts had a large library and Weezy discovered to her delight that they had a section on her own favorite interest, the Tudor period in England. She spent hours reading about Henry VIII and Elizabeth I and their times.

"So relaxing, sweetie," she said when Snooky questioned her taste. "So reassuring to read about other people's troubles, four hundred years ago. Nothing better. Plus, they're not just ordinary people, they're monarchs. When they have problems, it's so . . . so *satisfying,* somehow. I can't get enough of it."

The house was just as Snooky had described it: painted pink on the outside, with huge windows everywhere and a terrace leading down to white sand on a private beach. The water was halcyon blue, the sun shone every day in a cloudless sky, and Weezy would glance up from her book to find tiny lizards watching her from their perches, sunning themselves on the steaming rocks. Little white birds roamed the beaches, pecking at insects in the sand. Once a day Snooky would clamber up the trees and bring down coconuts which he split open on the rocks, scooping out the sweet white meat. Whenever she got too hot she would go for a swim in the crystal-clear water, where brilliantly colored fish swarmed through the shallows. Their hosts, Peter and Nancy McAllister, provided them with food and drink and left them alone, just as Snooky had promised. The house was so large that privacy was not a problem; the two of them had an entire wing all to themselves. Whenever Weezy felt sleepy, she would stretch out in the lounge chair and take a nap, the shadows of the palm tree playing over her face, the tropical breeze blowing in from the sea. Whenever she thought of this time, years later, it was in vivid colors in her mind: lapis blue, sundrenched yellow, blinding white, the jade-green of the water when a shadow passed over it. The days blended one into the next, and her life before she had arrived on the island seemed very far away, a mere pinprick in the distance, receding to a far horizon.

"Enjoying yourself?" Snooky asked one day, smiling at her indulgently. He felt that his plan had worked out better than he had ever expected.

She looked up from her book. Her hair was bleached in the sun and now shone with bright gold and amber highlights. "Oh, yes. Yes, you know I am. More than I can say. Peter and Nancy have been wonderful."

"Some other people we know could learn a thing or two from them."

"Well, Maya's pregnant, she's not supposed to be a great host right now. Anyway, these two must be absolutely loaded. I've never seen a house like this in my life."

"Yes, Nancy comes from old money. I'm sure she considers this house barely adequate."

"It's awfully nice of them to put up with us. I'm not exactly sure what they get out of it, to tell you the truth. Certainly not the pleasure of our company, as you said—we hardly ever see them."

He waved a careless hand. "Oh, it doesn't matter. They love having guests, imagine how empty this house would be otherwise. They spend part of the year here and they love it when people drop in. Which just goes to prove my old maxim, that you don't have to have money as long as your friends do."

"You bloodsucking leech," she said, turning a page.

"Sucking them dry," he said grandly, picking up his rum drink. "Sucking them dry. Ask Bernard, he'll tell you."

"Well, it's true that they don't seem to mind. They make me feel like we could stay here forever."

"I'm sure they'd be delighted to have somebody look after the property while they're away. Make it look lived in."

At night they would go out to a local restaurant, eating in a tree house nestled in the branches of a palm tree, or in a French restaurant on the bay where the sound of the water lapping against the dock formed a gentle accompaniment to their meal. Snooky ordered the same thing night after night: conch stew.

"Giant, rubbery slugs," he would say in satisfaction as the dish was set before him.

Weezy would look up from her grilled fish in amusement. "I remember when I used to be able to tolerate that stuff."

"Try it again, sweetheart, you'll go crazy. It's delicious. I never eat anything else when I'm here."

"So I see," she said, grinding pepper onto her rice. "So I see."

After dinner they would linger over coffee, watching the sun sink into the water, casting fiery tendrils of light across the bay towards them. They would hold hands and Snooky would tell her little anecdotes to make her laugh. Then they would drive back to the beach house, go up to their bedroom and make love. Weezy felt as if she were living inside a bubble: a giant, iridescent bubble, with glowing colors which spread and burst all around her like fireworks. She felt that her life had become beautifully round, full and creamy, like the perfect moon they had seen from the window of Maya's house that May night. That moon waned into nothingness and then came again, growing to a huge white orb which hung above the waters of the bay as they sat in the French restaurant, talking and laughing and holding hands. Weezy, in a happy daze, felt that time had lost all meaning for the two of them. The glowing Caribbean colors during the day, and the tranquillity of the nights, combined to produce in her a glowing, lazy satisfaction. She felt like one of the sand lizards basking on a rock.

When she tried to describe this feeling to Maya, there was a long, crackling silence on the other end of the phone.

"Your brain's been addled by too much sun, too much swimming and, I would venture to guess, way too much sex," Maya said at last.

"You're just jealous."

"I am jealous. It's July, and it's turned cold here. The nights are cold. Every time you talk about the Caribbean heat I feel like screaming."

"Your brother eats giant slugs every day. Does that make you feel better? Like you're not missing that much?"

"No."

"You could come visit us, both of you. Snooky said you could. He said our hosts wouldn't mind, and believe me, Maya, this house is so big I nearly got lost once. I ended up in a third-floor bathroom and thought I'd never see the beach again."

"No, no, you're having your own vacation, we don't want to intrude. Besides, Bernard hates the sun and the heat, he's like a bear, he can't take the sun."

"But you would love it, sweetie."

"What difference does that make?" Maya asked bitterly. "Since when do my wishes count for anything? All I am is a giant incubating machine. My own genes aren't concerned with me anymore, they've turned their attention to the next generation, so why should anyone else care about me? I'm obsolete . . . outmoded. Every day I feel calcium leaching out of my spine to make the baby."

Weezy shuddered. "How . . . horrible."

"Exactly."

Later, lying on the beach drinking papaya juice and watching the sunset, Weezy remarked, "Your sister sounds depressed."

"Oh, yeah?"

"Yes. She was talking about the baby sucking calcium out of her spine to make its own bones."

"What a disgusting idea."

"I can't wait for this pregnancy to be over. Are all pregnant women this way?"

"No. Maya's always been high-strung. Everything is always a cause for alarm."

"She's getting ready to take Lamaze classes. Should I tell her what my mother used to tell me, that anyone who refers to childbirth pain as 'discomfort' should be hit over the head with a large ice pick?"

Snooky was busy trying to train one of the lizards to respond to his commands. "Go," he said imperiously. "Come. Come back here. Go. Sit. Sit! Oh, damn."

"Never had a dog, did you?"

"No, and frankly, I've never gotten over it. Come here. Sit. Sit down. Stop. Go. That's right, go! Hey, Weezy, I think it's getting the hang of it."

Weezy watched him for a while barking orders at the sand

lizards as they swarmed around him, intent on their own errands. Finally she stretched luxuriously and gave him a peck on the cheek. "I'll be back at the house when you're ready to go out for dinner."

Bernard, alone in his office, with the windows pulled all the way up and the pungent smell of the pine tree outside his window drifting in, was having trouble concentrating. He had followed Sophie and Sylvie along on their adventures, in their quest for the lost path of the lobster migration, but now he had come to a standstill. He chewed on one fingernail, typed a few words, crossed them out with a large red pencil, then typed a few more. At last, with a heavy sigh, he opened the top drawer of his desk and took out the two letters Weezy had received.

He had found that these letters, even shut away in a drawer, had a way of disturbing him when his attention was supposed to be elsewhere. For the hundredth time since Weezy had gone away, he perused the envelopes carefully, then took the letters out and re-read them. By now he knew their messages by heart.

**I DESTROYED YOUR PAINTINGS BECAUSE YOU DONT DESERVE TO HAVE AN EXHIBIT   YOU HAVE NO TALENT   YOU ARE NO GOOD   DO YOU HEAR ME   YOU ARE NO GOOD**

**YOU THINK YOU ARE SUCH A BIG DEAL   YOU THINK YOU ARE SUCH A GREAT ARTIST   IM JUST AS GOOD AS YOU   IM BETTER   I DONT**

## KNOW WHO YOU THINK YOU ARE TRYING TO IMPRESS EVERYBODY

Again he frowned over them. The vicious messages stood out in stark contrast to the cheerful golden letters. He was puzzled, and angry at himself. There was something Weezy had said in his company . . . something she had mentioned, that had not made much of an impression at the time, but now was sitting in the back of his consciousness, scrabbling away at him, trying to get his attention. It was almost a physical pain to try to remember it, it was such a tiny thing, almost a throw-away line, and yet . . . and yet . . .

Bernard frowned, willing himself to remember. He closed his eyes, searching the black vault of his brain. It was useless. The memory would not reveal itself. He opened his eyes and put the letters down on the desk. It was maddening not to know who had sent them. In the hothouse environment of Weezy's art world, who was sufficiently driven by hate and jealousy to laboriously put these poison-pen messages together and mail them?

The door opened and Maya came in. He shoved the letters hastily back into the drawer. She perched on the edge of his leather armchair and kissed the top of his head.

"Reading those letters again?"

Bernard nodded guiltily.

"I imagine you must have them memorized by now, sweetheart."

"Yes."

"If you'll take my advice, you'll stop torturing yourself. You don't even know these people, Bernard. How can you possibly guess who sent it?"

"Snooky described them to me."

Maya met this with a contemptuous snort. "Snooky! All right, I agree he has a good eye and a way with people, but whoever wrote those letters must be very good at camouflaging themselves. Not even Snooky could pick it up. And who knows what's really going on? All artists are nuts . . . except Weezy, of course."

This was very much in line with what Bernard had been thinking. He nodded again.

"I just came back from watering Weezy's plants. I stopped off on the way back from the store. The house seems so deserted. I wish they would come back home."

"They can't, Maya. They're far too busy drinking rum and dancing in the moonlight."

"It's been over a month already."

"I'm sure it's good for Weezy. You've said how happy she sounds on the phone."

"That's true." Maya played with the button on the oversized shirt she was wearing, one of Bernard's. "Do you think we should go away, too?"

"Sure. Why not?"

"Where should we go?"

He put an arm around her. "Wherever you want."

"Oh, what's the use, anyway? What am I going to do, drag my massive bulk around the Berkshires or something? What kind of a vacation can you take when you weigh a ton?"

"You don't weigh a ton." He patted her stomach. "The doctor said your weight gain is fine. You look wonderful."

"I'm so hot all the time, Bernard, my body temperature is way up. I always used to be cold. Oh, look, the baby's kicking."

They sat for a moment in pleased silence, watching the shirt jump as the baby did underwater somersaults.

"How are things going with Sophie?" Maya asked.

"Not good."

"Are you still planning to call your lobster Sophie?"

"Yes."

"That's okay. I've decided I like Rebecca better. Don't you?"

"I like Rebecca."

"Or Rachel. And if it's a boy, I'm thinking Justin."

"Justin?"

"Justin. What's wrong with Justin?"

"Nothing. How about Leo?"

"Leo? Why Leo?"

"I had a friend named Leo. I like the name Leo. It's a strong name for a boy."

"Hmmmm," said Maya. "Okay. Justin or Leo. Or Jared."

"Jared?"

"Yes, Jared. Remember my friend from college, Suzie? She named her little boy Jared. I thought it was a nice name."

Bernard shuddered. "I have to get back to work."

"Well, I'm just saying. I'm just trying to have a discussion."

"Can we discuss names over dinner?"

"What, and spoil our appetite?" said Maya, heaving herself off the armchair and closing the door gently behind her.

# SEVEN

WEEZY AND SNOOKY stayed away all summer long. "We should go," Weezy would say at least once every few days, but they didn't go, they stayed in their island paradise. They outstayed their hosts, who flew to their home in Scotland in the middle of August. Nancy gave them the keys to the house, left them with instructions to enjoy themselves, and thanked them (as Snooky had predicted) for helping to look after the place.

"She must be kidding," Weezy said. "The housekeeper looks after this place. We just abuse it."

"No, no, I told you. They're grateful to us."

Meanwhile, in Connecticut, the summer days dragged by. The cold spell had passed and now the weather was unbearably hot and humid. Maya's body temperature rocketed when she went outside, so she spent more and more time in her bedroom, lying with five or six pillows strategically arrayed around her swollen body, watching TV for hours. Her apathy worried Bernard.

"We have to get away," he said one day. "I know you don't want to fly and you couldn't stand a long car ride. How about the Berkshires, after all?"

"I don't know," said Maya, lying in darkness with the

reflected TV image flickering over her face. "I'm sort of enjoying it here."

"We have to get away. The Berkshires are only a couple of hours. Remember the Ivanhoe."

The Ivanhoe was a beautiful little inn surrounded by mountains.

"I don't know," said Maya again. "Maybe. What would we do with Misty?"

"What did we do last time we went there?"

"We left her with Paul."

Paul Sanders was their next-door neighbor. He lived in a geodesic dome which had almost frightened Bernard away from the whole neighborhood.

Bernard's forehead crinkled. "We did?"

"Uh-huh."

"You sure?"

"Yes, Bernard. The Ivanhoe doesn't take dogs, remember?"

Bernard sat down on the bed. "I'm worried about Paul. He's ninety years old if he's a day."

"Eighty-seven."

"No way."

"Eighty-seven, sweetheart. He told me so."

"Then he's a liar as well as being old," said Bernard with energy. "He could die tomorrow and Misty would starve to death."

"He's in perfect health. He's more energetic than I am."

"I don't like it."

"Then we don't have to go."

Bernard cocked a worried eye at her. "No. No. We have to go. We have to get away from here. We have to breathe the clean mountain air. We have to walk on unspoiled paths. We have to commune with Nature."

"Oh, God," said Maya, stuffing another pillow under her

knees. "It sounds exhausting. Leave me at home. I'll take care of Misty, and you can go."

In the end, they surrendered the dog to the tender care of their next-door neighbor and spent a week at the Ivanhoe. They walked on unspoiled paths, breathed the clean mountain air and explored the local antique stores. Maya grew happier and more relaxed as the days went by. Their visit was marred only by the fact that the double bed was much too small for two adults and the number of pillows Maya required in order to get to sleep at night.

"I can't help it," she snarled at him one night, "I *need* these pillows. Do you have any idea how uncomfortable it is to have a stomach this large?"

"Do you want me to sleep on the couch?"

"No, no. Here. There's a space over here that's almost big enough for you. Just don't move around a lot in the night. And don't snore, I get so little sleep as it is."

"I do not snore."

"Bernard, I regret to inform you that you snore all night long. I never noticed before, but now that I have to get up to go to the bathroom four hundred times a night, it's struck me how much you snore. I lie awake listening to it."

"I'm sorry."

"Don't apologize. Just don't snore. Is there room enough for you now?"

"Don't worry about me," Bernard said heavily. "Two or three inches at the edge of the bed are all I need for a good night's sleep."

Despite his complaints, Bernard would fall asleep almost at once, exhausted from the long walks, leaving Maya to lie awake and watch the moonlight creep across the floor and spill onto the Victorian chaise. She would turn and twist, rearranging pillows, cursing under her breath, trying desperately to get comfortable. Lying on her stomach, her favorite sleeping position, was an impossibility. When she lay on her back, she felt as if she were drowning; as if a large hand had come down on her chest and firmly clamped off her supply of air. So she twisted from side to side, heaving her stomach back and forth, cursing her slumbering husband, far away in his dreams. At last she fell into a fitful doze, to awaken with a start, her mind filled with images of the baby: so solid and real, moving inside of her, and yet somehow not real at all.

One day in early September, when the weather was still sultry and hot, Bernard opened his front door to find Snooky and Weezy standing there.

"Weezy," he said. "Nice to see you."

"I'm back, too, Bernard," said Snooky.

"Yes, so I see."

"We're sorry we stayed away so long," said Weezy. "Where's Maya?"

"Upstairs." His gaze swept over them. They looked relaxed and happy. They were dressed in island white, which showed off their tans to advantage, and Weezy's hair had turned the most astonishing amber color in the sun. Her skin was golden and her hair was aflame in yellow and red.

"Weezy," he said, "you look like a torch."

She smiled at him. "Thank you. Are you going to move aside, sweetie, and let us come in?"

Bernard moved aside obediently. "I don't think you should let Maya see you. It's too depressing. It'll just set her off."

"Why?"

"You look . . . well, relaxed."

"She's not relaxed? How is she doing?"

"Does the phrase 'third trimester' mean anything to you?" Bernard went upstairs ahead of them. He knocked softly on the bedroom door. "Maya? There are some people here who I think you might want to see."

Maya looked up from a pile of pillows. Her face lit up as they came into the room. She stretched out her arms.

"Snooky," she said with a half-sob. "Weezy. You didn't . . . you didn't tell me—"

"We didn't have a chance," said Weezy, laughing and hugging her. She pushed the pillows aside and curled up on the bed. "We decided this morning. All of a sudden I said, 'Let's go,' and Snooky agreed, and so we packed up and went to the airport. It was time, anyway, with the baby coming so soon. I'm sorry we stayed away so long."

"You look wonderful, Missy," said her brother, surveying her with approval. "Fecund is the word, I think."

"I'm enormous," said Maya in despair, patting her stomach. "I never thought I'd be this big, honestly I didn't. The doctor says the baby is going to be over eight pounds. Eight pounds! How do they explain the other seventy-two?"

"Now, now, get a grip on yourself, Missy. You don't look like you've gained that much."

"No, no, not quite, but you know what I mean. In that league."

"And you're taking Lamaze classes? You and Bernard?"

"Yes, yes, they're wonderful. We do all this breathing together. It seems that if you breathe right, it doesn't really hurt at all. Not at all!"

"Amazing," said Weezy. "How amazing."

"Yes, and we've been practicing the breathing together at night. Breathing and pushing. I think we're almost ready. The nursery is all set up—you should see it, Weeze, with the little white crib and everything—and I even bought my first toy for the baby, a little white bear." Maya scrabbled among the pillows and lifted up the bear, which regarded them solemnly from its button eyes. "I keep it here, next to me."

She cradled the bear and burst into helpless sobs.

"Jesus," said Snooky later, after they had calmed Maya down and he and Bernard had retreated to the kitchen for a restorative cup of coffee. "I've never seen her like that."

"Eighth month," said Bernard, pouring two big mugs. "Thirty-fourth week. Only six more weeks to go." He handed Snooky one, and added cream and sugar to his own. He sat down at the table and leaned his head against his hand. The dog came wandering in, her toenails clicking against the tile floor, and lay down on his feet.

"Has it been this way all summer? She didn't sound this bad on the phone."

"No, no, it comes and goes. She felt pretty good during the middle trimester, but now she's uncomfortable most of the time. She can't wait for the whole thing to be over."

"Well, frankly, neither can anyone else."

"Really? The two of you don't look like you've been losing sleep over it."

Snooky grinned at him serenely. "No, we had a wonderful time."

Bernard grunted. He drank his coffee.

"Have you taken care of Weezy's place?"

"Maya watered all the plants once a week, even, may I add, when she wasn't feeling well, and—"

"Hold on. Why didn't you take over for her?"

Bernard threw him a contemptuous glance. "Do you think she'd let me take care of the plants? She knows I'm not a plant person. Naturally I offered, but she said she wanted to do it. She was convinced that without her loving touch all the plants would keel over and die. I spent quite a lot of time trying to disabuse her of that notion, but she didn't want to listen to me."

"Oh. That's true, I remember what happened when she gave you that little cactus. She told me you were the only person she ever knew who could kill a plant that didn't even need to be watered for half the year."

"Well, it damn well needed to be watered the other half of the year," said Bernard with asperity.

"Every living thing needs water sometime, you know. I mean, it's a fact of life. The universal solvent. Why don't you set up a Japanese stone garden or something? That sounds like it might be more in your line."

Bernard shrugged. "I followed all your long-distance instructions. I called Weezy's cleaning lady last week, and opened the front door so she could get in. We went by later and locked up. Anything else on your list?"

"Yes. I have to pick up Weezy's mail for the whole summer."

"She has to do that, they won't give it to you."

"I don't want her to do it. I was wondering if you would come with me. They know you down at the post office, and if Weezy called they might let you pick up her mail. Don't you think so?"

"I don't know. Maybe."

Snooky glanced at him uncomfortably. "What are the chances that there's another one of those letters there?"

Bernard drummed his fingers on the table. "Almost a certainty."

"I agree. That's why I want you to come with me. I don't want Weezy to have to be there when we get it."

Bernard sat thoughtfully for a few minutes. Then he nodded, drained his coffee and pushed back his chair. Misty grumbled at his feet. "All right. Let's go now."

"Now? Right now?"

"Yes."

"Nothing if not a man of action," Snooky said approvingly.

---

When they reached the local post office Snooky did most of the talking while Bernard, after saying hello, lapsed into silence. The postmaster put up only a minimum amount of resistance. Ridgewood was a small town and Bernard was a well-known figure at the post office, coming in from time to time to mail off his manuscripts and galley proofs. After a brief argument, the postmaster nodded. "There's a lot of it, though," he said over his shoulder, going into the back. "A lot."

He re-emerged with a large cardboard box filled with letters and magazines. "Here you go, Mr. Woodruff."

"Thank you very much."

They drove back to Weezy's house. It seemed strange and still and airless inside, like a buried time capsule. Snooky threw open all the windows and let the summer breeze come in. Then he and Bernard sat down in the living room and began to sort through the mail.

"Here's one," Snooky said almost immediately. He turned it over and glanced at the postmark. "July sixteenth."

"And here's another one," Bernard said a little while later. "Postmarked August tenth."

"Nearly one a month since we've been away."

"Yes."

Snooky opened the first letter and read it, his face impassive. Then he tossed it across the coffee table. "Take a look."

Bernard picked it up.

**I HATE YOU   I HATE YOU   I HATE YOU**

He turned the page over. That was the entire message. "More succinct than the others."

"Uh-huh. Distilled to the essence. What's the other one say?"

Bernard tore it open and removed the page inside. His

heart was beating fast. The letters were repellent, and yet he felt a great curiosity to find out what they said. It seemed incredible that someone like Weezy could be the focus of such hatred.

**YOURE NOT SUCH A GREAT ARTIST<br>YOUR PAINTINGS ARE NO BIG DEAL<br>IM JUST AS GOOD AS YOU  JUST AS<br>GOOD**

"Hmmm," said Bernard. He showed it to Snooky. "What do you think?"

"Redundant."

"Yes. The same message over and over. Trying to drive the point home, apparently." He watched as Snooky put the letters back in their envelopes and stuck them in his pocket. "Are you going to show them to her?"

"Yes. I don't want to, but she's already told me if there are any, she wants to see them. I just wanted to be the first line of defense, that's all."

"I hate to see her upset."

"Me, too. Bernard . . . do you think she's in any danger?"

"I don't know."

"I hate this," Snooky said vehemently. "I feel so helpless, I don't know what to do. Maybe I should hire her a real bodyguard." He looked dejected at this thought.

"Maybe you should."

"Do you think so?"

"I don't know what to think," said Bernard. "None of it seems to make any sense."

"That's what Weezy's said all along. She said she never bragged about her career or pushed herself forward. She can't imagine who could hate her so much."

"If she's in some kind of danger and we didn't do anything, I'd never forgive myself."

"Yes. If this person feels so tortured, maybe they think that killing her would be the answer."

Bernard nodded.

Snooky opened the drawer of a small cabinet and took out the telephone book. He opened it and began to thumb through the yellow pages.

"Where do I look? Under *B* for bodyguard?"

"No, I don't think so."

"*M* for muscleman? *T* for thug?"

"Try *S* for security. How do you survive in the world, Snooky? Don't you know anything at all? How do you function?"

"Not very well, apparently," said Snooky in a bitter tone, drawing the phone towards him and starting to dial.

"I don't want a bodyguard," said Weezy. She looked down at the letters in her lap. "I don't want a bodyguard."

Snooky took her hands in his, covering them with his warm, comforting grip. "I know you don't, sweetheart. But you have to. Look at those letters, it's getting more personal now. Even worse than before."

She nodded slowly. "But I don't want a bodyguard."

"I know, sweetheart. I don't want you to have one, either."

"This is so creepy. I'm afraid to go outdoors. My whole life has stopped." She leaned against him, and he put his arms around her. She had borrowed Maya's car to come and see her house, and he had shown her the letters. Bernard stood uncomfortably, a frozen statue, in the background.

"I know, I know," murmured Snooky.

"Can't we just go away again? Why can't we just go away?"

"We can, if you want to. Of course we can. It's not a bad idea."

"I was happy when we were away."

"Yes. Me, too."

"Let's go away again. Why can't we just live away? You do that, don't you? You never stay anywhere for long. Can't I go with you?"

He held her in a fierce embrace. "You can go anywhere with me. You know that. I'm not leaving without you."

"We could go back to St. Martin. I was happy there, Snooky. We could go back to the islands and I could paint like Gauguin. I've never wanted to paint like Gauguin, but you know what I mean. Island scenes, stuff like that."

"Okay. Whatever you want. I'll call Peter and Nancy tonight."

"Oh, no, no, no," said Weezy, suddenly irritable. "We can't impose on them again. I gave the housekeeper the key, I can't ask for it back. Don't you have any other friends?"

"I have lots of friends. Millions of friends. We'll go somewhere else. How does Majorca sound to you?"

"Majorca," Weezy said dreamily. "Yes. Majorca. You know somebody there?"

"Oh, yes. They love me in Majorca. We'll leave tomorrow."

"You're wonderful," said Weezy, and gave him a long, lingering kiss. In the background, Bernard twiddled in an agonized manner with the leaves of a large plant. He cleared his throat uncomfortably. "If I may say something . . ."

Weezy looked up. "Yes?"

"It's not a bad idea, going away for a while. Things might change while you're away."

"Wait a minute. I can't go. The baby's coming next month. Snooky, we can't go."

"There's plenty of time to see the baby," Snooky said. "Majorca is a great idea. It would be better if it were winter here, but never mind, it'll be winter soon. We'll stay away for a nice long time."

"Your friends won't mind? Wait a minute, why do I even ask? Your friends never seem to mind. I don't know where you find them."

"Oh, here and there, here and there. When you travel a lot, you find people who don't mind unexpected visitors. You'll love Diane and Frank, they're great. They've got two kids and these gigantic dogs that look like ponies. I don't know what they're called."

"Scottish deerhounds?"

"No."

"Irish wolfhounds?"

He shook his head. "Some exotic name. Unpronounceable."

"But anyway, what about the baby? I can't leave before the baby's born," she said fretfully, turning to Bernard. "What should I do? Maya will kill me. Stop playing with that philodendron, please, you're going to bruise it."

Bernard let go of a leaf. "Maya will understand. I think, if you don't mind my saying so . . ."

"Yes?"

"I think it's more important that you go away right now. We'll all be here when you get back."

Weezy nodded. She picked up the letters and crumpled them savagely, then threw them on the floor. "Can I ever come home, do you think?"

"This won't go on forever," said Bernard.

"Oh, really? Why not? What's going to stop it?"

Bernard had no answer to this. He remained silent. Weezy gave a brittle laugh.

"Woman without a country," she said.

That night Bernard had trouble falling asleep. He tossed and turned in bed, pulling the covers this way and that. He muttered to himself, dozing off fitfully and awakening a few minutes later. Maya, who barely slept at all anymore, switched on the light and regarded him kindly.

"Having trouble falling asleep?"

"Yes."

"Good," she said, switching the lamp off. "Misery loves company."

When he turned he woke her, and when she turned she woke him. They snarled and hissed at each other like cats in the night. Finally Maya fell asleep, her stomach propped up on two pillows, a pillow between her legs, a pillow behind her back and two more pillows under her head. She sighed as she slept, murmuring to herself.

Bernard lay awake, staring angrily into the darkness. He hated not being able to sleep. He could tell already that it was going to be a long night. He felt that sleep was far away, a land he had been to once but for some reason was not permitted to visit again. He wondered how he had ever been able to fall asleep, it seemed impossible. He turned over cautiously, rearranging the blankets, trying not to disturb Maya. She spoke suddenly, in a loud, interested tone.

"Didja?" she said. "Didja really?"

Bernard's heart nearly stopped, it was so unexpected, but she was sound asleep. She burrowed deeper into her pillows and her breathing became calm and regular again.

There was something bothering him. Something Snooky

had said today had triggered off that memory in the back of his mind again, and now it was jumping up and down, screaming at him. Something Snooky had said . . . something almost inconsequential, something Bernard knew already, something everyone knew, but they didn't realize how important it was . . .

He pulled up the covers and grumbled to himself under his breath. "What? What is it?"

The darkness did not answer. He felt disgusted with himself. What was it? Why couldn't he remember? He squeezed his eyes shut in an effort to recall. It was something so . . . so *obvious*.

At last Bernard dozed, a shallow sleep filled with nightmares. He was wandering in the woods . . . he was looking for a baby, but at every turn it eluded him . . . he knew the baby was his responsibility and he shouldn't have lost it, but it was getting away, fleeing farther and farther into the distance. He woke up with a jerk, snuffling and snorting miserably. With a trembling breath, he lay down again. Next to him Maya, for once, was sleeping peacefully. Bernard thought with some bitterness that he seemed to have absorbed all the insomnia and bad dreams from her, and tonight it was his turn. He was almost afraid to fall asleep again, but when he did dream, the images had changed. He was sitting at a table and eating . . . eating and drinking, but what was being served to him was something noxious, something thick and creamy and poisonous. He knew he shouldn't keep eating it, but he couldn't help himself, he ate and ate and ate, all the while knowing that he was poisoning himself, eating wildly with tears in his eyes. He consumed unbelievable amounts, amounts that in real life would have killed him. At last, with a snuffle, he awoke with real tears in his eyes.

Bernard loved food and he hated having bad dreams

about it. Food was one of his greatest pleasures in life. He shook himself all over in disgust and then lay still, listening to Maya's calm breathing.

At last, around five-thirty in the morning, when the sky was getting light and the birds were starting to sing, it came to him. He smiled. There was no one to see him, but he smiled anyway. The writer of those letters had made one mistake. It was a natural mistake, one that would not mean anything if Weezy had been a different type of person, but it showed that the person behind those letters did not know Weezy well at all. Bernard thought of her, asleep in Snooky's bedroom upstairs, and a contented feeling spread throughout his body. He turned over with a happy grunt and fell asleep.

At breakfast, Weezy and Snooky had an animated discussion concerning their plans for Majorca. Bernard listened silently. At last he put down his coffee cup with a loud clatter. "Weezy."

"Uh-huh?"

"Remember you said once that none of your students ever took much of an interest in your exhibit?"

"Yes? What of it?"

"Well," said Bernard, "I was wondering something last night. Did you ever tell any of them the name of the gallery where it was going to be held?"

She gazed at him, her mouth open. "No. No, I didn't. I never said anything about it, other than that I was going to have an exhibit. Nobody . . . well, nobody asked me."

"Did the gallery advertise?"

"No," she said slowly, "it was too early for that. The show wasn't going to be held for months."

"Then how did that person know which gallery to call?"

"I . . . I don't know," she stammered. "Word gets around . . . they could have heard from somebody . . . they could have called around the different galleries . . ."

Bernard shook his head. "There must be hundreds of galleries in New York. They'd have to be very lucky to hit the right one. Don't you think so?"

"I . . . I guess so . . . but if someone really wanted to find out, I'm sure they could do it somehow . . ."

"How?" Bernard asked patiently.

She was silent for a minute. "I don't know. I'm not sure."

"Did you tell anybody in your class? How about Elmo?"

"Oh no, Elmo didn't care. We never talked about it. We just argue about his work, that's all we do."

"Yes. You're not like most people, Weezy, you don't brag about yourself. You never talked about the exhibit. Snooky reminded me of that yesterday, and it made me think. Now listen to me. Was there *anybody* that you told about the show? Anybody you told the details to?"

Weezy's eyes widened. She glanced over at Snooky.

"Oh, my God," she said. "That day in New York. I couldn't help myself."

Snooky was nodding. His eyes looked very hard and bright, like a snake's.

"Harold," he said. "And Harold's girlfriend."

# EIGHT

SNOOKY AND WEEZY were quiet most of the way into New York. They held hands and Weezy looked out the window of the train.

"How did she sound when you called her?" Snooky asked at one point.

"Surprised," Weezy said briefly.

"You're sure it's her and not him?"

"Yes." Weezy looked up at him. "Say what you want about Harold, he's not the psychotic poison-pen type. Not the shiny gold letters, no, that's not his style. And he's perfectly thrilled being a doctor, he doesn't need to tear me down."

"Are you sure?"

"Yes, yes, yes. Harold may be a slimy disgusting toad who left me for somebody else, but he's not a canvas-slasher. He'd be too afraid that some paint might get on his very expensive Italian shoes."

"Okay, then. The gallery owner said he hadn't gotten any other calls about your exhibit?"

"Uh-huh."

"And the other galleries you called said they hadn't gotten any inquiries at all?"

She nodded.

"Which galleries were those?"

She rattled off ten names, most of which were unknown to him. "They're the obvious ones," she said.

"Okay." He squeezed her hand. "How're you doing?"

"Okay."

They got a cab outside of Grand Central and directed the driver uptown. Gabriela Loeser lived in a fancy co-op on East Seventy-third street, a tall building constructed of shiny dark glass. The doorman buzzed them up and she met them at the door of her apartment.

She was smiling. She wore a red silk dress with a black leather belt. She looked relaxed and perfectly put together, every blonde hair in place. "Weezy, how nice to see you."

Weezy made an odd, noncommittal sound. "I think you know my friend, Arthur Randolph."

"Yes, we met in the restaurant." She nodded to him and led the way indoors.

Her apartment looked like a photo essay from *Architectural Digest.* Hardwood floors, Oriental carpets, lace draperies framing the windows, and overstuffed sofas in a floral pattern. A vase of fresh flowers stood on a Mission Oak cabinet in the corner. Everything was beautiful and discreet and very, very rich, thought Snooky. She didn't buy and furnish this place on her salary from *People* magazine, he thought; whoever she was, she came from money. Lots and lots of money.

Gabriela indicated a place for them on one of the sofas. "Would you like coffee or tea?"

"No, thanks," said Weezy.

Snooky shook his head.

Gabriela seated herself in an armchair opposite. The chair was covered in a Turkish kilim fabric, and in her red silk dress, with her pale skin and her deep red lipstick, she made quite a striking picture. She leaned forward confidentially.

"I'm sorry about how long the article is taking. There's

always a certain lag time, of course, but in this case it's taking me longer than I thought to complete it. I hope you don't mind, I think it's going to be wonderful once it's done."

Weezy gave her a hard stare. "I didn't come here about the article."

"Oh. Well. When you called, I kind of assumed . . . ?"

"I came here because I wanted to find out why you've been persecuting me. Why you trashed my studio and wrote me these letters." Weezy reached into her handbag and took out the four letters, tossing them angrily on the table between them.

Gabriela's face went white. "Trashed your studio—!" she said, her voice wavering.

"Yes. And these goddamned letters. And the phone calls, and the dead flowers. I want to know why. I can't imagine why, and I want to know. You have Harold, who's the only thing we ever shared—otherwise you're a complete stranger to me. I'd like to know what in the world I've ever done to you."

Gabriela's face was flushed a deep rose. "Nothing . . . what . . . I can't imagine . . . !"

"You're not a very good actress," said Weezy witheringly. "I'm sure you're surprised that I found out who it was, but suffice it to say that I know it's you. Why did you do it?"

Gabriela stared at her for a long moment. Her hands had turned into claws, gripping the sides of her chair. She seemed to come to an inner decision.

"Because I hate you," she whispered.

Weezy leaned forward, her cat-eyes narrow. "I know you do, you goddamned bitch. I'm asking you why."

"Because Harold still loves you."

Weezy expelled her breath in a puff of air. "Harold?" She laughed shakily. "Harold? You really are crazy. Harold hates me. That's why he moved out, remember?"

"No," said Gabriela. "You're wrong. He still loves you.

Everything is Weezy this, Weezy that. Weezy does this better than you, Weezy does that better. Weezy used to like to go on walks, Weezy loved to cook for me, Weezy's such a great artist, Weezy, Weezy, Weezy!" She stood up abruptly and went over to the window, drawing the lace curtains aside and looking down at the teeming streets below. "It's too much," she whispered. "Ever since we ran into you in the restaurant he's been talking about nothing else. It was bad before, but now . . . ! Weezy is such a great artist, Weezy has such a wonderful talent, Weezy is so sensitive. You should see her paintings, you should see her work, oh well, you couldn't possibly understand, Gabriela, all you are is a crummy journalist. All you do is work for a yellow rag, your work is nothing, Weezy's work is everything. She does *art! Art!*" She shot Weezy a furious look. "I'm nothing and you're everything, yes, that's how it is, according to Harold."

"Harold never even liked my work when we were together," said Weezy.

"That can't be true."

"But it is. He never said a word about it then. I always thought he seemed embarrassed by it."

Gabriela shrugged in disbelief.

"And so all that stuff you said about being a big fan of mine . . ."

"Oh, I'd never even seen your paintings. I was repeating what Harold kept telling me."

"And the phone calls?"

Gabriela flushed and looked guilty, like a small child. "Oh . . . I don't know. I can't explain, really . . . it just made me feel better."

"What do you mean?"

"Well . . . I was so *curious* about you. There was Harold, babbling on about you all the time, and it made me feel so curious . . . so one day I picked up the phone and dialed your number. When you answered, I couldn't think of anything at all to say, so I didn't talk. I just waited. It made me feel scared, but sort of . . . I don't know . . . relieved, somehow. That I had finally heard you. After that, I would call every so often, just to kind of . . . I don't know . . ." Speech failed her. She came back and sat down on the sofa, tucking her skirt neatly under her legs.

"Frighten me?"

Gabriela waved a hand helplessly in the air. "I don't know. Not really. Just to keep in touch. It made me feel better, that's all. I mean, I knew all about you and you didn't know anything about me, and this was a way of—of keeping the balance, I guess."

"I see."

"But then I called and some man answered—was that you?" she asked Snooky.

"No, it wasn't."

"Oh. Well, somebody answered, and I guess you know what happened. He sat on the line as long as I did, and didn't say anything either, and . . . well, it kind of freaked me out. After that I figured I better not call anymore. You might have put a tracer on the line or something. I mean, I had been careful not to call too often, because I didn't want to get caught."

"Mmmm-hmmm," said Weezy. "Tell me something. How'd you get my number in the first place? Harold sure as hell didn't have it."

"Harold? Oh, no. I couldn't have asked him anyway. It was that article, you know. The one in the *Times*. It said where you were living, so I called directory assistance and got your number."

"I see. So then, after you met me in the restaurant . . ."

"I made up an excuse to see your paintings. I had to see what Harold was talking about. I pretended I was going to do an article on you. And you bought it. Pitiful. Did you really think I'd do an article on Harold's ex?" She shook her head. "I had to see what you were doing, that was all, those famous paintings. Your wonderful talent."

"My brilliant career," Weezy said bitterly.

"Yes."

"And the lovely bouquet of flowers?"

Gabriela flushed again. "Oh, well . . . actually, Harold gave them to me for my birthday. I mean, when they were new. I kept them for weeks. I couldn't bear to throw them out. He used to tease me about it whenever he saw them here. 'Why are you keeping that bouquet?' he used to say. 'Throw it out, I'll buy you another if you like it that much.' You know, that's how he is. Generous."

"A prince among men," said Snooky.

Gabriela looked over at him in a puzzled way, as if she was having trouble placing him. "Yes. Well, anyway . . . I called you up for that interview, and when Harold heard about it he hated the idea. He told me he didn't like the two of us getting friendly. I suppose nobody likes their girlfriend and their ex getting together. But I said that if you were so talented, then you should be getting more publicity, and he shut up after that. After a few days he seemed to . . . I don't know, to change his mind, I guess. We had dinner one night, and he spent the whole time talking about how wonderful an artist you are, and that's when I decided to send you the flowers."

"I see." Weezy tilted her head to the window and lapsed into a contemplative silence.

Snooky leaned forward. "You used a word processor to address the label."

"Yes. Yes, I did. I have a printer here."

"Why didn't you use it for those letters you sent? It's a hell of a lot easier than sticking on all those gold letters."

"Oh," said Gabriela. "I don't know. I thought maybe printers could be traced. I didn't think so, but I wasn't sure. So I used the gold letters. I thought it would be safer."

"Okay," said Snooky. "So you came up for the interview after that. What did you think of her work when you finally saw it?"

Gabriela paused. She lifted one hand and began to chew on a fingernail. "I thought it was good. I thought . . . I thought it was wonderful. Harold was right. It was everything he had said. I . . . I couldn't get over it, it made me want to kill you. It'd be one thing if he was just making it up, but when I saw the paintings—!" She shrugged. "I didn't know what to do."

"Apparently you managed to think of something," Weezy said in a low voice. "You came up and slashed them."

There was a long pause.

"Yes." Her voice was faint. She gave Weezy a furtive, guilty glance. "Yes. I . . . I'm sorry."

"I'm sorry? That's it? I'm sorry?"

"I didn't mean to."

"Excuse me?"

"I came up to talk to you," Gabriela said, lifting her hands helplessly. "Just to talk. I don't even know what about. I couldn't get you out of my mind. I was sort of . . . well . . . obsessed. I kept thinking about you, and Harold kept talking about you, and I felt like I had to talk to you myself or go crazy. I drove up one day on an impulse. I got in the car to do some shopping, and when I got out of the city I just kept going. When I got there you weren't home, but when I tried the front door, it opened. I figured I'd go in and wait for you. I thought I'd get another look at your paintings. So I went into your studio and started looking around. And . . . and I don't know . . ." Her voice trailed off. "I saw one painting . . . of a girl . . . I don't know, all of a sudden I went crazy, I guess.

I couldn't stand it. I had this penknife I carry in my handbag . . . I took it out and I . . . I . . ."

"You pitiful moron," said Weezy. "That painting wasn't even mine. It was one of my students'. Remember I told you at the interview that they were off to one side? I asked you if I could include them in the photos? Don't you remember?"

Gabriela looked frightened. She lifted one hand to brush a lock of hair off her face. "No . . . no, I don't remember. I wasn't really listening during the interview. I was . . . I was looking at you and at the paintings."

"She destroyed my studio and my exhibit because of Elmo's painting," Weezy said to Snooky, almost matter-of-factly. "I told you he was better than me."

"No, no, that's not true."

"Oh, yes it is. This proves it." She turned back to Gabriela. "I have another student whose paintings were the only ones you didn't touch. Why was that?"

Gabriela looked at her blankly. "What?"

"One of my students' paintings. They were stacked together in the far right-hand corner, away from the others."

Gabriela shook her head. "I don't remember. I don't know. I really don't know."

"All right. What about the letters?"

"After . . . after I . . ." she couldn't finish the sentence.

"Go on."

"Yes, I . . . I ran out and drove away. I didn't think anybody had seen me, but you never know, especially in a small town like that. I waited, but you never got in touch, so I figured . . . well, I figured you didn't know who it was. I felt so guilty and crazy and horrified, I didn't know what to do. But then Harold kept on talking about you. I thought getting rid of your paintings would make me feel . . . I don't know, different, but it didn't. One day at work I called up the gallery to make sure they knew there wouldn't be an exhibit. The owner didn't seem to know that anything was wrong. And I got scared . . . I thought maybe there were more . . . maybe I hadn't gotten all of them . . . maybe . . ." Her voice trailed away again. "So I started writing the letters. It made me feel good for a while, but not for long. Nothing made me feel good. Nothing worked. And now I feel . . . just . . . wretched." She hung her head and put her hands in her lap, like a guilty child. "I'm sorry," she said, her eyes filling with tears. "I really am sorry. I . . . I didn't think of you as . . . as *real.*"

"What did you think of me as?" asked Weezy, watching her. "Styrofoam? Insensate? With no feelings?"

"You were just Harold's ex, that's all, period. That's all."

"Harold's ex? That makes me nonhuman?"

Gabriela shrugged hopelessly.

"You stupid idiot," Weezy said, emphasizing every word. "You stupid idiot. You're blaming me for what that moron Harold is doing. He used to try it with me, about his ex-wife. Stacey was this, Stacey was that. Just what you're describing to me. Stacey was perfect, I was less than nothing. The thing is, I never blamed Stacey, I blamed myself. Which makes three stupid women. Stacey for marrying him, me for blaming myself when he talked about her, you for blaming me. And so far nobody's blamed Harold."

Gabriela began to cry.

"But at least I never wrote Stacey any disgusting letters or tore up her stationery store down in the Village," said Weezy. "You need help. You need some kind of help I'm not qualified to give you. You know, if I had been home that time that you came up, I could have told you about Stacey."

Gabriela covered her eyes and began to sob.

"I hope you feel bad."

"I do, I do," she wailed, rocking back and forth.

"I've been living in fear ever since this started. Keep the

letters, it'll remind you what you've done to me. Come on, Snooky, we're leaving."

They stood up and went to the door. Gabriela followed them, her hands weaving in the air in front of her face, as if she had suddenly gone blind.

As they left, she reached out and grabbed Weezy's arm in a clawlike grip.

"Are you . . . are you going to tell Harold?" she whispered, in a choked voice.

Weezy shook her arm free irritably. "No. Let go of me."

"You're not?"

"No."

And she shut the door in Gabriela's surprised, tearful, anguished face.

On the way back to Ridgewood on the train, Weezy sat looking out at the blue distance. Trees ran past, skimming over the ground, balancing with their branches held out like tightrope walkers. The train chugged and rattled its way north.

Snooky put an arm around her shoulders. "Well?"

"Well?"

"What do you think of that little interview?"

"Oh, I don't know. It was painful and disgusting and horrible, of course, but in a way . . . well, in a way I found it gratifying. That's an awful thing to say, I guess."

"No, it's not."

"Here I've been killing myself over Harold, feeling so humiliated and everything, and all the time he was holding me up as a paragon of virtue to his next girlfriend. When he did that to me about Stacey I didn't realize it was a pattern. I just thought she was great and I was awful."

"Harold sounds like quite a gem. As I told you in the beginning."

"Yes, so you did."

"And may I mention that I also suggested all along that Gabriela might be jealous of you. I said that Harold might be talking about you. I said it was a possibility."

"Well, you were right. As usual, nobody paid any attention to you at all, but you were right." Weezy patted his hand.

"How do you think the students will take the news?"

"Well, I can't wait to tell Elmo about 'Girl in White,' how it triggered her into a destructive frenzy. He'll be absolutely furious, but on the other hand, it'll appeal to his enormous ego. I'm sure he can easily imagine someone going nuts over his work." She laughed softly.

"And Alice?"

"Poor Alice, how we all maligned her. She's touchy and paranoid and horrible, but not as horrible as somebody else I could mention. It's such a relief to know my instincts were right all along, it wasn't her."

"You did say that." He gave her shoulders a squeeze.

"Yes, I did."

"We still don't know who messed up her paintbox."

"Well, now that I know that it's not the same person who did everything else, I have a very good idea who it was."

"You do?"

"Uh-huh." She chewed her lip.

"Want to tell me?"

"Let me make sure first."

"Okay," said Snooky. "So you're not too upset?"

"Well, I'm upset, naturally I'm upset. I mean, I've been through hell over this. It's been awful. I had to cancel my class and go away for months because of it."

"That wasn't so bad."

"No, no. But you know what I mean. I hated feeling like I was running from something. Like I was afraid to go home."

"Yes."

"And those letters and everything . . . !" She shuddered. "Harold got what he deserved, he really did. He found himself a real winner this time."

"Harold," said Snooky, "is an idiot. A stupid, insensitive, loutish idiot who knows nothing about women. A man who gave up the chance of a lifetime when he broke up with you."

Weezy smiled lazily and leaned her head against his shoulder. "That's nice. I don't get to hear the word 'loutish' nearly often enough these days."

"The English language is going down the drain. Such a rich, varied vocabulary, and no one uses it anymore."

They rode for a while in comfortable silence.

"So it doesn't look like the article in *People* magazine will be forthcoming," said Snooky. "Are you devastated?"

"Oh, no. Of course I'd like it, but I don't need it. And I'm already thinking that I might try to do something new for the Genuardi Gallery next year, instead of duplicating the paintings that were ruined. I think I'll try something different . . . a whole new look . . . something I've been thinking about for a while, but I didn't have the energy before . . ." She turned back to the window in absorption, her eyes wide and unseeing.

"That's good," he said, but she was no longer listening. She was watching a carousel of forms and colors rotating gently inside her head.

Weezy called up her students on the phone and told them that she was teaching again. At the beginning of the first class, she announced that the person who had wrecked the studio had been caught, and that they were all off the hook.

"For which I hope you'll be suitably grateful," she said. "And, by the way, Alice's paintings were simply overlooked, that's all. The person who did this never met any of you. I don't want to go into this, but it's someone who knows me and nobody else."

There were expressions of relief, and a palpable easing of tension in the room. Alice, in particular, looked smug. "I told you it wasn't me."

"So you did, my dear."

The class went well; everyone was on their best behavior. Mrs. Castor said to Weezy, "You look happy again."

"I am, thanks."

"Enjoyed your vacation?"

"More than I can say. Snooky told me it was your idea for us to get away from here. I can't thank you enough."

"You were looking tired," said the old lady. "I'm glad to see you looking so well now."

After class, Weezy asked Elmo to follow her into the living room for a private chat. He stood with his arms folded, surveying her quizzically. "Yes?"

"Elmo, you shithead," she said affably. "Why did you mess up Alice's stuff?"

He did not argue. "How'd you find out?"

"As soon as I figured out that somebody else had done the major damage, it was clear to me that only you would have the nerve to do that to Alice. I know you pretty well."

"Yeah."

"So tell me."

Elmo scratched his cheek guiltily. "I'm sorry, Weeze. I was sure she had cut up 'Girl in White,' and it was killing me. I figured she was the only one nuts enough to do it. And then she kept picking on Jennifer, hinting that if Jen used one of her brushes she'd paint better, that kind of stuff. I saw red, that's all. One day after class I opened her case and messed everything up. It was easy, I just went over and did it. I don't think anybody saw me, other than Jen, and to tell you the truth, she was thrilled."

"Nikki saw you, you bumpkin."

"She did?"

"Yes, but don't get all red in the face, she didn't tell. She said to Snooky that she was glad somebody had done it."

"Yeah, well, that's how everybody felt. Alice is a mean little bitch."

Weezy looked at him thoughtfully. "Okay. But she would never have cut up 'Girl in White.' You know that."

He shrugged. "She was the only one, Weeze. I figured it had to be her. Who was it, by the way?"

"None of your business, junior."

"That private, huh?"

"Yes. Nothing to do with any of you—nothing. A ghost from my past."

He shrugged. "If you say so."

"Try to control yourself from now on, will you? Are you still mad at Alice?"

"Nah."

"You could always apologize to her."

"Don't press your luck, Weezy."

"If you don't, she'll keep on thinking that Jennifer or Nikki did it."

He thought this over. "Yeah. Maybe. I'll think about it. I'm not promising anything. I think she doesn't deserve to know what happened."

"That's my good, kind, forgiving boy," said Weezy. "Now listen, there's something else I have to tell you. It's something you need to know."

"What?"

"Well, I don't know how to say this, but the person who slashed all the paintings was triggered off when she saw 'Girl in White.' She thought it was my work, and it was so good that it sent her into a homicidal frenzy. I'm sorry, Elmo. I know it's a strange thing to hear. I really am sorry."

"She thought 'Girl in White' was your work?" Elmo said slowly.

"Uh-huh."

His face turned slowly red. "She must have been a moron, Weeze. You've never done anything to touch my 'Girl in White.' "

Weezy patted his face. "That's what I thought you'd say," she said, laughing.

"Cheers," said Maya, raising her wineglass.

"Cheers," echoed the other three, and they all drank.

"Yuuccch," said Snooky, shuddering. "Do I have to drink grape juice? It's such a letdown after that wine you served to me last time."

"Now, now," said Weezy. "It's not fair to drink good wine in front of Maya while she's pregnant, you know that. I still feel bad about last time, I don't know what I was thinking. Now stop whining."

"I like to whine."

"I know. More pasta, anyone?"

She had decided to have a little dinner party, just the four of them, before the baby was born. "Because goodness knows when we'll be able to get together again afterwards, Maya. I mean, not to depress you or anything, but having a baby makes it harder to have these little intimate meals."

"I know, I know," Maya said unhappily.

"How are you feeling these days?"

"Like a great whale, moving slowly and ponderously through the ocean. Like a sea animal on land, gasping for air."

"Like a mighty mastodon, lumbering across the primordial veldt," said Snooky.

Maya glanced at him in annoyance. "Oh, shut up, Snooky. Honestly."

"This is why I'm having a dinner party," said Weezy. "Because we could all use some entertainment. And because I haven't cooked for someone as appreciative as Bernard in months."

Snooky had laid the table with crystal and silver, all of Weezy's best. The grape juice glowed in a decanter on the sideboard. "I refuse to decant it, it's not wine," Snooky had said.

"Pretend," said Weezy. "Use your imagination. I'm not serving it in the bottle it came in, I'll tell you that."

There had been a momentary snag in the proceedings when Snooky, emptying a steaming pot of vermicelli and boiling water into a colander, had watched in horror as the colander tipped slowly over, spilling its precious contents all over the sink. Weezy had sat down on a chair and laughed helplessly.

"Ohmigod, Snooky, what do we do now? Send out for pizza?"

"We can still save it. Give me a hand here." He was scooping it back into the colander. "We'll wash it out, they'll never know the difference."

"We can't serve them soapy vermicelli, Maya's pregnant."

"Oh. Right."

"We'll have to start over. Fill up that pot again, will you? Let me check and see if I have any other kind of pasta."

She found two boxes of linguini and said they would do. "Not as good as the other kind, but Maya and Bernard will never know. Do you want to tell them dinner will be a little later than planned, or should I?"

"It's my fault, I'll do it."

Over dinner, Maya asked, "How's the class going, Weezy?"

Weezy shrugged cheerfully. "Oh, the usual. You know. Bruised egos and frayed tempers. But nothing serious, nothing outrageous. I must say it's been a different world since I came back. I think they're afraid I'll leave again if they get too difficult. Does anyone want more sauce on their linguini?"

"I do," said Bernard. He watched in satisfaction as she ladled hot meat sauce laced with garlic onto his plate. "Thank you."

At the end of dinner, Weezy raised her wineglass again. "To friends."

"To friends," said Maya.

"To friends and good food," said Bernard.

"Friends and good food," they said, clicking their glasses. "Cheers!"

A month later, on October eighteenth, two days before her due date, Maya went into labor.

She began to feel an uncomfortable feeling in her stomach, like gas pains, on a bright and sunny Saturday morning. At first she thought she had eaten something that disagreed with her, but as the morning went on, it finally dawned on her that the pains were spaced regularly apart, every ten or fifteen minutes.

"This is it, Bernard."

Her husband leaned down and kissed her. "Okay."

"You ready?"

"No."

"Good. Me neither."

As the day went on the pains gradually became stronger and closer together, just as she had read in all the books. Maya was worried.

"It's taking too long," she said, fretfully thumbing through one of her birthing manuals. "Too long, Bernard. Is something wrong? It's been eight hours, shouldn't the pains be every five minutes by now?"

"I don't know." Bernard had paid attention during the birthing classes, but as this long day passed he felt all his hard-won knowledge seeping away from him, sliding gently away and over the horizon, out of his grasp. "I don't remember anything. Did we take those classes? Do you remember when we're supposed to call the doctor?"

They decided to call the doctor, who was reassuring. "Just stay home and keep timing the contractions. Call me when they're five minutes apart, or if your water breaks."

Neither of these things happened. Day turned into night. Maya could not lie down or sleep because of the pain, and yet the contractions were still eight or nine minutes apart. At midnight, over her weak protests, Bernard bundled her into the car and drove to the hospital.

"This is normal," said the labor nurse. "Don't worry. This happens all the time."

"You're only at three centimeters, Mrs. Woodruff," said the resident. "I can't admit you until you reach four centimeters. I'm sorry."

"But the pain—!"

"Call me if it gets worse. We don't want you all alone at home, screaming."

Bernard and Maya got in their car and drove back home, silent and miserable. "I feel rejected," she said. "Rejected by the medical establishment. How could I not be at four centimeters yet? I've been in labor forever. How could they turn me away?"

"Maybe if we walk around, it'll help," he said, remembering one fact from the hours of lectures.

They walked around the streets of Ridgewood for the rest of that long, dreary, agonizing night. At daybreak, Maya clung to him and sobbed.

"Let me go to the hospital," she wailed. "I want to go to the hospital. Please don't make me walk anymore. I can't walk one more step. I want to go to the hospital, Bernard. I want the pain to stop and I want to lie down."

Bernard put her in the car again, along with her little valise that they had carefully packed three weeks earlier, with her toothbrush, a towel, a washcloth, some magazines to read during labor, and two adorable little baby outfits which Maya had lovingly picked out from the white chest of drawers in the nursery. He drove her to the hospital and demanded that she be admitted.

"She's in pain," he told the labor nurse, a tiny woman with a wise old face. "A lot of pain. You can't send us home again."

"Is she going to have drugs?"

"We weren't planning to."

The labor nurse looked at Maya sympathetically. "You sure, honey?"

"We took Lamaze," Maya gasped. "Another one's starting, Bernard."

After they held her hands through the contraction, the labor nurse said confidentially, "Not to burst your bubble, hon, but Lamaze is what you do while you're waiting for your epidural."

"No, no," said Maya, shaking her head. "No. I can take it. Oh, God, here comes another one. I can't stand it, Bernard, I can't—" Her breath was cut off and her face turned white.

"Think of peasant women," said Bernard. "Think of cave women. Think of horses in the fields."

"Shut up, shut up, shut up," sobbed Maya. "Leave me alone. Go away. Where are you going? That's right, leave me all alone here, having your baby. That's right, just abandon me in the hospital. Oh, God, here comes another one, I can't take it, it hurts sooooooooooooo muuuuuuuuch!"

"There's something wrong," she confided to him later,

once she had finally been admitted ("four centimeters, Mrs. Woodruff, congratulations") and ushered upstairs to the labor room. They were met by a pleasant-faced young woman named Amber who checked Maya over, then sat down with a cheerful air to read a magazine. "I think it'll be a while, Mrs. Woodruff. Try to conserve your energy. You'll need it for delivery."

"What energy?" Maya sobbed. "I have no energy. Leave me alone, Bernard, stop touching me, I hurt everywhere."

When she whispered to him that something was wrong, he was seriously alarmed. He looked down at her pale, anguished face. "What? What is it?"

"It shouldn't be taking this long. It shouldn't be hurting this much. They never said it would hurt like this. They said it would be a beautiful, natural experience, Bernard. They—" Her voice was cut off in an inarticulate wail. Later, she whispered, "I'm dying here. I'm dying, and nobody cares. Something is terribly wrong."

"You're not dying. Nothing is wrong."

Maya bared her teeth and snarled at him. "A lot you know about it. It just kills me that this is your kid too, and your entire role is to sit there and bring me ice chips. It just kills me."

At eight centimeters she threw the paper cup at him, screaming, "NO MORE ICE CHIPS!" at the top of her lungs.

At nine centimeters she had lost all trace of human dignity.

At ten centimeters, the doctor came in, nodded and said, "Now push."

The rest of the beautiful, natural experience was lost upon Maya, who pushed until she felt like her guts were pouring out of her and spilling onto the floor. She pushed for an hour and a half, and then was bundled down the hallway into the delivery room, white sheets flying, exposed to half the hospital, not caring, wishing she were dead. She was surrounded by medical personnel and admonished to push.

"PUSH! PUSH! PUSH! PUSH!" they chanted, in unison.

To Maya, it sounded like some kind of arcane tribal rite. She was far away in a daze of pain. If she had been able to, she would have killed the instructor who had talked about "pressure sensations during the birth experience." She was sure something was horribly wrong. It shouldn't be this bad. It shouldn't hurt this much. Nobody had told her. She was used to being prepared for the experiences in her life, and there was no preparation for this. It did not feel like the birth of a baby. It felt like a brush with death.

"PUSH! PUSH! PUSH!" shouted voices around her, above her, far away. Bernard seemed far away. She couldn't tell where he was, exactly. She wondered wistfully where he was. She thought he was holding her hand, but she wasn't sure.

"PUSH!" shouted her doctor, a familiar voice. She pushed, and the baby came out. There was a happy collective sigh in the room.

"It's a girl," said a voice, a woman's voice, above her and far away. Maya blinked. "A girl, born at two oh five P.M. Congratulations!"

Bernard gripped her hand. She could feel him now.

"A girl," he breathed. "A girl, Maya."

She looked up at him, standing pale and wild-eyed over her. His hair was tousled and he looked distraught.

"A girl," he repeated, as if she hadn't heard the first time. "A girl."

"I'm thirsty," said Maya. "Do you think they'll let me have some water now?"

---

Weezy came to the hospital with a flat box wrapped in silver paper with a large pink bow. Inside was a newborn sleeper outfit in pink and white.

"Oh, thank you," said Maya, holding it up. "It's adorable."

Snooky came carrying Mabel the bear, and a large green noisemaker. He stood at the foot of Maya's bed and blew it as loud as he could.

"Hurray!" he shouted.

Maya regarded him with distaste. "Go away. Stop making so much noise."

"What should I do with Mabel?"

"Mabel is three times the size of Rebecca, you realize that. Take her home. Put her back in the nursery. Rebecca will play with her when she's five years old."

Snooky sat down next to her bed. "Weezy made me promise I wouldn't tell you that you look awful."

"Thank you, Weezy."

"You're welcome."

"How do you feel?" asked Snooky.

"Awful."

"Still in a lot of pain?"

"Oh, my, yes. Yes, indeed."

"Thinking about having any more kids?" he asked brightly.

"No, no, no, no, no," said Maya. "I don't think so. Not any time in the near future. No, no, I don't think so."

"We went to the nursery before we came here," said Weezy. "Rebecca is gorgeous. Absolutely, fantastically gorgeous."

Maya smiled at her. "Isn't she, though?"

"Oh, absolutely. And I'm not lying to you, Maya. You know I would say it anyway, because you have to say that kind of thing to a new mother, but I really mean it."

"She favors our side, thank God," said Snooky.

"Yes," said his sister, "that's what Bernard says. He thinks she looks like me."

"Thank God."

A faint crease appeared between Maya's brows. "She could look like Bernard, I wouldn't mind. I would like it."

"Well, I wouldn't."

She frowned at him. "Are you deliberately trying to aggravate me?"

"No, no, don't be aggravated. Listen, I'm dying to hold my beautiful little niece."

"Not until we leave the hospital, Snooks. She has to stay in the nursery during visiting hours."

"That's a shame. We left Bernard standing guard over her like a Tyrolean watchdog. He was frightening a few fond grandparents away from the glass window. They were afraid to stand there with him glaring at them."

"Yes, he never leaves her alone. It's a comfort, really, I don't have to worry that she's crying and I don't know about it. He would stand there all night long if the nurses let him."

"Rebecca Constance is the prettiest name," said Weezy dreamily. "I just love it."

Maya smiled over at Snooky. "We thought you'd like Constance."

"I wish Mother could have seen her," he said, taking her hand.

"Yes."

After a pause, Snooky said, "Which brings me to a more macabre topic. When is William slinking into town with his hated wife and loathsome offspring?"

"Oh, he called this morning. They're planning to come in the day after tomorrow. He's combining it with a business trip to New York."

"Go figure that. Day after tomorrow, you say? I would

leave town, but it would look so obvious. And I want to stay around to hold Rebecca once they spring her from her glass prison."

"Yes, please stick around, Snooks. I don't want to have to handle William by myself. I'm not up to it quite yet."

"I understand. Anything I can bring you, Missy? Anything from the outside that you crave?"

"I'd like some more painkillers, if you see a nurse anywhere. Do you think I'll ever walk again?"

"You'll walk," Weezy said. "My mother had four children, and I distinctly remember her walking."

"We had no idea what it was going to be like. We didn't understand. Do you know what I brought in my bag for the hospital? A tape of canoe sounds on the river. You know. Loons crying, crickets chirping, that kind of thing. Gentle paddling noises, the rushing of the water. It was supposed to calm me down during labor." She uttered a cracked, hysterical laugh. "Calm me down during labor!"

Weezy nodded in sympathy. "Bernard told us that you didn't get much of a chance to read those magazines you brought along, either."

"No, no, I was screaming too loud to enjoy them," Maya said tiredly. "Don't go yet. I love seeing both of you. Stay and tell me stories."

Weezy looked at her doubtfully. "But you seem so tired, sweetie. Why don't we let you nap and come back later?"

"No, no. Please stay. Did you really think Rebecca was as outstandingly beautiful as you said?"

Inside the glass walls of the nursery, a large bearded man glared at the curious faces pressed against the window. He stood protectively over a little crib that said WOODRUFF in pink letters. Nestled inside the crib, a tiny mite of humanity squirmed and wriggled. She rubbed her eyes, glared up at her father with a gaze as fierce as his own, and began to squeal.

Bernard felt a fluttering of alarm, a nervous palpitation of his heartbeat that occurred whenever his daughter began to cry. He left the nursery, closing the door securely behind him, and went down the hall to Maya's room.

"She's crying, Maya."

"Oh. Okay. Help me out of bed, will you?"

She hobbled down the hallway, leaning on his arm, and settled herself with a groan on a chair in the corner of the nursery. Rebecca began to nurse.

"I like this," said Maya. "Exposing my breasts in front of countless strangers with their faces pressed against the window. This is nice."

"They're not looking at you, they're looking at their own babies," Bernard said, patting her shoulder. He moved between her and the window, his brows beetled, his look so fiercely unwelcoming that several people lost their nerve and drifted away down the hall. After what seemed like a long time, Rebecca gave a happy hiccup and fell asleep. Maya rearranged her hospital gown, handed her back to Bernard and limped off towards her room.

"Call me if she needs me."

Bernard needed no reminder. He held his daughter tightly for a moment before putting her back into the crib. She was a mystery to him, he thought; where had she come from? What was she doing here? He rarely waxed philosophical, but her birth, which had been one of the most hair-raising experiences of his life, had got him thinking. He and Maya had created her body, but not her essence. He had known that the moment she lifted those dark blue eyes to his.

He tucked her in tenderly, arranging the soft pink blanket around her so that she would be comfortable. Rebecca looked comfortable, splayed out on her stomach like a frog, lost in the quick shallow sleep of infancy, her chest fluttering up and down. When he was finished playing with the blanket, he stood for a moment stroking her downy head, covered with fluffy dark hair, not as light a brown as Maya's nor as dark as his own. It was another way, he mused, that she was already different from them. It was not love that he felt for her, really: more like a tremendous responsibility and protectiveness. He patted her head tenderly and straightened up, to find Weezy watching him with amused eyes through the glass. Snooky was next to her, grinning at him and holding Mabel. Bernard stiffened and gave them an offended look. *Don't disturb my privacy,* the look said. *Leave me alone with my baby daughter.*

Weezy nodded, her eyes soft, and blew him a kiss. Snooky waved the teddy bear's arm, and as Bernard resumed his watchdog stance, the two of them moved away hand in hand, down the corridor and out of his sight.